GETTING AWAY WITH MURDER

RUSSELL WATE

CRANTHORPE
MILLNER
PUBLISHERS

This book is a work of fiction. Names, characters, places and incidents are either products of the author's imagination or are used fictitiously. Any resemblance to actual events or locales or persons, living or dead, is entirely coincidental.

First published by Cranthorpe Millner Publishers (2026)

ISBN 978-1-80378-367-3 (Paperback)

www.cranthorpemillner.com

Cranthorpe Millner Publishers

Printed and bound by CPI Group (UK) Ltd
Croydon, CR0 4YY

FSC www.fsc.org
MIX
Paper | Supporting responsible forestry
FSC® C013604

The DCI Alexander McFarlane Crime Mysteries

Greed is a Powerful Motive – 2021

Missing But Not Lost – 2022

Death at Chateau Peveril – 2023

Body Overboard – 2024

FOREWORD

This is a story about a detective, his skills and the process involved to investigate homicide. It shows us that detective as a man, his family and his life. The book is also a travelogue as seen through his eyes.

∞

The investigation branch within the Foreign, Commonwealth and Development Office (FCDO) described in this novel is fictional and is not currently or will ever be real in the format I have described within the story. They do have very gifted police superintendents who work there on a seconded basis as liaison officers, and they do all they can to support families and police forces. They work with a murder and manslaughter team within the FCDO.

∞

My absolute thoughts and wishes go to all those families who have lost loved ones abroad and the nightmare they face in trying to come to terms with and understand it, as well as having to plan for their loved ones to be returned to the UK.

Chapter One

Five days earlier

The hotel room that Inspector Otto Wagner of the Vienna District Police was peering into was probably no different from thousands, if not tens of thousands, of hotel rooms around the world. There was though, in this one, a significant difference. Lying on the couch in the room was the body of a young man.

Standing in the corridor beside him was an agitated, stressed and constantly talking hotel manager. Otto put his hand through his hair – well, what hair he had left.

'Please could you just be quiet for a moment so that I can think,' Otto said, rubbing his face with both hands and looking straight at the manager.

'I will, but' – the hotel manager did not stop as Otto had asked and carried on talking – 'this is not the man who is staying in this room.'

'What do you mean?' Otto's eyes darted back and forth between the dead man on the couch to the manager.

He sincerely hoped there was no strange business going on here. Who was the person in the room? Was he a sex worker? Or a thief?

'The occupant of this room,' the manager said loudly, to ensure he was heard and understood, 'should be a Mr Andrew Barrington. He is an Englishman who is at least fifty years old and I was there when he checked in this morning. I saw him and this person is not him.'

From what Otto could see, the dead man was probably only in his early twenties. Certainly not anywhere close to fifty.

Otto sighed. He was now regretting taking the call to attend the Neuer Markt hotel, but as he had been only ten minutes away at the police station near St Stephen's Cathedral, he had responded to the request for attendance to this dead man found in the hotel room.

He had walked there, enjoying the fresh air and the sunshine that they had that day in Vienna. He was going to get a coffee and a pastry from a nice shop just off the Neuer Markt, but he hadn't had a chance. Yet another thing he was now regretting – he'd had hardly any breakfast and had not eaten since.

There was a noise in the corridor behind him and, on looking round, he was delighted to see two of his finest detectives arrive, DCs Mia Eckhart and Johanna Gruber. Although they were young, only in their twenties, they were enthusiastic, bright and efficient. Otto felt blessed to have them on his team.

While glancing at them in the corridor, Otto was pleased to see a CCTV camera on the ceiling behind them.

'Good,' he said aloud, 'that will help us find out what happened. Mia and Johanna, please take the manager to his office. I understand the cleaner is waiting in there, traumatised by what he has seen. Please take their statements. Also get someone to come to the hotel and download the CCTV footage for the entrance and reception area, then this corridor.'

Otto wondered why the manager started frowning at him when he mentioned the CCTV.

'Yes, boss,' was all the detectives could say, before a man came into the corridor from the direction of the stairs.

He was moving at speed and was all in a fluster. Mia grabbed hold of him by his arm to make sure he didn't go any further towards the hotel room.

'What's going on?' the man shouted. 'Where's Arthur, my son? He was resting in my room.'

'Change of plan, Mia. Can you please escort who I presume is Mr Barrington back to the police station? I will join you all shortly.'

The hotel manager started shouting and pointing. 'That's him. That's him, he is the man staying in this hotel room.'

Otto really felt at this point he needed a hotel room to lie down in himself.

The man, Mr Barrington, didn't want to go, and Johanna had to try and calm him down, helping Mia by taking his other arm.

'If you come with us, sir, we will explain what is happening.'

Together, they expertly steered him out of the corridor and, deciding not to wait for the lift, proceeded to descend the staircase. Mr Barrington could be heard shouting loudly the whole way down.

He was clearly distraught, and as they led him out of the corridor and down the stairs, Otto could hear him saying to Mia and Johanna, 'Has my son collapsed or something? Has an ambulance been called? Why won't you let me go and see him? Please, let me see my son.'

For the first time since he had arrived at the hotel, the worried look Otto had been wearing disappeared. It looked like nothing untoward had happened here. The man in the room had died from some sort of natural cause, if what Mr Barrington had said was true.

Otto's phone buzzed and he looked down to see he had received a message from Johanna.

Should we tell this man that his son was found dead in his room?

Johanna was, quite rightly, asking whether they were *sure* it was Arthur Barrington who was in the room, and whether they should give his father what they called an 'agony message', telling him his son had died.

Otto replied:

Ask Mr Barrington to show you a recent picture of his son. If he sends it to you, and then you to me, I will confirm. Don't tell him until I confirm.

With that settled, Otto returned to the matter at hand. Realising he now had no staff left to interview the hotel manager and the cleaner, he turned to the manager.

'I will need to take control of this room for the next day or so. I might not be able to find anyone to take your statements for a while, so you can send the room cleaner home.' Realising he had been talking in a rather abrupt tone, Otto added softly, 'Tell him I am sorry, and we will see him later.'

The hotel manager went off, leaving Otto alone outside

the room, but not for long. Two crime scene investigators soon turned up, already in their forensic paper suits, carrying cases and with cameras slung around their shoulders.

The hotel corridor now felt very cramped and crowded again.

'What sort of job do you want doing, boss?' asked Paulina, the older of the CSIs. Now in her fifties, she had been round the block many times during her time working with the police service. 'Eckhart told me the death isn't suspicious, probably an illness or something like that? Is that what we're thinking?'

Running his hands through his sparse hair and then over his face, Otto realised just how tired he was. The endless sixty- to seventy-hour weeks were taking their toll. His wife, a school teacher, had started complaining that she hardly ever saw him. Yet however tired he was, and however much he wanted to go home, Otto knew he was always the one to do the right thing. He needed to pull it together for the sake of this young man and his father.

'Full job, please. We owe it to him,' he said, pointing into the room at the body. 'Young men are not meant to die, are they?'

Paulina nodded, and the CSIs went into the room, proceeding to take photographs and visual recordings, including a 360-degree video. The younger CSI took some tapings along the entranceway in the room.

'You can come in now, up to the place where the room opens up,' he said to Otto.

Having put on a forensic paper suit himself and double gloved as requested by the CSIs, Otto pulled up the hood and entered the room. The first thing that struck him was how hot it was in there.

'Have you got an estimate for when the forensic medical examiner is going to arrive?' he asked.

'Ten minutes or so,' Paulina told him. 'I know what you're thinking: it's far too hot in here and not just because we have suits and hoods on. The body will start to decompose before we know it. Why do they have hotel room thermostats set so hot!'

The room was in semi-darkness, the curtains pulled across the windows, and despite the noise of the business of the CSIs, there was an eerie silence hanging over the space. The disconnect between the visual of the young man's dead body lying before them and the faint hum of the busy shopping area of Kärntner Straße nearby only added to the eeriness – life's normality relentlessly continuing on outside while this hotel room remained suspended in time.

Arthur Barrington was lying half on, half off the couch, the position unnatural, like he had fallen onto the couch rather than laid himself down.

Otto's phone buzzed again. The picture he had received from Johanna of Arthur Barrington was definitely a match for the body he was looking at now. Gosh, he looked so young; younger than Otto's own children.

As he looked up, he saw there was a chair and a small coffee table beside Arthur's body that had been knocked over. Maybe this wasn't going to be as straightforward as he had originally thought. There *had* been a recent spate of hotel room burglaries in the city centre. Had Arthur been disturbed by the Albanian teenagers they currently had as their main suspects?

On another table were two used coffee mugs that the younger CSI was photographing, then putting into bags as exhibits to be examined later.

The bed, a large king-size, was fully made, and on one of the bedside tables was a book, a pair of glasses and a laptop. Maybe it wasn't the burglars then – surely, they would have taken any tech lying around?

A large black suitcase was lying open on the floor, filled with clothes.

The medical examiner arrived then, and after some resistance – he never liked to put on the forensic paper suit unless he was sure it was a murder – he did as instructed by Paulina, who took no messing. With the help of the two CSIs, he took off the dark green jumper Arthur was wearing. They examined and photographed his body, then turned Arthur over.

'No sign of any injuries,' the doctor said. 'Bag his hands and head though before he's moved.' Then, looking directly at Otto, he added, 'Do you want me to take a blood sample for toxicology and get the hospital pathology department to examine it for infection or disease before we consider an autopsy?'

'Yes, please,' Otto replied.

He was feeling more relaxed about this death again now; there was a good chance it was non-suspicious. He left the others to finish their examinations and headed off to the police station.

Firstly, he needed to talk to his boss, then to the state

prosecutor to tell him about the blood sample they were taking, then finally someone in the British Embassy in Vienna. But before any of that, he knew he must go and talk to Mr Andrew Barrington.

Chapter Two

On a dreary Monday morning, the week following Arthur Barrington's death, a team meeting for the Consulate Investigation Team at the Foreign, Commonwealth and Development Office (FCDO) in Whitehall, London had just finished.

DCI Alexander (Sandy) McFarlane, who had chaired the meeting, was pleased that the team had not alerted him to anything requiring his immediate attention. He and his colleague, DS Juliet Ashton, had only just returned from a case they had been working on in Barbados, and if they played their cards right, a short trip to Austria beckoned.

This trip to Vienna was only a possibility though, as his boss, Detective Superintendent Jane Watson, had been quite firm with Sandy earlier that morning that he was not going to Vienna unless she – and Jane repeated the word with emphasis, *she* – received a formal request from the Austrian police for their and his involvement. Otherwise, they were not going to get involved.

While Sandy (the name his family and friends called him) had been in Barbados at the time, he had received a call from his paternal grandfather John McFarlane, who was a retired family court judge but still worked on a part-time basis as a barrister, and also lectured occasionally on law at the University of Cambridge.

John had told Sandy that he had been approached following one of these lectures by one of his students, Freddie Wainwright, who had asked for his advice about the death of a friend, Arthur Barrington, who had been found dead in a hotel room in Vienna. Freddie had told John that he and his sister, Emily, Arthur's fiancé, were extremely distressed by Arthur's passing, and they were both desperate to know what had happened, but that no one was telling either of them anything.

Now that Sandy was back in the UK, a meeting with the two siblings had been arranged, and Sandy needed to find out a bit more information before this meeting took place in Cambridge later that Monday afternoon. He looked through the emails on his laptop and found what he was looking for. The British High Commission in Vienna had contacted him to say the person dealing with the British citizen's death was a senior inspector, Otto Wagner.

When the number he called for Otto was answered, Sandy immediately introduced himself. 'Inspector Wagner, this is DCI Alexander McFarlane from the FCDO in London. I am calling about' – Sandy looked through his notes – 'Arthur Barrington, twenty-two years old, who died last week at the Neuer Markt hotel. Can you fill me in on some details please?'

'Please, call me Otto. I will do my best to answer your questions.'

Unbeknownst to Sandy, Otto was less than pleased to be receiving his call. He had been enjoying *not* thinking about the death of Arthur Barrington for the past few days.

'Call me Sandy, then. It's what most people call me. I

have a meeting this afternoon with Freddie and Emily Wainwright.'

'Who?' Otto asked, earnestly scrambling about looking all over his desk for the meagre file he had for the death of Arthur, whilst at the same time opening up the electronic investigation file on his computer.

'I understand from my grandpa—'

'Your grandpa? What's he got to do with this?' Otto interjected, now totally confused by this British detective and all these new names he hadn't heard of.

Realising he wasn't explaining this very well, Sandy lopped back. 'Apologies, let me start at the beginning. My grandpa is a lecturer for the law department at the University of Cambridge and he was approached by one of his students, Freddie Wainwright, asking for advice about Arthur's death. Apparently, Freddie was a close friend, and his sister Emily was Arthur's fiancé. They both want to know what happened to him.'

'Right,' Otto said, scanning Mr Barrington's statement. 'I'd been wondering about the girlfriend. Her name is not included in the statement from the father, Andrew Barrington, which is why it is new to me, but there was mention of a girlfriend who the family had been trying to convince him to break up with. Arthur had been talking about marrying her this summer. I wasn't aware he'd proposed.'

'Glad to be of help,' Sandy said, pleased that Otto was putting the pieces together. 'Just to explain where I fit in: I work for the Foreign Office in London, and on occasion investigate suspicious deaths of British citizens abroad.'

Otto's tone took on a hint of excitement. 'Can you fly to

Austria then and take over this investigation?'

Sandy wondered whether he was eager for someone to pass this investigation over to. 'Not take over, but we can assist. You will need to make a formal request to my boss, Detective Superintendent Watson.'

Otto hummed in acknowledgment, then paused as he searched for an update from toxicology, but they had yet to send him any results.

He explained this to Sandy. 'His father said Arthur was ill. If you could find out from his friend and fiancé if they knew anything about this, that would be very helpful. We are awaiting some test results, which I am hoping will show that he died of some natural disease. If that is the case, there will be no need for any of us to do anything more regarding this investigation. I will keep you informed.'

∞

Exiting the train station in Cambridge, Sandy knew he was not going to succeed with any suggestion to Juliet that they should walk to the city centre. Even proposing that they take a bus to Drummer Street bus stop was going to fall on deaf ears, so they took a cab to the entrance to Trinity College and went in through the Great Gate.

The college was certainly the wealthiest of all the Cambridge colleges, and just like St John's College, where Sandy had been a student, it had existed since Tudor times. In fact, some of the buildings at Trinity originated from centuries before this, though Juliet did not share Sandy's interest in their history, and he had long since learnt not to mention it.

The Porter at the gate told them that Sandy's grandfather was waiting for them in the Wren Library, and as they made their way towards the building, Sandy couldn't help but admire the over three-hundred-year-old clock face that adorned King Edward's Gate, though Juliet's brisk pace gave him little time to take it all in.

As they climbed the stairs to enter the library, he was surprised to see not only his Grandpa John, but also his other grandfather, Tom, waiting for them at the top.

'What is he doing here?' Sandy mused, before it suddenly dawned on him that the porter at the gate had likely been referring to Tom when he said Sandy's grandfather was waiting for him.

Tom was a retired detective inspector from the local constabulary, and a number of the porters in the Cambridge colleges were also retired police officers, so many of them knew Tom well, and Sandy by association.

'He's here to help,' John explained. 'Young Freddie came to me first, and I decided to call you. If I want to ask Tom to assist as well, that's my choice, not yours.'

Ignoring Juliet sniggering away beside him, Sandy sighed. 'Not anymore, Grandpa. This is now police business and we need to speak to the two young people by ourselves, without you two butting in. Am I clear?'

John and Tom looked at each other.

'He was always stubborn.' John muttered, 'but now he's getting assertive with it. We had better do as he says.'

Seeing the sad look on Tom's face, Sandy addressed him,

whilst continuing to ignore Juliet, who was now outright laughing. 'I presume you drove here, Grandad? Why don't we catch up after this meeting. You can drive Juliet back to the train station, then me home to Ely afterwards. That'll give us plenty of time to debrief.'

Sandy's grandfathers nodded in unison, before heading back down the stairs, leaving Sandy and Juliet to take a seat at the far end of the library.

The Wren Library was always quiet in the late afternoon, with the public not allowed in after 2:00 p.m., making it the perfect place for this meeting – casual enough to not be intimidating, yet devoid of onlookers. As they waited for Freddie and Emily to arrive, Sandy looked around, recalling that the library had been built in the 1700s, named after its architect, Sir Christopher Wren. The numerous bookcases and alcoves were made to Wren's designs and were all decorated with incredible woodcarvings, made of limewood so as to stand out against the darker oak and cedar wood that they adorned – an intentional choice by their creator, Grinling Gibbons.

Before Sandy could immerse himself too greatly in the library's history, two dark-haired young people entered, looking similar enough that he could only assume these were the Wainwright siblings.

'Freddie and Emily Wainwright?' he asked.

The two nodded, and Sandy gestured for them to take a seat.

'I am DCI McFarlane and this is my colleague, DS Ashton.' Juliet nodded on the mention of her name. 'Can we call you Freddie and Emily?'

'Everyone calls me Em,' the young woman said.

She was dressed in a dark green dress, and glancing at the ring finger on her left hand, Sandy saw a small solitaire diamond ring, presumably given to her by Arthur Barrington.

Pushing away a wave of sadness for the young couple, he pressed on. 'Well, everyone calls me Sandy, so you are both welcome to do the same.' He turned to Freddie. 'Would you mind telling me how you came to be friends with Arthur?'

'We went to school together,' Freddie said, looking at Emily as he did so. 'Arthur was the year above me at Stamford School and three years above Em.'

'Were you friends at school then, or only once you came here to Trinity?' Juliet asked.

'We were close at school, but as soon as I came to Trinity, we became pretty much inseparable.'

'What about you, Em?' Sandy asked.

There were tears welling in her eyes as she fiddled with her engagement ring. 'I met Arthur at school, but he never really noticed me back then. I was just Freddie's little sister… three years is a lot when you're that age.'

Clasping Emily's right hand in his, Freddie interjected, 'Em, he adored you, even back then. But you're right, three years *is* a lot when you're young. That's why he waited until you were sixteen before he told you how he felt.'

The inevitable tears began to fall from Emily's eyes. Juliet passed her a tissue.

Taking over the conversation, Freddie added, 'There has only been one girl for Arthur and that is my sister.' He smiled sadly at Emily. 'They got engaged on her nineteenth birthday.'

'What was Arthur doing in Vienna?' Juliet asked, trying to support Emily by moving to a different topic.

'Arthur is…' Freddie paused, clearing the lump in his throat. 'Sorry. He was a brilliant violinist, and he had secured a job for a year there as a relief violinist in the Vienna Philharmonic. There are so many music groups and concerts on in Vienna, he was able to play every week.'

'Did he study music here at Cambridge then?' Sandy asked.

'No, English Literature, like me. He went every weekend to the Royal Academy of Music though, and had a tutor here in Cambridge.'

'What was he going to do when he came home this summer then?' Sandy asked.

'He had been offered a job in London, again as a relief violinist,' Emily explained, her voice rough with tears, 'but I told him I couldn't move away from Mum and Dad.' She looked to her brother for reassurance. Seeing him nod, she went on. 'They both have mental health issues, and with Freddie still studying, I decided to stay close by, so I can help look after them and the house.'

Taking on the story from his sister, Freddie explained, 'Arthur and Em had decided to get married this summer, and Arthur had just turned down the job in London. He was in the process of getting work and a place to live in Stamford.'

'His dad was so angry that he was throwing away his talent and his life that he flew to Vienna to convince Arthur otherwise.' Emily's voice dropped, and Sandy struggled to hear what she said next. 'He rang me on the way to meet his dad in his hotel room, telling me how nervous and scared he was, but that he was going to fight for us. He told me not to worry, but…' Emily's body began to shake again with grief. '… now he's gone, and I can't help but think the worst must have happened in that hotel room.'

Sandy and Juliet looked at each other, startled at this revelation.

'What we have heard from the detective in Vienna is that they think Arthur died of an infection,' Sandy told them. 'But… are you saying you think his father might have murdered him?'

That was *exactly* what they were insinuating.

CHAPTER THREE

After dropping Juliet off at the train station, Sandy and his grandfather, Tom, made their way slowly out of Cambridge. The traffic was always awful at this time of day.

'When are you going to ask me what this case is all about, then?' Sandy asked his grandad.

'I thought it was none of my business, since I'm no longer officially a police officer,' Tom said, trying to sound offended, but failing – he couldn't resist smiling back at his grandson.

Sandy chuckled. 'You can take the man out of being a detective but you can't take the detective out of the man.'

Before he could say anything else, his phone vibrated, telling him he had a call incoming from Otto Wagner.

'Hello, is that DCI McFarlane?'

'Yes, Otto. Sandy McFarlane speaking.'

'I've just had the toxicology report sent to me for Arthur Barrington.'

Sandy looked at Tom and gave him a thumbs up. It looked like the case would be over almost before it had started.

'I presume you're going to tell me Arthur died of an infection?'

'No,' Otto said, clearly frustrated by the results in front of him. 'Although there are traces of virus in his system, these are of a fairly common strain of influenza, which did not – I repeat, did not – contribute to Arthur Barrington's death.'

'So why did he die then?' a confused Sandy asked, subconsciously running his free hand through his hair.

'The toxicology report doesn't say. I'll need to organise and get permission for an autopsy in the next day or so. Are you able to come over and help?'

'As I said, if you send an email to my boss Detective Superintendent Jane Watson, asking for my assistance, she should be able to authorise it.'

'On it,' Otto replied.

'Oh, before you go, Otto, we saw Freddie and Emily Wainwright this afternoon. Although they have no evidence, they insinuated that Arthur's father may have killed him. Or, at least, he had reason to.'

The pause on the other end, then the heavy sigh, was heard by both Sandy and his grandad.

'There was no evidence on Arthur's body of any struggle,' Otto explained, 'but there *was* an overturned table and chair in the bedroom. This investigation is going the opposite way that I would wish. How soon can you get to Vienna?'

'How soon can you get your request in to Jane Watson?'

∞

Sandy's mother began to interrogate them both as soon as they walked through the door of her riverside house by the Great Ouse in Ely.

'What are you two doing here? I thought you' – she pointed at her father – 'were visiting John McFarlane in Cambridge, and you' – she pointed at her son – 'are meant to be staying in the flat in London with your father.'

Before Sandy or Tom could answer, mostly because they were speechless, Katherine continued.

'I am having a quiet night in by myself and suggest that if you want anything to eat, you go to The Cutter Inn.'

After dropping his bag off, Sandy and Tom sheepishly walked the hundred yards to their local public house and ordered a beer each and dinner.

'I think I've got the gist of what the case might be about.' Tom paused and took a long sip of his beer. 'I had a case when I was a young police officer of something called sudden adult death syndrome.'

The food arrived and Sandy waited for the waiter to put the plates down and move away before addressing his grandad's hypothesis.

'I've never heard of that before. Is it similar to sudden infant death syndrome? Or "cot death" you might have called it back then?'

'Yes, very similar I am led to believe. This could be the case here. Living away from home in a bedsit, not a lot of money, not sure what his nutrition was like, getting infections, etcetera. It's certainly possible.'

'Alternatively, his fiancé might be right,' Sandy offered while finishing a mouthful of his dinner. 'It could be murder... there's certainly motive by the sounds of it.'

Tom had stopped eating and was gesticulating with his knife. 'If it *is* murder, and the father is the one who saw the victim last... it's him you should be looking at as your main suspect.'

∞

The following afternoon, Sandy and Juliet were on a flight to Vienna. Late in the evening of the previous day, Jane Watson had called both Sandy and Juliet to give them permission to fly out to Vienna for a few days to assist with the case – only a *few* days, though, she had emphasised.

This suited Sandy just fine – he wanted to be back in the UK by the weekend anyway, so he could spend time with his girlfriend, Hannah. He couldn't get the sight of Emily Wainwright's engagement ring out of his mind, and as he sat on the plane, he found himself fiddling with the small box he kept in his pocket. He took it everywhere, but it wasn't *him* who should be keeping the contents of the box.

After Jane's call the previous night, Sandy had also been contacted by his Grandpa John, wondering if Arthur Barrington had died of sepsis. John had apparently done some research and there had been forty-eight thousand deaths in the UK alone from sepsis the previous year. This, he told Sandy, was more than the combined deaths for breast, bowel and prostate cancer per year. Well, that was according to the Sepsis Trust, but given the statistics, it surely could be the cause of the death if Arthur had some sort of infection.

Sandy had told him this was unlikely given the toxicology report, but offered the suggestion Grandad Tom had given regarding sudden adult death syndrome. John had told him to find out whether anyone else in Arthur's family had experienced it, or sudden infant death syndrome, as though it was an unlikely cause of death, it would be more likely if there was a family history.

Sandy loved both of his grandfathers dearly, but just

sometimes – to be fair, it was no more than sometimes – he wished they were not so keen to get involved in his investigations. It was highly likely neither sepsis nor sudden adult death syndrome had killed Arthur Barrington, but now they had mentioned the possibility, he had to investigate those options.

Juliet had arranged for Arthur's medical records to be emailed to her that morning from his family doctor in Stamford, before they got on the flight, but they only revealed that Arthur had been seemingly healthy and fit, and had never complained of any heart or breathing issues – well, not that had been reported to them, anyway. When the surgery had checked his other family members, they couldn't see anything that would assist.

Once Sandy and Juliet had landed, the city airport train got them into the centre of Vienna in sixteen minutes. Juliet hadn't grumbled when she saw how quick it was, but she sure was grumbling now as they trundled along with their carry-on cases behind them. It was only about a kilometre, Sandy kept reassuring her, but his platitudes weren't working. Fortunately, the architecture that lined their walk made up for it, and Sandy managed to drown out Juliet's grumbling, which was getting louder and louder, especially whenever they encountered a street made of cobbles. The streets got busier and busier with people as they got closer to the city centre, where the police station was situated.

Just before they got to Stephansplatz and the cathedral that dominated that plaza, Juliet suddenly noticed that they were passing their hotel, whose name was translated the "King of Hungary". It wasn't surprising that she hadn't immediately realised – the business admin team at the FCDO didn't normally book this sort of hotel. It was stunning, and Sandy knew from his research that it dated back to the 1700s.

Having decided that they had time before their meeting, they checked in quickly, before heading off to meet Inspector Otto Wagner, Juliet steering Sandy quickly past the cathedral to stop him spending too much time admiring it.

Almost immediately on arrival at the police office, they were shown up to Otto Wagner's cramped office. The desk was littered with paperwork, strange given that so many modern investigations relied on digital records, not paper ones.

'I like paper,' Otto had explained when Sandy had asked, after the customary introductions and handshakes, before leading them through the main office thoroughfare towards a more suitable meeting room, since Otto's office didn't have enough space for the three of them to sit.

Opening the door to a spacious, well-lit meeting space, Otto walked around to the other side of the large table, placing down a slim folder he had brough with him before writing the name "Arthur Barrington" in large letters across the whiteboard.

'I presume you also have the notes relating to this suspicious death displayed in your major incident room?' Sandy queried, looking firstly at the slim folder and then at Arthur's name on the board.

He was beginning to worry that this might be the sum total of the investigation material collected to date.

'They are overrun with other long-term investigations at the moment,' Otto explained, 'but we believe this case is one with a natural cause of death.' He looked at Sandy and Juliet for confirmation, frowning at their expressions. 'We do, don't we?'

A short discussion then took place regarding possible sepsis and sudden adult death syndrome. Otto smiled and nodded, visibly relaxing at the knowledge that this was the priority hypothesis for the cause of Arthur Barrington's death.

While this conversation was taking place, into the room walked Otto's colleagues, DCs Mia Eckhart and Johanna Gruber. After introductions, Otto stood up to lead the briefing. He was wearing his usual grey suit, his usual white shirt, top button undone, and his usual dark blue tie, lying half unknotted, which all added to his appearance of weariness.

'Arthur Barrington's autopsy is scheduled for tomorrow morning, so we should know more following that. DS Ashton, if you could please forward me Arthur's medical records, I will send them over to the pathologist.'

'What time tomorrow? And where?' Sandy asked, making notes in the notebook he had for this investigation.

'Around 8:30 a.m., so if yourself and DS Ashton could meet me here at 8:00, then we can head over to the Center for Forensic Medicine together. It's part of the Medical University of Vienna. Should only take ten minutes or so to get there.'

'Please, call us Sandy and Juliet,' Sandy insisted.

The rest of the team nodded, and Mia and Johanna suggested they too should go by their first names.

Otto looked at his two detectives. '*You* can both call me sir, but you two' – he turned to Sandy and Juliet – 'are welcome to call me Otto.'

This prompted an echo of laughter throughout the room, easing the remaining tension.

'The examining magistrate has agreed to the autopsy following the result of the toxicology and the medical examiner's report,' Otto added.

Sandy hadn't researched what the local processes were, which was unlike him, but he presumed the examining magistrate was like a combination of the British Coroner and Crown Prosecution Service together, although he couldn't be sure. *A question for Otto later*, he thought.

Otto resumed his briefing. 'We need interviews and statements from the hotel manager and the room cleaner.'

'Sir,' Johanna said, emphasising the word "sir", 'they are both in today until 5:00 p.m. and are expecting us. We would need to go soon to make sure we catch them.'

'Juliet, could you and Johanna visit them now then, please? And grab the CCTV from the hotel while you're there.'

There were nods from both Juliet and Johanna.

'We have a statement from Andrew Barrington,' Otto continued, pulling out a document from his folder and holding it out, 'taken by Mia on the day of the death. What contact have you had with him since then, Mia?'

'I've been on the phone with him every day. He's moved to a hotel across the square in Neuer Markt, the Hotel Europa. His wife, Arthur's mother, is with him. Her name is Faith.' Mia consulted her notebook, making sure she was getting the names right. 'The youngest son, Henry, was here until Monday, but has now gone home, and Andrew told me this morning that he and his wife intend to do the same, either tomorrow or the next day.'

'Right. Mia, you and Sandy go to see them now, and if you haven't already told Mr Barrington about the autopsy' – Mia shook her head – 'then inform him and his wife that it is taking place tomorrow.'

With their meeting wrapped up for now, everyone stood to leave.

'Oh, Otto, is there any chance I can visit the hotel room, even if you haven't retained it?'

Otto took the final piece of paper out of his now empty folder: the CSI report from Paulina Steiner of the room examination.

'We still have the scene, no guard on it, but all locked up. I have the key in my office.'

'I always find it helps me to visit scenes. It allows me to focus my thinking – knowing that someone died there and I must do all I can to find out how they died and, if unlawfully, who killed them.'

Otto nodded in understanding, placing the papers back in the folder and handing it to Sandy so that he could have a read of it. He then led them back to his office.

As they walked through the open-plan office, Mia went off to collect her bag.

'Only thing of note in the folder,' Otto mentioned as they walked, 'are the fingerprints on both the glasses in the room – both are different and with no trace on our database. It's the same with the DNA from each of the glasses: two separate profiles, neither on our database.'

As the detectives left the police station, walking together the few minutes to the Neuer Markt, Juliet gave Mia a warning.

'Don't let him go wandering off into the cathedral or get distracted by any fancy architecture you come across – he'll be lost to us once he starts down that road.'

Sandy made no reply. After all, there was a lot of truth in what Juliet was saying.

Chapter Four

The walk from the police station to the hotel was as short as Otto had said it would be, though the Kärntner Straße, the main shopping street in Vienna's city centre, was heaving with a sea of people, relentlessly going both ways up and down the street. Once they turned right onto the Neuer Markt, the quiet and tranquillity was a welcome contrast to the bedlam of the shopping district.

As they passed the Neuer Markt hotel on their left, Juliet and Johanna peeled off and went inside. The square itself had hardly any people in it. Mia told Sandy it was one of the oldest squares in all of Vienna. Sandy noticed the fountain in the middle, which had a statue, and further along there was a church to the far right ahead of him. *Worthy of further exploration if I get a chance*, he thought.

As the Barringtons were staying there, the receptionist at the Europa knew about the dead young English man and who his parents were. She organised a discreet and quiet table in the first-floor restaurant and personally collected Andrew and Faith Barrington to come and see them.

'This is the lovely, kind and thoughtful young lady that told me Arthur had died,' Andrew said to his wife, before turning to Mia and taking her hands gently in his. 'Thank you for calling every day to make sure I'm all right.'

The Barringtons looked to be in their early fifties. Based

on their dress and manner, they gave the outward appearance of a professional couple, though the deep sadness and trauma of the last few days were evident for all to see. Their grief was etched across their faces and the way they held their bodies, looking all stooped and weighed down by the death of their eldest son, spoke volumes.

It seemed that they barely noticed Sandy standing at Mia's side.

'When can we see Arthur?' Faith asked Mia. 'When can we take him home?'

Identifying this as the perfect opportunity to introduce Sandy, Mia stepped to the side and explained that DCI McFarlane, from London, could tell them more.

Sandy shook both the Barrington's hands, gesturing for them all to sit down. 'I will try and find out for you, but…' He hesitated, knowing how upsetting this next part always was for the loved ones of the deceased. '… though we still believe Arthur died of natural causes, we haven't yet managed to identify what the illness, disease, infection or whatever it was happens to be.' Seeing that the Barringtons were taking in his every word, Sandy paused for a moment, before delivering what he knew would be a blow. 'We are having an autopsy tomorrow to see if that can help to establish his cause of death.'

Faith's whole body rocked backwards in anguish. 'Please don't cut my boy's body up. Surely you can take blood tests or X-rays or scans to find out how he died? Andrew says he seemed quite ill during the short time they had here together.'

Sandy wanted to hold Faith's hand to try and reassure her, but instead, he continued, albeit softly and patiently. 'What you are describing is a non-invasive post-mortem. We do have them sometimes in the UK, though I am not sure what happens here in Austria, but it wouldn't apply to a case like this. Our blood tests at the moment do show he had a strain of flu, though.'

Andrew looked at his wife. 'Sweetheart, they must do everything they can to find out why he died. That is all I want to know: how our son died.'

'And we will do our upmost to find out as quickly as we can,' Sandy said, before sliding out Andrew's first statement from the folder Otto had given him. 'Can we just recap, Mr Barrington? You flew here to try and convince Arthur not to marry Emily Wainwright, is that right?'

Andrew looked startled. 'No, that's not why I came.' He glanced across at his wife.

'Poor Em, she's so young. I hope this doesn't ruin the rest of her life,' Faith said in a mournful and soft voice. 'They were very much in love.'

'I wanted to convince Arthur not to give up his violin job in London,' Andrew explained. 'He would have had the opportunity to play with the most incredible musicians in the world, playing the most wonderful musical scores.'

Faith interrupted. 'But Andrew, he had only just got his job as a teaching assistant at Stamford School. He would have made such a wonderful teacher. He and Em would have been happy.' Faith's tears flowed freely now.

Undeterred, but taking hold of his wife's hand, Andrew continued. 'I rang Emily's dad, Douglas, and told him I was going to Vienna to talk to Arthur and get him to postpone the wedding so that he could keep the London job. I don't think

Douglas knew about the new plan for them not to live in London but to stay in Stamford.'

He looked at his wife, who shook her head and whispered, while using a tissue to mop her tears, 'No, Em's mum and dad knew nothing, but Freddie did – her brother.'

After a moment of quiet as a member of staff came into the restaurant, saw them, then turned quickly around and went out again, Andrew went on, clasping both of his wife's hands.

'I don't know Douglas all that well, but he said he would come with me. I told him the flight times I had booked, but there was no sign of him at the airport or on the plane. To be honest, I wasn't surprised he didn't turn up – from what I have heard about him, he is very unreliable.'

'In your statement,' Sandy said, pointing to the document in front of him, 'you say you checked into your hotel room and Arthur arrived almost immediately, looking very unwell. You then had a row and you stormed out and went to that bar.' Sandy pointed to the bar, Le Bol, across the Neuer Markt Square, which they could see easily from their seats.

Andrew shook his head, on the verge of tears. 'Saying *we* had a row isn't true. It's just not true. *I* shouted at Arthur, told him that he was throwing his music career away for a young girl. Arthur was not at all well, and he kept saying how much he loved her and that he was going to marry her no matter what I thought. I kept shouting, and when I saw I was getting nowhere, I left him to rest and stormed out of the room. Arthur, my beautiful son, was not part of the rowing. It was all and only me, shouting at him.'

As Andrew started crying in earnest, Sandy decided to

bring the conversation to a close. 'We will stop now and I will ring you after the autopsy tomorrow,' he said gently, before heading down to the reception area, leaving Mia to finish talking to the Barringtons.

When he got to the reception, Sandy slipped outside and walked towards the middle of the square. He looked at the fountain that he had spotted earlier: the Providentia fountain, featuring a statue of Providentia herself in the centre. Built in the 1700s, it had survived the heavy allied bombing of Vienna during the Second World War, when the Neuer Markt had been hit. Apt really, given that Providentia was the goddess of good foresight and governance.

A short while later, Mia appeared, and Sandy immediately checked in, making sure she was OK. It was an emotional job, dealing with grieving families. Family liaison officers were an incredible and essential part of any homicide or suspicious death investigation, and Sandy respected the role that Mia was carrying out.

Once she had assured him she was holding up, and had confirmed that she had taken fingerprints and DNA from Andrew for elimination purposes, they headed back to the Neuer Markt hotel.

They could see no sign of Juliet or Johanna, so they went straight up to the room where Arthur had died. Outside in the corridor, Mia pointed to the camera that was positioned on the door, now with an alarm that Otto had installed to protect any unknown entry into the crime scene.

As Sandy donned the forensic protective clothing that Mia had brought along for him – the paper suit, gloves, mask and over shoes – Mia called the control room to tell them that he was entering the scene.

As soon as he walked inside, Sandy could see the couch where Arthur had been found dead. He stood and took in the enormity of the tragedy of such a young person dying in that spot. After Sandy had taken a few moments to picture it all, he vowed under his breath to Arthur that he would do all he could to find out how he had died.

He looked around the room, which was not large but an above average-sized hotel room. The table and chair that had been knocked over were now righted and back in, Sandy presumed, their original position. On the side shelf next to the table were CSI markings, where Sandy assumed the cups had been found and removed for forensic examination, and from which the team had yielded the mystery fingerprints and DNA.

Glancing around the bed, it was clear it hadn't been slept in. Lying on the floor next to it was an opened small carry-on suitcase, the wheeled type. On view inside were clothes and a wash bag.

The curtains were drawn, making the room dark and eerie, especially as it was light outside.

After he had left the room, and placed his forensic suit into an exhibit bag, Sandy and Mia walked downstairs to find the manager's office. Sandy knew there had been nothing gained by his scene visit, but for him, the visiting of scenes, and in particular the scene of a death, was an essential part of an investigation.

The manager's office was situated at the back of the small reception area, and the door to the office opened just as they arrived. A short Asian man came out first, followed by a man who introduced himself to Mia and Sandy as the hotel manager. Both of them promptly left, allowing Sandy and Mia to join their colleagues inside the office.

As they sat down on the two remaining chairs, Juliet looked over at them. 'Do you want the bad news or the really bad news?'

'Go on then, the bad news first,' Sandy replied while getting his notebook out of his backpack, before realising he probably didn't need it and dropping it back in again.

'The room cleaner, who has worked here for six years, having moved to Austria from the Philippines, didn't see or hear anything.'

'I thought he was working in the room next door and heard the noise?' Mia asked.

'I will come to that in a moment,' Juliet said. 'He was on the next floor up and responded first to a radio message from the hotel reception about a disturbance.'

Sandy had now decided he *did* need his notebook after all and promptly got it out.

'On entering the room,' Juliet continued, not even glancing at the statement that Johanna had written, 'he found Arthur lying lifeless on the couch and moved straight out of the room, where he collided with the manager, who was arriving at just that time.'

'He had nothing further to add,' Johanna said, before sharing a look with Juliet.

The two immediately started giggling, leaving Sandy and Mia looking on in confusion.

'Now to the manager!' Johanna said.

Sandy could only assume that said manager was the

source of their hilarity.

'Been here man and boy for twenty-two years,' Juliet added, clearing her throat. 'He became the manager only in the last few months. Sandy, if you picture Basil Fawlty' – she looked directly at Sandy and started giggling again – 'well, that's who he must have modelled himself on!'

'The hotel has got a regular guest called…' Johanna looked at the statement momentarily to get the name right. '… Ursula Proll. She was working in the room next door and called the hotel reception to report a disturbance in the room. The manager went straight there.'

'Running up the stairs, two or three at a time,' Juliet added, smiling. 'His words, not mine.'

'He bumped into the cleaner as he went to go into the room as the cleaner was coming out,' Johanna said, before Juliet interjected.

'The manager kept saying, "Can't believe he beat me, I was virtually sprinting". "I can't believe the cleaner wasn't on the same corridor. He must have been to beat me". He just *kept* saying it.'

'Apparently, he eventually checked Arthur for a pulse, found none, then came straight out and called the police,' Johanna said. 'And we know Inspector Wagner was the first police officer to respond to the call.'

'What about the CCTV?' Sandy asked. 'Have they secured that for us?'

Juliet and Johanna looked at each other and started laughing again.

'He kept saying, "Why does it always happen to me",' Juliet said, in between her laughing. 'I swear he's exactly like

Basil Fawlty off *Fawlty Towers*, it's uncanny.'

Sandy chuckled, then tried to shift the conversation back to the matter at hand. 'CCTV?' he asked again.

'Broken for the last two weeks. It was on his to-do list to fix,' Johanna responded. 'It is fixed now, apparently, but obviously it's too late.'

'You're telling me there was no CCTV across the whole hotel at the time of Arthur's death?' Mia said, shaking her head. 'Who's going to tell Inspector Wagner? It's not going to be me.'

Sandy shook his head, as did Juliet, leaving Johanna to say, 'I suppose it will have to be me then.'

Having done all that they could that day, they agreed with Mia that she would bring a digital forensic investigator with her in the morning to trawl through the square, in particular the bar that Andrew said he went to straight after his row with his son. They would also check the hotel's wireless router for both Arthur and Andrew's phones, to see when they connected and disconnected from the router.

It wasn't much to go on, but at least it might help them create some sort of digital trail to match up Andrew's statement with what actually happened.

Chapter Five

The drive the next morning to the Medical University of Vienna was exactly as Otto had said: it only took them ten minutes.

'Where did you eat last night?' Otto asked as they parked the car near the forensic medical centre entrance.

'I think it was called Reinthaler's Beisl,' Sandy said, looking at Juliet for confirmation, but she just shrugged. 'We had to queue outside for a few minutes and it was very crowded and cosy when we got inside. Food was great though. Johanna recommended it.'

'No doubt you had the wiener schnitzel and the sauerkraut?' Otto said. 'And don't tell me, the apple strudel to follow? Gosh, very touristy.'

Both Sandy and Juliet nodded.

'Washed down nicely with a couple of beers too,' Juliet added.

As they entered the examination room in the forensic medical centre, they could see the forensic pathologist, who introduced himself as Professor Franz Von Tripp. Sandy misheard the surname initially, and thought he had said Von Trapp. He had briefly considered asking him whether he was related to the family of the *Sound of Music*, and was glad he'd decided against it, once he realised his mistake. That would not have gone down well.

The room was much bigger than any post-mortem examination room Sandy had experienced before, and had a few banks of seats on the sides at both ends, no doubt for students. They took a seat at the nearest point to the examination table being used that morning. Around the table were Paulina Steiner, the CSI whom Otto had been using for the investigation, and Johanna, who was going to take exhibits. The professor and two of his assistants were also there. All of them were clothed in green scrubs and had on hat coverings and masks. They were all also double gloved.

The room itself was a lot brighter than other examination rooms Sandy had been in before. Even so, Professor Von Tripp, one of his assistants, and the CSI had bright, movable ceiling-mounted lights beside them that they were using to scrutinise Arthur's neck.

As this was the first time he had seen Arthur, Sandy was struck by how young he looked – still just a boy, really. His very small physical frame and the lack of hair on his head, with it having been shaved ready for the autopsy, only added to this image of youthfulness.

'Was this bruise to Mr Barrington's neck visible when you saw him at the hotel, Inspector Wagner?' the professor asked, pointing to a blue-yellow tinged bruise on the right side of the neck. He turned the head, and there was another area of bruising the other side of the neck, but it was less defined.

Otto and Paulina looked at each other and shook their heads. They had both seen Arthur's body, and Paulina in particular had closely examined him. The report from the medical examiner hadn't mentioned it either, but he had only completed a fairly cursory examination, looking for signs of life and any visible trauma wounds. This bruise had clearly come out during the time after death.

'There appears to be bright blue woollen or synthetic-type fibres in and around the bruising on the right side,' the professor said. 'But I can't see anything visible on the left.'

Paulina was diligently taking photographs of the neck, including some marks at the rear of the neck, which the professor suggested might be finger marks. The professor continued talking, but mostly to Paulina and his assistants, rather than the detectives.

'I don't want to use tape on this area to lift the fibres,' he said, again indicating to the area around both of the bruises. 'Can I have a couple of those swabs we use to get glass and fibres out of hair please?'

Paulina went off to her CSI case to see if she had any with her, which luckily she did. She passed them to Professor Von Tripp.

'What does this mean?' Otto asked, his anxiety clear for all to see.

The professor looked at him. 'This, I believe, indicates blunt force trauma to the tissues of the neck, possibly caused by a ligature. Did you find anything that would fit with that in the room?'

Otto could only shake his head.

'Then my initial suspicions are that young Mr Barrington was strangled using an advanced choke-type hold.'

It was strange that nothing had been seen at the scene that fit the colour of the fibres. Sandy knew that Otto had diligently applied the principles of "The Golden Hour", acting early to secure any seemingly significant material that might otherwise be lost to the investigation. He could see Otto's anxiety increasing with the realisation that he might have missed something.

'This kind of chokehold,' the professor continued, 'is most commonly used by special forces in the army and police officers. They called it the "carotid restraint hold" back in the day. It can at times be fatal, so it's not used much by law enforcement anymore – they just use guns nowadays, don't they.' He chuckled. 'Let's see what the rest of the autopsy brings and whether I can support my suspicions.'

Though Sandy couldn't see his mouth due to the mask he was wearing, he thought he was smiling by the twinkle in his eyes. The professor was clearly enjoying himself.

Once the swabbing and more photographs had been completed, the autopsy began in earnest. Professor Von Tripp was a pathologist who liked to talk as he worked, no doubt due to him being a very accomplished lecturer in his field of forensic medicine.

He spoke to the detectives throughout. 'As you know, we've had toxicology completed, which showed no sign of disease other than a common strain of influenza. The X-ray showed no broken bones.'

'Have you ever come across sudden adult death syndrome?' Sandy asked, remembering his conversation with Grandad Tom.

'I have.' The professor stopped what he was doing to look directly at Sandy. 'Have you?'

'No,' Sandy replied uneasily. 'But my grandad was a senior police detective and he mentioned to me a case that he had involving this.'

‘I always think there is a cause to be found somewhere.’ The professor had returned to his preparation for his first incision, which looked likely to be in and around the throat area. ‘Probably heart, maybe a rare chromosome or a liver issue.’ He then looked around at one of his assistants. ‘When will the results of the CT scan be with us? Helpful before I start on the brain in particular, but also the other major organs and the soft tissue around this neck trauma.’

The assistant scuttled off to the corner of the room where there was a desk, on which stood a computer monitor.

The professor pointed around the eyes of Arthur Barrington and a small area above the bruising.

‘See here and here, there is petechiae bruising.’

Although Sandy couldn’t see what he was talking about, as he was not quite close enough to the body to see this tiny detail, he knew what the professor meant.

He continued with his lecture. ‘This is pinpoint bruising, which can indicate asphyxiation or strangulation or other causes, so it is helpful in this case but not by any means conclusive support.’ He pointed the bright portable light into Arthur’s right ear. ‘No bleeding in here. Only sometimes found in these sorts of cases.’

The professor then opened Arthur’s mouth as wide as he could, which Sandy found, as he was sure anyone else would, very disconcerting.

‘There are a number of recent papers and studies that talk, unhelpfully in this case, about drowning, but they do say that reddening to the teeth and gums might also support strangulation or asphyxiation.’ As he pointed to the teeth, he continued, ‘See here?’

Sandy couldn't see what he was pointing to.

'There is definitely some reddening, but the research isn't confirmatory and there are research papers that equally dispute this as a finding. Quite frankly, I think it is a load of rubbish.'

This brought a laugh from the room. The professor was no doubt an entertaining lecturer.

'Where does this take us then?' Sandy asked.

'All adding to the picture, that is where it takes us, young man,' the professor said, definitely smiling.

'The CT scan analysis has arrived in your inbox, Professor,' the assistant said.

He walked across and looked at the screen and read the report. 'As I thought.'

'What is your thought?' Otto asked.

'The deep tissue around the neck trauma fits with my initial thoughts and the brain shows signs of encephalopathy.'

'What do you mean by that?' Otto asked, looking totally confused.

Sandy knew and wanted to answer, but quite rightly thought it best for the professor to do so.

'Damage to the structure of the brain,' the professor said, before he focused back on his autopsy.

During the next couple of hours, he worked hard, taking samples and asking for photographs to be taken.

On one occasion, he said, 'A crack to the hyoid bone. How very interesting. Paulina, photographs please. Johanna, exhibit bag please.'

Sandy watched in amazement at the master at work. The professors notes were beginning to have an order to them, and the evidence of an unnatural death was building up considerably.

At the end of the autopsy, Professor Franz Von Tripp took his gloves off, placed them in an evidence bag and walked over to the table that Johanna was working from. He took the pen she offered and proceeded to sign all the exhibits to make certain that continuity was ensured.

The assistants were still busy at work washing Arthur and the stainless steel table his body was lying on. One of them was stitching away at his head and all around the neck, where a lot of samples had been taken.

What a surreal sight, Sandy thought. You had to compartmentalise seeing this sort of thing; if not, it could eat away at you.

Before the professor went out to get changed, he came over to the detectives. 'Pending further pathological examination, my initial findings are that Arthur Barrington died by strangulation.'

'Not by hands around the throat strangulation, but by this arm around the throat-type mechanism – the chokehold?' Juliet asked.

The professor called over one of his assistants and stood behind them. He placed his right arm around the assistant, pushing his bicep into the neck area, with his left arm almost clamping it in place across the throat area.

'This is what I mean,' the professor said, as he swiftly let go of his assistant, who wasn't smiling in the least.

'So, it would have taken a strong man to be able to kill using this movement?' Otto asked.

'Trying to understand or make sense of the actual pressure

applied to the neck is not as useful as you would think as it is variable. The amount of strength required to compress the jugular vein and carotid artery is less than you think. It can vary from one person to the next, depending on development of the neck muscles. Arthur, as you can see, was a very slight man.' The professor looked over at Arthur and his assistants at work. 'He also would probably have been, at the time of his death, weak due to the influenza. So, I can't help with the amount of strength needed or the amount of time that it would have taken to cause the trauma that caused the fatality, especially if the assailant knew what they were doing. A small boy or girl, if Arthur was sat down at the right height, could have caused this death.'

'We are definitely looking at this being a murder enquiry then?' Otto said, rubbing anxiously at his face and head.

'You will have to wait for my full report for confirmation, but absolutely, yes. I believe that, based on my findings to date, this young man' – he pointed at Arthur's body – 'Mr Arthur Barrington, was murdered.'

CHAPTER SIX

As they left the examination room at the university medical centre, Otto called out to Johanna and Paulina. 'Small meeting room in one hour, please.'

He didn't wait for a reply from them as he carried on striding out of the building, with Sandy and Juliet struggling to keep up.

Before they reached the car, Otto was on his phone. 'Mia, small meeting room in one hour. There have been developments.'

Not one word was exchanged between the three of them on the drive back to the police office.

Once he had parked, Otto turned to them. 'Sorry, I am more than a bit distracted. I need to see my boss, Superintendent Isabella Mahler, immediately. Grab some lunch and I'll see you both shortly.' He again didn't wait for a reply, leaving Juliet and Sandy almost speechless outside.

As they were close to St Stephen's square, they decided to head there for a bite to eat, and ended up sitting outside a café with coffee and baguettes.

'That was a surprise,' Juliet said. 'I was sure this morning when we left our hotel we wouldn't get any answers from the post-mortem. Unascertained was the most likely outcome, wasn't it, Sandy?'

'Absolutely,' Sandy replied before biting into his next

mouthful. 'He was good though, Professor Von Tripp. I look forward to seeing Inspector Wagner's plans, but he has realistically only got a suspect pool of one at the moment, doesn't he?'

Once they had wrapped up lunch, they headed back to the police station.

The walk to the small meeting room took them past Otto Wagner's office, which had a window looking into it and a glass door. They heard him even before they got to it.

'What do you mean there is no CCTV? What do you mean it wasn't working?' His voice got louder. 'I don't believe this!'

Otto was clearly a man under immense pressure, and the stress was showing.

As they went past the office, Johanna came straight out and followed them, shaking her head, indicating that it hadn't been a pleasant experience.

Already in the meeting room was Mia, a man who was presumably the digital forensic investigator, Paulina, and now the three of them. A uniform inspector followed shortly afterwards, just before Otto arrived.

The briefing began and Otto outlined briefly for Mia, the uniform inspector, and the digital forensic investigator what had been established at the post-mortem.

'Who are our suspects?' Otto asked, though this was clearly rhetorical as he carried on talking. 'Andrew Barrington is the last known person to have seen his son alive, so he is our prime suspect.'

'What about the two Albanian boys that you mentioned yesterday as currently suspected of breaking into hotel rooms?' Sandy asked, while he frantically looked through his notes to see if he had written down their names, but as he couldn't find them, he suspected he hadn't been given them.

'Superintendent Mahler told me to go careful with the boys – there is some other intelligence building that they may be in the picture with. Although she hasn't been told exactly what this is, she thinks it best we don't cause an issue until we have something more definite to indicate they are involved.'

Well, Sandy thought, *that shuts down any further discussion about them as suspects.*

Looking at the uniform inspector, Otto continued. 'I would like you to send two officers to arrest Andrew Barrington for the murder of his son. He should be at the Hotel Europa in Neuer Markt with his wife Faith Barrington.'

Although fully understanding that this was obviously the right course of action, Sandy was concerned for the two parents that he had seen only the previous day.

'I wonder if Johanna, who has met them, and Juliet, ought to go as well. I think this would be better for both of the Barringtons, Mrs Barrington in particular.' Thinking that he was in for a strong discussion about this as a course of action, Sandy kept talking. 'We can treat parents who have lost their child with sensitivity but still have an investigative mindset, can't we?' He looked around the room and saw nods, including from Otto. 'Andrew Barrington may well be guilty, but he might not be.'

'Yes, that makes sense,' Otto agreed. He nodded at Johanna and Juliet for them to go. 'Look for a blue jumper as well please, so we can compare the fibres with those found at the autopsy on Arthur's neck.'

After the uniform inspector, Johanna, and Juliet had left, Mia outlined what CCTV they had recovered. The bar, Le Bol, that Andrew Barrington had told them he had gone to after storming out on his son, had some good CCTV, which they now had possession of for the relevant times. There was also a restaurant closer to the Neuer Markt hotel that had CCTV that went out into the square and almost covered up to, but not quite, the doors of the hotel. On the opposite side of the square, the Hotel Europa, which the Barringtons were now staying in, also had CCTV that went into the square. One camera looked towards, but didn't quite reach, the Neuer Markt hotel.

The digital forensic investigator was going to examine the footage and print off any relevant still photographs for them. Hopefully this would help piece together Andrew Barrington's movements.

∞

Johanna knocked loudly on the Barrington's hotel room door. It was a knock that meant business. Juliet was standing next to her in the tight corridor, and at the end of the landing by the lift and staircase were two constables, carrying their weapons just in case they were needed.

When the door opened, Andrew Barrington stood there with a shocked and worried expression. On recognising Johanna, his face relaxed.

'Come in,' he said, gesturing for the detectives to enter the hotel room. 'We have been worrying about what happened at the post-mortem this morning and we were debating how long to wait before calling Mia or DCI McFarlane.'

As they entered the room, one of the uniformed constables came up behind them and surreptitiously placed their foot in the door to stop the door closing.

Faith Barrington was sitting upright in bed, a magazine on her lap. It looked like Andrew had been sitting by the table in the room, looking at his phone, which was lying on the tabletop. On seeing the detectives, Faith jumped to her feet.

'Mr Barrington, there is no easy way to do this,' Johanna said, clearing her throat as she did so and summoning up all of her courage. 'I have come to ask you to accompany us to the police station.'

Andrew Barrington nodded and placed his phone in his pocket as he slipped into a pair of brown shoes.

'It's not quite like before though,' Johanna added. 'I have to tell you that I am arresting you for the murder of your son, Arthur Barrington.'

Johanna didn't have a chance to caution him – on the word "arrest", Faith fainted and dropped like a stone onto the carpeted floor.

Andrew Barrington, who hadn't quite got his right foot into his shoe, hobbled over to her and went down onto his hands and knees, putting his wife's head gently in his hands. 'Faith, Faith, it is going to be OK.' He looked up at Johanna for reassurance. 'It is just normal procedure. We both know I would never harm our son.'

The noise had summoned the uniformed police officers at speed, and the hotel room was now not only very hot, but extremely overcrowded – not in the slightest bit conducive to help someone who had fainted.

Taking her own phone out of her jacket pocket, Juliet phoned Sandy.

'Mrs Barrington has fainted. Can you get Mia to come to their hotel room as soon as possible please?'

Juliet didn't wait for a reply and ended the call. Looking at Johanna whilst trying to reassure Andrew Barrington, she said, 'I will wait here with Mrs Barrington until Mia Eckhart arrives, so if you all go now it will be less crowded and I can make Mrs Barrington more comfortable.'

They all left the room as a now stirring Faith Barrington was helped onto the bed by Juliet.

Andrew Barrington paused at the door and looked at his wife. 'Don't worry about me, I'll be fine.' His face, though, looked anything but fine, with worry, concern and a certain amount of fear etched all over it.

After they left, Juliet put the kettle on for a hot drink for them both. She asked Faith where Andrew's clothes were, so that she could look through them for the blue jumper that they were after. He was wearing an orange one at the moment, so there was a chance she might find it in his suitcase.

Whilst she wanted to find out what had happened to Arthur, a part of her hoped she didn't find anything. A father killing his own son would be a true tragedy.

∞

Sitting in the interview room at the station was Andrew Barrington, Johanna, and another detective that had been seconded to help with the interview. There was no lawyer present – Andrew had said he didn't want one telling him to make “no comment”. He wanted to do all that he could to help find out how his son had died, and if it was an unlawful act, to find out how that had happened.

The rest of the team were able to downstream monitor the interview from the meeting room. Initially, only Otto and Sandy were in the room, but they were soon joined by Mia and Juliet.

‘How come you’re back so quickly?’ Sandy asked Juliet.

Mia responded before Juliet could, as they both took their seats to watch the interview. ‘Mrs Barrington wanted to be here to support her husband, so she’s sitting downstairs in the small room off the reception area.’

‘Did you find the blue jumper?’ Sandy asked.

‘No, nothing in the hotel room, anyway,’ Juliet answered.

Looking at Mia, Otto asked, ‘Did you notice if there were any bins on the way to or from Le Bol that he might have dumped it in?’

‘No, I didn’t,’ Mia replied, standing. ‘I will go and check now.’

Juliet went with her. It was only five minutes or so to the Neuer Markt, so they would have an answer for them soon.

‘The initial findings from the post-mortem,’ Sandy heard Johanna say, reading from her notebook, ‘are that the forensic pathologist believes Arthur was strangled using a chokehold.’

Andrew Barrington almost rose from his chair. ‘What! Who would do that to my beautiful, sweet and innocent boy?’

‘We suspect that someone might be you, Mr Barrington,’ Johanna said softly.

‘Of course it wasn’t me! I have never laid a hand on him or my other son in my life. If they needed any discipline, it wasn't me but my wife who took that role on.'

'So, you deny that you did this?'

'Yes, it wasn't me. I left Arthur to sleep. He felt quite unwell,' Andrew replied, now with his head in his hands. 'Who could have done this?'

A tear or two was falling from his eyes and rolling down his face. He rummaged about in his pocket and found a hanky to dab his face with.

'You told me and DC Eckhart that you had lost your temper with your son and had shouted at him. Did that loss of temper go further and you strangled him in your rage?' Johanna probed gently again.

'Absolutely not.' Andrew was now indignant.

'If not you, who then?'

'I have no idea,' Andrew said, shaking his head. 'I was only gone thirty to forty minutes at the most. I don't think he had fallen out with anyone. When we visited his room and spoke to his work colleagues there, they expressed how much they had liked Arthur.'

Back in the meeting room, Mia and Juliet had returned and shook their heads. There were no bins in the square or any publicly accessible ones in Le Bol, and no jumper left behind there.

The digital forensic investigator walked into the meeting room with a number of photographs of Arthur Barrington arriving near the hotel and then Andrew leaving and returning forty minutes later. In the photographs, Andrew Barrington was wearing an orange jumper, the same one that they could see him wearing on the screen in front of them from the interview downstream.

Otto stood. 'I'm going to go down and get him released. I am not saying it can't be him, if the blue fibres are a red herring, but let's not keep a grieving father in custody longer than we should.'

'Agreed. It looks like that orange jumper is the only one he's got,' Sandy said, which prompted a slight chuckle from Mia and Juliet. 'Shall I go down with Mia and explain to Andrew and his wife, after he has been released, what the next steps are likely to be? Might be worth taking possession of the orange jumper too, just in case. Though we'll have to check he has another one – wouldn't want him freezing to death on our watch.'

CHAPTER SEVEN

After releasing Andrew Barrington and speaking with him and his wife, Sandy and Mia headed through the city to Arthur's lodgings, to see if they could speak to some of his colleagues. As they walked, they passed part of the Spanish Riding School, where the famous Lipizzaner breed of horses were kept. The majestic white horses had been bred in Vienna for several hundred years, and as they looked out over a paddock where some of the horses were going about their paces, Sandy couldn't help but be in awe of the magnificent creatures.

As they walked closer, he realised Juliet and Johanna were also standing, watching the horses. They clearly hadn't made too much progress getting to Arthur's lodgings.

'How did you get on with Mr and Mrs Barrington?' Juliet asked, as they set off together.

'Fine. They are distraught, as you can imagine,' Sandy replied, trying to quicken their pace as Mia and Johanna stormed ahead. Juliet did walk exceptionally slowly, and added to this, her heels did not suit the cobbled streets. 'When I asked for his jumper, he said gladly, he would give us anything we wanted to help find out what had happened to his son, even his right arm.'

'Are they going back to England or staying?' Juliet sounded slightly out of breath.

'They are going home tomorrow, but only if they can see Arthur in a chapel of rest before then. If not, definitely the next day. I promised to call Professor Von Tripp in the morning, which Otto was happy with.'

They headed down a quiet side street, making their way to a typical, historical Vienna townhouse – the house where Arthur had been staying. The door was open and Mia and Johanna had already entered. The noise from the people that lived there, or were visiting there, was not what you would expect from talented musicians. Indeed, it was jarring, with different pieces being practiced all at the same time.

Deciding to split up, Johanna and Mia went to talk to the residents, to see what they could find out about Arthur and the year that he had spent with them, and if there was anyone that may have had a grudge or fallen out with Arthur. Sandy and Juliet, meanwhile, headed to Arthur's former bedroom, to look through his belongings.

The room that Arthur shared with two others was cramped; Arthur's bed was unmade and his few belongings sat in a couple of holdalls, one large and one small. The clothes were not folded, just thrown inside. His violin was lying on his bed in its case with a document case next to it, which, when examined, contained reams of sheet music.

'Oh my word,' Juliet gasped, a tear rolling down her cheek. She had in her hand a large folder that looked full of handwritten letters, which she had removed from the small holdall. 'These are love letters from Emily. I feel like I'm intruding; these show a clearly very passionate, caring and undeniable love affair between the two of them.'

'Can you read them, Juliet?' Sandy asked, not wanting

to look at them himself. He felt only one of them needed to intrude by doing so. 'There may be something in them that might help us explain what happened. I can give them back to Emily when I visit with an update. I'm not going to mention their existence to Arthur's parents.'

As they finished looking through Arthur's belongings, Sandy realised that he had never once sent or received a handwritten letter from his own girlfriend, Hannah. Letter writing was an almost forgotten method of communication, taken over, certainly in Sandy and Hannah's busy lives, by WhatsApp and text. How lovely for Emily and Arthur to have shared their love for each other this way.

Once they had finished looking through Arthur's belongings, they went to wait in the street outside the house, looking sorrowfully at Arthur's last place of residence.

It wasn't long before Mia and Johanna joined them.

'Not one person had a bad word to say about him,' Mia said. 'Arthur was extremely well liked by everybody.'

'They also told us that Arthur had an incredible talent and a great career ahead of him,' Johanna added.

'No one had a grudge because Arthur had got a part at any time that they felt they had deserved instead?' Sandy asked, hoping there was at least another line of enquiry or suspect they could investigate further.

'No, nothing like that,' Johanna said, while looking at Mia for confirmation, who just nodded in agreement.

'I will come back in the morning to pack up Arthur's things and see what his mother and father want to do with them,' Mia said, before heading back into the house.

She came back moments later with Arthur's violin in its case.

'I will take this to them now on the way back to the police station and see how they are after Mr Barrington's traumatic arrest.'

'It wasn't a traumatic arrest, Mia,' Johanna said, backed up by Juliet. 'I was so sweet about it.'

'So much so that Faith Barrington fainted,' Mia retorted, unconvinced.

Before Johanna could reply, a call came in from Otto. He told her that he had received a call from the manager of the Neuer Markt hotel. Ursula Proll, the lady who was in the hotel room next to the Barringtons, was back in Vienna and at the hotel now, if she could go and see her.

'I am going to see Fräulein Proll if either of you two want to join me?' Johanna said. 'And if the manager of the hotel says sorry to me once more for the CCTV not working, I think I will swing for him.' She started laughing. 'Better I do it than Inspector Wagner.'

'I'll go with you,' Sandy said. 'Juliet, if you go with Mia to see the Barringtons at the Hotel Europa, I will meet you back at our hotel before we go out for dinner.'

∞

An extremely elegant-looking Ursula Proll was waiting in the lounge area for them. The manager was luckily nowhere to be seen, but the detectives were sure he was lurking somewhere, ready to jump out at them.

After introductions, it was plain to see that Fräulein Proll was every bit the high-flying business woman. She was articulate and intelligent and had charismatic interpersonal skills that had the detectives following her every word.

'I returned to my room from a meeting in the city,' Ursula said, sipping from a glass of white wine. 'I went up in the lift with the man I have been told is Mr Barrington.' She looked at Johanna. 'The father of the victim, I understand?'

'He was the man in the room next to you, is that right?' Johanna asked, looking longingly at Ursula's wine.

'Yes, that's right. We said hello to each other, and I had no sooner kicked off my shoes when I heard a knock on the door. I opened it, but it was in fact his door being knocked on by a young man, who I now know to be the young Mr Barrington. I watched as they embraced – so warm, it was. Beautiful, the love of a father and son.'

The two detectives looked at each other. This fitted with Andrew Barrington's account exactly.

'I know it was several days ago now, but do you remember what the father was wearing?' Sandy asked.

'Yes, I do actually. Well, not his trousers.' Ursula paused for a moment while she was trying to picture the scene. 'I can only say dark-coloured trousers, but he had on an orange jumper, which I thought looked very stylish – that is why I remember.' She smiled a devastatingly beautiful smile.

'How soon after that did you hear an argument?' Sandy asked, busy taking notes but always looking at Fräulein Proll when he asked any questions.

'At that time, I didn't hear an argument as such. I just heard one voice, which I am presuming was the father's voice, raised almost to a shout. Then the door came open and slammed shut.' Ursula, looking a bit sheepish now, added, 'I couldn't resist looking out of my door, and saw the father going into the lift and stair entrance.'

'What happened then? Did you hear him come back or anyone else arrive next door?' asked Sandy.

'Not for a little while,' Ursula said.

She took her time to think and remember what had exactly happened. It appeared sipping her wine helped her thought process. Sandy was now also longingly thinking about alcohol. It had been a long day and a post-mortem was always an uncomfortable experience. Alcohol helped him to blot all that out; to compartmentalise.

Putting down her wine glass, Ursula continued. 'I got changed out of my work suit into a loose-fitting dress, then put my headphones on and started my laptop up to complete some online training.' Ursula looked at the detectives. 'How long would that have taken, ten minutes or so? Oh, wait, I made myself a cup of coffee before sitting down at the desk.'

No words were said for a few seconds, and both Johanna and Sandy nodded encouragingly at Ursula to continue.

'Then over the sound of the voice in my headphones, I heard a loud shout and what I would describe as a crashing sound.'

'Had you heard a knock on the door before that?' Sandy asked.

'No.' Ursula paused again. 'There may have been one, but the noise from my headphones would have drowned it out.'

'Was the shout in English?' Johanna asked.

'I don't know that either. It was a loud voice that I heard. Might have been more than one voice, thinking about it now.

It did all go quiet for maybe a few minutes. I had by now turned off my laptop. I was listening intently, but no more sound came from the room.'

'What happened then?' Sandy asked, encouraging Ursula to continue.

'After a short while, I heard the door slam. I phoned reception immediately and then looked out of the door, but there was no sign at the lift and stairs entrance of anyone. They must have run out very quickly – I was just a few moments on the phone to reception.'

The detectives thanked Fräulein Proll for her help, and Johanna told her that she would bring a written statement based on what she had said for her to sign before she left Vienna again.

'You will have it all on CCTV anyway, the comings and goings from the room, won't you?' Ursula said to the smiles and shaking heads of the detectives.

As they stood to leave, they saw the hotel manager lurking behind some house plants in the corner of the lounge area, pretending not to look at them, even though he clearly was. Sandy stifled a laugh. He really was a comedic caricature.

Chapter Eight

The next morning, since Otto was tied up in meetings until lunchtime and Mia and Johanna were at a court hearing with another case, Sandy convinced Juliet that they should do some sightseeing. Otto didn't need them until two p.m., and there was nothing else that they could do that morning regarding the investigation, so this was, in Sandy's eyes, a perfect way to spend their time.

They started their day by taking a short walk to the Hofburg, the Imperial Palace, which according to Sandy's internet search was the number one tourist attraction in Vienna. It had been the main home of the Habsburgs, one of the longest lasting and most important royal families in Europe. As one of their main residences, the Habsburgs had spent a fortune on making the palace one of the most impressive in Europe, it's majesty preserved for Juliet and Sandy to see on their guided tour.

The tour had been Juliet's idea – unbeknownst to Sandy, she had decided it would be the best way to keep him moving forward at a decent pace and prevent him lagging behind, looking at all of the exhibits.

Sandy was delighted with their visit: seeing the apartments of Emperor Franz Joesph and his wife Empress Elizabeth had been a treat, as he had been fascinated to learn that the palace buildings also housed both the offices of the Federal

President of Austria and the Chancellor of Austria. *They truly are fortunate to have such a beautiful location steeped in such history as their day-to-day offices,* Sandy thought.

As they walked back to the hotel to collect their laptops before the afternoon briefing, Sandy received a call from Professor Von Tripp.

'Professor, thanks for returning my call,' Sandy said, adjusting the phone from one hand to the other. He had tried to call earlier, but the professor had been lecturing. 'Two quick things. Firstly, the Barringtons. Arthur's mother and father would like to visit. I presume you have a chapel of rest so they can see their son. Is that possible?'

'Of course. My technicians have done a marvellous job of reconstructing Arthur. I know how traumatic it is for families, but the body itself won't add to the trauma as is sometimes the case,' the professor replied. 'Let me pre-empt your next question, if I may. How long is it going to take to complete all of the different tests? The autopsy was only yesterday – give me a chance, young man!'

'No, that wasn't it actually,' Sandy said, laughing with the professor. 'The family want to know when they can have their son repatriated to England?'

'From my point of view, I have all the photographs, X-rays and scans that I need, plus all of the samples that I need as well, so I have no problem releasing Arthur's body.'

'I will tell the family and our consulate offices here in Vienna to start thinking about how to organise that then,' Sandy replied, knowing how pleased Mr and Mrs Barrington would be for this small crumb of comfort.

'Hold your horses, young man,' the professor said

forcefully. 'You must let them know that we have those samples and that they won't be returned for some considerable time, if there is even anything left after our tests. They may wish for us to ethically dispose of the samples for them. Besides, it is not only my agreement you need. It is Inspector Wagner's for one, and as I am sure you have found out by now, he is an anxious man. Of course, the final agreement comes from the examining magistrate.'

A decision for our team meeting this afternoon, Sandy thought, as he approached his hotel room.

No sooner had Sandy pressed the key card on his door lock and opened the door fractionally, when he knew something wasn't right. It was like a second sense; he could only describe it as if there was a disturbance in the air. Of course, he wasn't like the fictional Jedi warriors in the *Star Wars* movie franchise, but he knew, he just knew, something was amiss.

He opened the door further and saw that the curtains had been drawn. He had opened them when he left, but the cleaner might have pulled them across. What this meant was that the room, although not quite in darkness, was so dim that he could see hardly anything.

Before he could step in any further to investigate whether he was just imagining it, he was grabbed and forcefully shoved out of the way of the door.

His attacker seized their opportunity, opening the door and racing quickly out into the hotel corridor.

Regaining his footing almost immediately, Sandy ran after them, and was able to tap tackle the person to the floor, hitting them hard on the ankle, a move he had perfected during his years of playing rugby.

His attacker, dressed in a blue hoodie, dark trousers, and a dark blue woollen balaclava, went sprawling on the floor. Sandy was on his feet immediately, and in a forward movement, he jumped and sprawled on top of the person, who by the looks of it was a young man. He had a hold of Sandy's backpack that he kept his laptop and notebook inside.

As if he was grabbing and wrestling a rugby ball from an opponent, Sandy managed to prize the backpack from the thief.

Just as he was in the process of calling out to Juliet for help, as they were directly outside her room, Sandy was grabbed from behind and was put into a choke-type hold by another person, who had come up behind him.

Struggling against their hold, Sandy was able to move his head fractionally, and realised his new attacker also had on a blue balaclava. The fabric had shifted up his neck, revealing three star-shaped tattoos: the outside two both the same size and silver coloured, and the larger one in the centre a faded red.

In his current position, despite the chokehold from behind, Sandy had an advantage, and was able to shift his neck and head to loosen the second attacker's hold whilst also keeping hold of his backpack and the person he was lying on top of, who was writhing about viciously while trying to get free.

Realising the chokehold wasn't freeing his friend, the attacker behind Sandy let go and stood up, taking a step back. With all of his might, he kicked Sandy hard in the ribs. The pain was unbearable, and Sandy screamed out in pain, his grip on the person he was holding starting to loosen. Another kick followed, forcing him to release the first attacker as he concentrated all his efforts on holding onto his backpack and trying to defend himself.

As the youth he had been holding got to his feet, he took aim for Sandy's head, when suddenly, Juliet's door opened.

At the sound, the youths ran off at speed along the corridor, down the stairs, and presumably out of the hotel.

Sandy was still lying on the floor and unable to stand as Juliet leaned over him, full of concern.

Eventually, they managed to manoeuvre Sandy into a seating position. With all the commotion, numerous people had begun to appear in the corridor. One of the hotel management told them they had called for an ambulance, much to Sandy's dismay. He kept saying he would be fine, but the pain to his ribcage was telling him the opposite – that in fact, he wasn't fine at all.

At least I managed to keep hold of my backpack, thought Sandy. He might not have been able to apprehend the thieves, but he had been able to retain his property, and had got a decent look at his attackers.

He would bet good money on them being involved in Arthur's death.

∞

The multitude of painkillers the doctors and nurses had given Sandy were making him feel groggy, but he was thankful that at least they were dimming the pain in his side.

He was lying on a bed in a curtained off area of the closest hospital's emergency department. He didn't know the name of the hospital; he didn't remember much of the journey there, to be honest – he had been too busy trying to block out the pain by concentrating on the rhythmic sound of the oxygen coming out of its cylinder.

The emergency department was full of people, much like in the UK, and because he had arrived in an ambulance and on a trolley, it appeared that he was able, to a certain extent, to jump the queue.

He was glad there were no monitors attached to him. It meant he could move about freely on the bed. Well, as freely as the pain in his side allowed. His hideous hospital gown crinkled as he moved – a necessary evil for them to take X-rays, an ultrasound, and a CT scan of his chest and stomach area. Sandy was not sure where his clothes were or his backpack, but he hoped Juliet had possession of them.

He could see his phone, lying on the table next to him. The table only contained a water jug and an empty glass, which he filled up. He was very thirsty. Also on the top was a clean vomit pot. Sandy did remember being sick as soon as he had got to the emergency department. Gosh! That had hurt so much – so much so that he vowed to do all that he could to fight that feeling and not be sick again.

Glancing at his phone, he saw that the time was now past four p.m. He must have been in the hospital for well over two hours. His phone had also gone crazy with messages and missed calls. They were from his boss Jane Watson, his girlfriend Hannah, his mother and father, his two sisters and his grandfathers. Gosh! Juliet *had* been busy telling everyone she knew that Sandy had been beaten up by two youths. He knew he shouldn't, but he currently felt very embarrassed.

The first people he saw were Juliet and Mia.

'What happened in the team meeting?' Sandy asked.

'Nothing,' Juliet answered. 'Inspector Wagner cancelled it until tomorrow morning. Forget about work, how are you feeling?'

'Groggy and in pain,' Sandy said, while indicating to his side.

The next person to walk in was Otto Wagner.

'How are you feeling, Sandy?' he asked.

'He's just answered that,' Juliet said. 'He's fine. Not sure what he's doing lounging about like this.'

'I am so sorry, Otto, that I couldn't keep hold of at least one of them,' Sandy said, looking forlornly at Otto. 'They must be your hotel thieves, and I suspect probably the murderers of Arthur Barrington, certainly based on their blue outfits and the chokehold one of them tried on me.'

'Not strong enough,' Juliet said, chuckling.

'I am! I was!' Sandy said indignantly. 'I had a hold of one and kept the other off me until he started booting me.'

'I would have kept hold of both of them,' Juliet said smugly. 'You know I'm stronger than you.'

They were all laughing now and this light-hearted moment had lifted the mood nicely, even if it was hurting Sandy dreadfully to laugh.

'Don't worry,' Otto said. 'We have reliable intelligence as to who they are, and I think if we push the informant, we will be able to house them quite easily.'

'Do you know who the informant is?' Sandy asked.

'I don't. It is all being kept very secret. Something big is going on.' Otto looked out of the curtain to see if anyone was nearby that might hear their conversation. 'My boss and I are being kept in the dark, but she has a meeting either this evening or tomorrow morning where she'll be briefed on as much as she is allowed to know.'

The doctor arrived and instructed everyone other than Juliet to leave.

'You have been very lucky, young man,' she said, smiling. 'No internal injuries and, incredibly, no broken bones.'

'So, am I free to go then and get back to work?' Sandy asked, grinning. This was good news. As he shifted, the bruising at his side twinged. 'I'll need some heavy-duty painkillers though.'

'Not so fast, young man. You have extensive bruising already and you need to wait for a nurse to strap you up.' She looked at Juliet for support, even though she didn't know their relationship. 'In my view, no work for two weeks and no physical activity for four weeks or so.'

Sandy sighed. It looked like this would be the end of his time in Vienna. He was gutted he was going to be deprived of the opportunity to arrest those thugs that had assaulted him, who were also undoubtably the number one suspects for the murder of Arthur Barrington. What a let-down.

Chapter Nine

Leaving the hospital that evening had taken an inordinate amount of time. The nurses were rushed off their feet and it took almost two hours for one of them to attend to apply the strapping to Sandy's chest. It then took almost as long for the medication to arrive.

On returning to his hotel room, Sandy wondered if he ought to feel a bit uneasy after what had occurred there only that afternoon, but it didn't seem to be affecting him at all.

He looked down at his phone. None of the calls or messages that he had received had been answered yet. He was, and always had been, very grateful and thankful that he was a member of such a loving and close family, but he didn't and never had liked it when all of their attention was focused on him.

Propping himself up in bed on the plentiful hotel pillows, the pizza slice and drink that Juliet had bought for him on the table by his side, he set about calling the three women he knew had to contact first.

'Hey, how are you?' Sandy said as Hannah picked up his call.

'What do you mean, how am I? How are *you*?'

'I'm fine,' Sandy assured her, leaning over to take a bite of his pizza and wincing loudly – too loudly.

'You're definitely *not* fine, I just heard you groaning in

pain,' Hannah said in a concerned voice. 'Good job Juliet has been keeping me updated on what's been happening with you, because you would just brush it off, saying "I've had worse playing rugby".'

'I have though,' Sandy said, trying not to laugh. He knew that would only hurt him more. 'I'm just so cross with myself that I wasn't able to hold onto at least one of them.' He paused. 'They're the priority suspects for the murder of Arthur Barrington. I could have put them behind bars then and there, but when one of them started booting me it was impossible to hold on.'

'The Vienna police will get them, don't worry. You just get yourself home.'

'I'm going to call the boss and see when that can be.' Sandy paused again, this time to have a sip of his drink, stifling his body's need to groan at the motion. 'I know what she's going to say though, so can I see you at the weekend please?'

'You try and stop me, Sandy McFarlane,' Hannah said. 'And call me in the morning before I have to go into court – let me know what sort of night you had.'

He finished his pizza and drink before he rang his mother, to make sure he didn't set her off by accidentally groaning in pain. He asked her to let his father, sisters and grandfathers know that he was fine, which she said she would, even though she knew that wasn't the whole truth. As his mum, she just wanted him home rather than far away in a hotel room alone.

Detective Superintendent Jane Watson was next on his list, and as expected, she answered the phone immediately.

'Jane, I'm sorry it's so late, and to have caused you so

much grief,' Sandy said. He was now standing up and pacing in the small space that his hotel room allowed. He hadn't been comfortable lying in bed and felt he needed to move about.

'No need to apologise,' Jane replied. 'Though you have caused quite the diplomatic stir – I've had our Austrian ambassador, Dame Lillian O'Brien, on the phone to me this afternoon, asking why she wasn't informed that members of the FCDO were on operational deployment in Austria.'

'Oh no,' Sandy groaned. 'Am I… are we in trouble?'

'No, of course not. Well, I don't think so. I've not heard from our minister querying anything, nor have I heard from his private office. I told Dame O'Brien quite firmly that you were injured as a result of a robbery, not due to work, and the Embassy had been previously informed about the death of a British citizen.'

Sandy could hear her flicking through her notes.

'Whose name I can't remember now. It's been a long day.'

'Arthur Barrington.'

'Yes, that's him. Anyway, I told her we were assisting at the written request of the Vienna District Police Department. That seemed to satisfy her.'

'Thank you,' Sandy said, relieved.

'You and Juliet are booked on tomorrow's British Airways afternoon flight to London, and I will not be seeing you in the office until two weeks on Monday. Am I clear? If you do get bored and insist, you can do the odd bit of computer work or calls from home only in a few days' time. But not before.'

Sandy sighed. It was going to be a long two weeks.

∞

The night had been as sleepless as Sandy had expected – the pain was immense, even with the painkillers, which hadn't relieved it as much as he'd hoped. The walk to the police station with their bags had been painfully slow, not because of Juliet this time, but because of Sandy. As they passed the cathedral, Sandy felt very disappointed that they hadn't been able to carve out the time for even a short visit.

'The priority for the briefing this morning is to plan the arrest and interviews of Flamur Hysa and Marin Ismalaj,' Otto said once they were all settled, as Johanna showed the two youngsters' pictures on the screen in the meeting room.

'How old are they?' Sandy asked, looking at the pictures of what looked like two children. 'And who is who? Do we know which of them had the stars tattoo?'

'Flamur has the tattoo. He is the one that tried to strangle you and kicked you, causing the injury,' Johanna said, showing another picture of Flamur with his star tattoo showing. 'I will add that you now know his name to your statement, when I have time to write it for you.' She looked at Otto, as if he was to blame for how busy she was. 'And they are, of course, both guilty of the attempted theft of your bag.' Looking at the details on some papers in front of her, Johanna continued, 'Not sure of their exact ages. They have been stopped a few times and arrested a couple of times. No charges have ever been brought against them. They keep giving different details, but best estimate, fifteen or sixteen years old.'

'How did they come to be in the country on their own at

that age?' Juliet asked. 'Is it child trafficking by a criminal gang?'

'Absolutely,' Otto said. 'We haven't got a huge problem with child trafficking – I don't think so, anyway – but it does exist. I would be lying to myself if I pretended it didn't.'

'Otto, we have the same in the UK,' Sandy said. 'Child trafficking and child criminal exploitation is happening in every city and in every small town in our country. Mostly moving drugs around using something we call "county lines", but it is awful. We're trying to do more to prevent it happening, but it's difficult.'

'Have there been instances of murder as well, like these two might have been involved in here?' Mia asked Sandy.

'Yes, there are some cases of murder due to serious youth gang violence,' Sandy replied. 'Do you know who Mr Big is? The head of the criminal gang, I mean?'

'Possibly,' Otto said. 'The piece of kit they were using to bypass the room key card is, I am told, exceptionally expensive to buy, even off the dark web. Not many criminal gangs are that sophisticated, other than one or two that we know of locally.'

'Do we know where these two are living?' Juliet asked, pointing to the images on the screen. 'I know I'm booked on the same flight as Sandy to go back to England, but I could delay it. I am very keen to get my hands on them.'

As Sandy was about to speak, Juliet gave him a look.

'No, Sandy, I know what you are going to say, and I know you outrank me, but you are not even meant to be here at this meeting. Our boss and the doctor told you to take two weeks off, so not another word out of you!'

Glancing at his phone, Otto cleared his throat. 'Well, my boss went to a meeting this morning and was going to tell me the details of possible addresses as soon as the meeting finished.' Picking his phone up again, he added, 'Nothing as yet. I will give her a call in a moment and we can plan our arrest strategy for tomorrow morning – first light, I would say.'

'While we are waiting, can I ask you about the release of Arthur Barrington's body?' Sandy asked. 'Professor Von Tripp is happy for the body to be repatriated if you and the examining magistrate agree.' Sandy looked at Otto, who started rubbing his hands through his hair and over his face again.

'Not just yet, is my view. Let's see what the other pathologists think about the samples, then I will talk to the examining magistrate.' Pausing to think further, he confirmed, 'No, definitely not at the moment.'

When his phone rang, Otto took the call, mouthing to them as he stepped out that it was Superintendent Mahler.

'What!' they heard Otto shout loudly.

They could see him storm off to his office, holding his phone to his ear. They all looked at each other, not knowing what to say.

Paulina, the CSI, eventually broke the silence. 'Not sure what that's all about, but the fingerprints and DNA on one of the coffee mugs has come back as Arthur's, and there is no trace on our systems or those we have access to across Europe for the prints and DNA on the other coffee mug.'

'Have they checked Andrew Barrington's fingerprints and his DNA sample that Mia took?' Sandy asked.

'Yes, negative,' Paulina replied.

'What about the fingerprints and the DNA database in the UK?' Sandy asked.

'We haven't got ready access to that since Brexit, so no, not yet,' Paulina said, shaking her head, not wanting to ask what Sandy or Juliet thought about Brexit.

Coming back into the room and putting his phone away in his pocket, Otto, whose face was quite red, let out a frustrated huff. 'We're not allowed to touch the two boys.'

'What?' Sandy stood up too quickly, making himself yelp in pain. 'This is a murder enquiry. That must trump any organised crime enquiry, surely?'

'Apparently not.' Otto was raging now. 'We are to put this part of the investigation and the assault and theft against you to one side for the foreseeable future, only picking up again once we are given permission from those at the top.'

'That's crazy!' Sandy said, Juliet agreeing with him – in fact, everyone in the room agreed.

'They are getting away with murder!' Mia exclaimed.

Otto ran a hand through his hair again. 'Go back to England, Sandy and Juliet. I will ring you when I have more news and we can move the investigation forwards again.'

Chapter Ten

On the flight back home, Sandy and Juliet found out coincidently that the Barringtons were on the same flight. Very little was said to each other, but Faith Barrington was inquisitive as to why Sandy was now walking tenderly and holding himself so carefully. This was something that Sandy was most certainly not in the right head space to discuss with them, nor did he feel it appropriate to talk to the parents of Arthur Barrington about the actions of other possible suspects to his murder.

On his arrival home in Ely, he found his parents and younger sister, Aileen, waiting for him. As his mother and Aileen fussed over him, his father suggested they go to the pub along the road, The Cutter Inn, for a drink.

'Everything always feels better', his father said, 'after a couple of pints with a few friends.'

Sandy declined, choosing instead to escape to his bedroom, leaving them to it. He had arranged for Hannah to come over in the morning to see him, as she had only just got back to Cambridge from her week away in court.

As he lay in bed, Sandy heard the front door open again. It was starting to feel like Piccadilly Circus in their riverside home beside the River Great Ouse. This time, it was his two grandfathers who had arrived. With a big sigh, Sandy decided he had better go down and see them both.

Making themselves at home in the conservatory, with hot drinks provided by Sandy's mother, the three of them settled in for what the grandfathers hoped would be a good discussion about Sandy's case. Sandy, on the other hand, hoped to tell them as little as possible, though he acknowledged that this was a futile thought.

'Definitely murder you say?' Grandad Tom said. 'How exciting. Obviously not for the parents, but for the thrill of the investigation.'

'What was the cause of death then, Sandy?' Grandpa John asked, while taking a large sip of his coffee. 'Can the pathologist be sure? They are known to change their minds, you know, when you get down into the more micro pathology.'

'I had a case,' Tom said, at which neither Sandy nor John rolled their eyes as other family members often did when Tom uttered this phrase. 'Following the post-mortem, the forensic pathologist said that the baby had died from shaken baby syndrome, or as they prefer to call it now, abusive head trauma.' He could see he had the other twos' attention and, taking a large mouthful of his coffee from his mug, he paused for effect. 'However, after the neuro and ophthalmic pathologists had done their examinations and specialist toxicology had come back, it was found to be a rare form of meningitis.'

'You hadn't arrested anyone though, had you, Grandad?' asked Sandy.

'Oh yes – the father, and given him bail, with a condition not to be in the family home as well. Nightmare!'

'Well, Professor Von Tripp was quite clear as to what he thought had happened,' Sandy replied. 'He said it was strangulation, with bruising externally and internally to support this.'

'I presume that the father is your main suspect?' Tom said. 'He was the last known person to see Arthur alive.'

'I think we've almost eliminated him,' Sandy said confidently, thinking about the orange jumper he had been wearing. 'Our prime suspects are undoubtably the two boys that broke into my hotel room.' He didn't want to get into too much graphic detail about the attack and worry his two grandfathers.

'Will you get the chance to go back to Vienna when they are arrested?' Tom asked.

'We have been told to leave them alone for the moment. Something important is brewing that involves them,' Sandy said, shaking his head. He was still in disbelief.

'What can out-trump a murder investigation?' Tom exclaimed loudly. 'This wouldn't have happened in my day.'

Ever the lawyer, John smiled mischievously. 'What about the offence of treason, then?'

Not one to roll over easily to his friend, Tom countered. 'Seriously, John! Two teenagers who are nothing more than thugs. No. It is not treason. It is a serious and organised crime investigation and no doubt it is a more assertive detective leading that enquiry who has won the day.'

'Who knows,' Sandy interjected, wanting to shut down the conversation now and head off to bed. He knew his grandfathers would be arguing long into the night if they were given the chance.

∞

The next morning, Hannah arrived early, having been driven there by Grandpa John, who happened to be her mentor.

He really is spending an awful lot of time at the Ely house these days, Sandy thought.

Relieved to see Hannah, Sandy pulled her into a hug, though her responding embrace was tentative.

'I don't want to hurt you!' she explained.

Sandy, on the other hand, just wanted her to hug him. It had been a traumatic last couple of days in Vienna for him, and he wanted a proper hug.

When Grandad Tom turned up a short while after Hannah and John, Sandy was even more confused. *What is going on with these old men? They spent all evening here yesterday!*

Knowing they would hound him about the case unless he and Hannah escaped, Sandy suggested the two of them go to Cambridge for the day. With a glint in his eye, he added, 'Let's go to The Oak Bistro for a late lunch.'

'That sounds wonderful, Sandy, it's such a lovely day.' Looking at him worryingly, Hannah asked, 'Are you going to be OK to drive?'

'Not really at the moment,' Sandy replied sheepishly. 'I thought you could drive.'

Before Hannah could say anything, Tom piped up, looking at John while he did so and speaking loud enough for everyone to hear, especially Sandy.

'Gosh, he really must love Hannah, mustn't he, to allow her to drive his precious car.'

Sandy had a red Morgan Roadster. The car was his pride and joy.

‘I thought he loved that car more than anything or anyone,’ John said, enjoying the leg pulling of their grandson. ‘Obviously I was wrong!’

They were all laughing as Sandy quickly led Hannah upstairs out of the way of the two old men, on the pretence of getting himself organised to go out.

When they came downstairs, ready to leave, Tom, ever the policeman, asked Sandy quietly, ‘You have got Hannah insured to drive your car, haven’t you?’ He had a worried look on his face.

Seizing his own opportunity to tease his grandfather, Sandy said, ‘No, of course not, Grandad. No one bothers with insurance these days!’ Seeing the anxious expression on both of his grandfathers’ faces, Sandy paused only momentarily for maximum effect, before he revealed the truth. ‘Of course I have. In fact, I added Hannah to my insurance over a year ago.’

‘What? Then why haven’t you let me drive your Morgan before now!’ Hannah exclaimed.

Both the grandfathers grinned at each other, but before they could say anything, they spotted Sandy’s mother shaking her head at them, making the sign to button their mouths firmly shut.

‘I could have used it whenever you were working abroad,’ Hannah chuckled.

‘No chance! Don’t push it,’ Sandy replied.

They drove away from the garage at the back of the house with Hannah jerking the car violently to start with, which worried Sandy and made him question whether letting Hannah drive his prized possession was such a good idea, especially as the movement was hurting his ribs greatly.

Fortunately, her driving swiftly improved, and as they pulled out of the side road to head up through Ely city centre to head off to Cambridge, they saw Aileen and her two boys walking towards the McFarlane home.

Hannah violently stopped the car.

'There's your sister. Let's go talk to her.'

'Let's not,' Sandy said. 'Quick, move, before she sees us.'

'How rude. I love your sister, and all of your family,' Hannah grumbled as they drove away.

As they moved out into the countryside around Ely, Sandy kept repeating, 'Slow down, Hannah.' Especially as they sped round the tight, winding Fen roads.

When she told him, 'I haven't driven for almost two years, just getting the hang of it again!' this only added to Sandy's worry.

Fortunately, it wasn't long before Hannah got the hang of the powerful Morgan Roadster.

'How is your investigation in Vienna going?' she asked as they sped along.

'Mia reckons the youths that assaulted me are getting away with murder. We've had to park their side of the investigation for the moment because the bosses there are blocking us.'

'Mia?' Hannah asked, a puzzled frown on her face.

'One of the detectives working with us on the investigation.' Seeing the frown disappear, he added, 'What I've learnt over the years with these sorts of investigations is that you need to be patient, tenacious, and always ready to react to any investigative opportunity that might arise. So, that's what I am doing.'

∞

Following a disagreement about where to park the Morgan in Cambridge – Hannah wanted to park in the Grand Arcade, but Sandy insisted the spaces were too narrow, or, as Hannah put it, he didn't want someone to accidently scratch his precious car – they eventually parked just off Hills Road and walked the short distance into the centre of Cambridge.

A cup of tea and coffee at the Fitzbillies café overlooking King's Parade was their first stop, then a visit to the brilliant new Bodies in the Bookshop, co-owned by Richard, a man Sandy knew from Heffers, where he had spent large amounts of time during his days at St John's college. As a crime specialist bookshop, there were plentiful excellent options to choose from, and Sandy bought a couple of crime fiction novels to while away the time over the next couple of weeks, given he was restricted to being at home.

Hannah laughed at him. 'Busman's holiday books,' she said.

As they were slightly early for their lunch reservation, they sat on a bench overlooking Parker's Piece and reflected on this being identical to their first ever date, which had also involved sitting on Parker's Piece and a meal at The Oak Bistro. Hannah was looking particularly lovely in her white cotton dress emblazoned with various-sized red poppies all over it, and Sandy had on his best cream chinos and a pink long-sleeved shirt. They looked every bit the smart professional couple that they were.

It's perfect, Sandy thought. *Today's the day.*

Entering The Oak Bistro a short while later, they found

it packed with diners, many of them accompanied by mounds of bags. A busy shopping day had been happening in Cambridge! Sandy was just thankful they had snagged a table positioned away from the busyness.

After they had finished their main course and their plates had been taken away, Sandy nodded at the restaurant manager, whom he had managed to sneak in a quiet word with earlier. Upon seeing the manager get into position, Sandy very slowly and gently lowered himself down to the ground… onto one knee.

An incredible silence descended around the restaurant.

'Hannah Abigail Tobias,' Sandy asked, his tone reverent as he gazed up at Hannah, 'will you marry me?'

In his right hand was an open blue ring box, a gold band with a large diamond solitaire in the centre glittering from within. The atmosphere in the restaurant became even more still as the gasps of people realising what was happening silenced. They all wanted to know what the reply was going to be.

Hannah looked firstly at the ring, then only at Sandy.

'Yes, it will be my life's pleasure to marry you, Alexander McFarlane.'

As she dropped to her knees to hug Sandy, there were claps and whoops of delight all around the restaurant.

'What took you so long?' she whispered into his ear.

'What can I say? I'm an idiot.'

'*My* beautiful idiot, though,' Hannah said, kissing him passionately and prompting more cheers and claps from the watching diners.

It was perfect.

Chapter Eleven

The excitement of the engagement took a surprisingly short time to quieten down.

Once the restaurant had resumed business as usual, Hannah began to talk excitedly about their plans. The first step, of course, would be to look at buying a house together, then once they'd officially moved in together, they could start planning for the wedding, though Hannah needed to finish her long-running trial first before she could fully clear her mind to be able to work through house-hunting.

The video that the manager of The Oak Bistro had taken of the proposal had worked out brilliantly, and they both circulated it to family members and friends with a short message from them both. From his side, only Sandy's mum and dad had been aware that he intended to propose at some stage. Ever the traditionalist, he had also followed the convention of asking Hannah's father for permission to marry his daughter. This had all taken place several weeks ago, and he knew his parents and Howard Tobias had probably started wondering whether he had changed his mind.

He had also told Juliet on the plane home. He'd felt it was important to explain that the reason he had held onto his backpack so strongly was not because the FCDO laptop was inside it, but because his engagement ring for Hannah was.

There was no way he was letting that go, and now, he was

glad he hadn't.

After all this time, he was finally marrying the love of his life.

∞

The restricted two weeks working at home were monotonous, boring and driving Sandy stir crazy. Towards the end of the second week, he had convinced his boss to let him travel a comparatively short distance to Stamford to see both the Barrington family and then Freddie and Emily, to update them on the investigation and to return the love letters back to Emily that she had written to Arthur.

He had amazed himself that he hadn't given in to curiosity and read the letters whilst being cooped up at home, but it just hadn't felt right. Juliet had read them, and he wanted to keep the privacy of them between Arthur and his fiancée.

Not quite being able to drive just yet, Sandy had enlisted one of his grandfathers to drive him to Stamford. They had decided to both come along, naturally, and were even happier when Sandy said he would buy them a late lunch at The George Hotel in the town centre.

Sandy had told them both that they would need to leave early, as he was scheduled to meet the Barringtons at 9:00 a.m. and the Wainwrights at 10:30 a.m. But when Sandy's two grandfathers arrived to pick him up, he was surprised to find them dressed in suits and ties.

'What do you both think your involvement in this trip is?' Sandy asked, looking at them. Before they could reply, Sandy continued, 'Your role is to drive me there and that is all. Neither of you are taking a step inside either of the houses I am visiting.' He looked at them as sternly as a grandson could. 'Have I made myself clear?'

They both nodded sheepishly and John, the judge in him always needing to have the last word, said to Tom, 'I looked The George Hotel up on the internet and it's a posh place. I am surprised Sandy hasn't got a tie on. Shabby, if you ask me!'

Rolling his eyes, Sandy climbed into the back seat of John's Mercedes. He thought he looked smart enough in his tan chinos, light blue shirt and blue checked jacket. *What do those two old codgers know*, he thought to himself.

The drive through the Fens to Stamford was pleasant enough, with the three of them enjoying each other's company, even if the two old codgers in the front spent most of it moaning about the cost of living and how much it cost to heat their homes, even though both of them, especially John, were relatively well off.

Arriving in Stamford, Sandy wondered why he had rarely visited. It was a beautiful place, and definitely somewhere to bring Hannah for a day out. Tom, as usual, had a case from many years ago that had brought him to Stamford. He wanted John to drive around so that they could find the house he was talking about and show them the police station, but Sandy needed to get on, so they parked in the Cattlemarket car park and Sandy headed off, telling his grandfathers to amuse themselves and that he would meet them at The George Hotel in time for lunch.

As he walked along the Meadows and into the town centre, he admired the profusion of old stone houses, the limestone buildings dating back over two hundred years in many cases. It was market day, so the streets were bustling, thriving stalls lining the walkways. There was a cosy feel to the town, and Sandy delighted in the hubbub as he made his way to the Barringtons home, just beyond the town centre near one of the five churches, which Sandy had recently learned were all medieval. He would have to make some time to admire them later in the day.

He had barely knocked on the Barrington's door beforc it swung open. Faith Barrington had clearly been waiting for him.

'Come in, DCI McFarlane. I saw you admiring the church. We live in a lovely area, don't we?'

Realising this was probably a statement rather than a question, Sandy just smiled and went into the house, which he was pleased to discover was one of the Georgian houses he had been admiring on the walk. From what he could see of the house, it was kept in immaculate condition.

Sat in the front room was Andrew, who gestured for him to take a seat while Faith went off to make Sandy a cup of tea.

'I'm sorry I've not been in touch,' Sandy said, sitting down on the sofa.

'I've had a couple of calls from DC Mia Eckhart, just checking how we are. She tells us there have been no further developments with the case,' Andrew said, looking at Sandy, clearly hoping that he might have something to tell him and Faith.

'I do have a bit of news to share with you on that front. We have another couple of possible suspects,' Sandy said, but before he could say any more, Faith came into the room and placed his cup of tea on a small mahogany table next to Sandy.

Looking directly at Sandy, and very close to tears, she said, 'What do you mean another suspect? The other suspect is Andrew, isn't it? You suspect he killed our son.' The tears were flowing from her eyes now.

Sandy paused a fraction too long.

'I can't believe you!' Faith screeched before he could respond. 'We're supposed to trust you, yet you sit here in our home and tell us that Arthur was killed by his father.' She pointed aggressively at her husband, then collapsed into the vacant chair.

Andrew was up in a flash, holding her against him and comforting her.

'I'm one of the last people who saw him alive, love. Of course I have to be a suspect until they find out who really did it,' Andrew whispered to his wife in a soft, comforting tone.

'Mrs Barrington, I can't deny that Andrew is one – and I stress, *one* – of our suspects,' Sandy said slowly and carefully, while he thought through what and how best to say things. 'As your husband has said, according to the information we have at the moment – though we are working on developing that further – he was the last person to see Arthur alive.'

Faith wasn't looking at Sandy, just staring into her lap, but she had stopped crying. Andrew didn't seem to be looking at him either.

'Unfortunately the CCTV wasn't working in the hotel corridor either.'

That did make them both look at Sandy.

'Why ever not?' Andrew asked. 'Or were they just dummy

cameras put up to try and fool people?'

'They were real,' Sandy explained. 'The system was down, sadly. The main suspects we have are two young lads.'

'Young lads,' Faith said, definitely interested again now. 'How young?'

'Maybe fifteen years old.'

'I saw something on the news about a group of fifteen-year-old boys stabbing each other the other week… that isn't what happened to Arthur, is it?' Faith asked. 'Or is there something else you haven't told us?'

'Arthur did not die of a stab wound. I was at the autopsy and can assure you of that. The pathologist believes that Arthur died of compression to the neck. I hope to have a conversation with him and Inspector Wagner next week to be updated on any developments.' Seeing sad nods from Arthur's parents, he added, 'These boys are suspected of stealing from hotel rooms. One of my reasons to visit today, other than to see how you are both doing, was to ask whether you had anything stolen from your hotel room, Mr Barrington?'

'No, and we had Arthur's wallet returned to us, so that wasn't stolen either.'

'Well, that is the link we have to them at the moment,' Sandy said, not wanting to tell them about his encounter with the two boys. He looked around the room and saw it was littered with cards emblazoned with the words "condolences", "sympathy" and "we are thinking about you". Seeing the display of these cards only made him more aware of the grief, trauma and sadness Mr and Mrs Barrington were experiencing. Sandy felt it was best now to go and leave them to grieve on their own.

As he walked away, he pondered whether he was right not to tell them or dismiss Andrew Barrington as a suspect. He decided he was, even though he appreciated that the timing from the CCTV at the bar didn't fit. On the way to Stamford, his Grandpa John had suggested that the wool fibres could have come from clothing that Arthur himself was wearing, and that needed checking before Andrew could be ruled out. His Grandad Tom had reiterated to Sandy about the danger of using something like the fibres as the sole elimination criteria. Tom had told them of a case where there was a suspect's DNA found, and as the suspect had an unusual name, and their DNA had been recorded on the National DNA Database, this evidence was used to eliminate them. Unfortunately, it transpired that there were two people with this name and the unusually named person that was on the database at that time was much older than the offender with the same name who, when caught, had committed dozens of further serious offences that could have been prevented.

Even when the evidence pointed away from a suspect, you had to tread carefully.

Chapter Twelve

Needing to talk to someone after his meeting with the Barringtons, Sandy called Juliet as he walked towards where he was due to meet Freddie and Emily,

'Just met up with Arthur and Faith Barrington. They are understandably incredibly sad. It was tough.'

'Are you OK?' Juliet asked in her best caring tone. 'I am sorry I couldn't come with you. My children need things doing with them today and I don't want to not be here for them, especially when I have a chance to be at home and not working abroad.'

'I'm all right. Just on my way to the Wainwrights to talk to them, and also to return the letters to Emily,' Sandy said, lightly patting his backpack where the letters were nestling inside. 'You said there was nothing in them that suggests Arthur has been telling her of any problems he had with anyone in Vienna?'

'No, nothing. Those letters are just full of Emily's love for him, and from what she says, the letters she received from him must be full of his love for his own family, including his father. What there *is*, though, is Emily expressing how tough her home life is. Her dad seems a tyrant and her mum, well, the whole family in fact, live in fear of him.'

'Let's hope he's not home when I visit in a moment then,' Sandy said.

‘She hadn’t told her mum or dad yet about the proposal, as far as I could see in her last letter to Arthur, or that they were going to stay in Stamford. She did write that she wanted Arthur to come back home and for him to be absolutely sure that he was happy with the decision to move before she told them,’ Juliet said. ‘Take care, Sandy, and give me a call later. An early meal beckons for me before I have to head out.’

The Wainwright family home was of a similar age, style and stone build to the house that the Barringtons owned, but that was where the similarity ended. The front garden to the house was unkempt – the weeds had overtaken the flowerbeds. The white wood-framed windows were in desperate need of repair and then painting. It was clear they hadn’t seen a paintbrush in a good number of years.

Walking up a short path, Sandy knocked on what would have once been a bright red front door – now faded and clearly rotten at the base.

Freddie opened the door and led Sandy into the front room, where Emily was sitting waiting on the sofa. Also sat in the front room was a woman, who Freddie introduced to Sandy as his mum, Hazel Wainwright. A slight smile on her lips was Hazel’s way of acknowledging Sandy. She wore a light blue dress and had a darker blue silk-type scarf secured around her neck.

Sandy sat as directed by Freddie on one of the single chairs in the tired-looking front room. The furnishings clearly hadn’t been updated for some considerable time, maybe even decades.

Jumping up as he sat down, Hazel asked, ‘Would you like a cup of tea, young man?’

Emily immediately stood up. 'I'll do it, Mum. Sit.'

'That would be lovely, Mrs Wainwright,' Sandy said, gesturing for Emily to sit down. When Hazel left the room, Sandy removed the stack of love letters from his backpack. As soon as Emily saw them, she went bright red. 'I've brought these to return to you.'

'You haven't read them, have you?' Emily whispered, her hand going up to touch her very red face.

'No,' Sandy reassured her, 'but my colleague, DS Juliet Ashton, has checked through them for anything that might be pertinent to the case.'

'Thank you,' Emily said, taking them from Sandy and getting straight to her feet. She quickly left the room and could be heard running upstairs, presumably to her bedroom.

'I need to tell you, Freddie,' Sandy said quickly, before Hazel Wainwright returned with his cup of tea, 'that we believe Arthur was murdered.'

'What!' Freddie stared at him in horror. 'Are you sure?'

'The pathologist is pretty certain but still needs to give us a formal conclusion. You and Emily's instincts that something untoward had happened to Arthur were right.'

As Emily came down the stairs and Mrs Wainwright came into the room with the cup of tea, the front door flew open and a man stormed inside, grabbing the cup of tea from Mrs Wainwright.

'Don't mind if I do.' He strode into the lounge area and walked to the chair that Sandy was sat in. When he saw Sandy, he came to an abrupt stop. 'Who are you?' he demanded loudly.

Sandy took in the man, who was evidently Douglas

Wainwright, given his familiarity with the space and how his family reacted to his presence. He had short grey hair and a straggly off-white beard. His eyes were strikingly blue, the same as Freddie and Emily's, but unlike his children, Douglas Wainwright's piercing gaze came across as unnerving and threatening.

'I am DCI McFarlane from the Foreign and Commonwealth Office,' Sandy offered.

Before he could explain further what he was doing in the house, Douglas bellowed at his wife, who was now cowering in the doorway.

'How dare you allow a spy into my house!'

Hazel instantly scurried off back to the kitchen.

'Dad,' Freddie said bravely, standing from his seat, 'he's here because of Arthur.'

'You're as bad as your mother. You know they're listening to all of us. Listening through the walls.' Douglas gestured all around him. 'Why does no one in this family understand me! There are people out to get me!'

'I'm definitely not a spy,' Sandy tried to reassure him, moving to stand alongside Freddie. 'I work for a different government department.'

'What, not MI5? It must be MI6 then. You can't hurt me in my own home. I won't let you.'

Douglas moved quickly and faced Sandy. He was slightly smaller, but not by much, and he went to square up, fists raised. Sandy decided he needed to quickly de-escalate the situation, so he immediately stepped backwards and sat down. Freddie took his lead and also sat, which led to Douglas pausing for a moment, looking confused, not knowing what to do next. He then sat down as well.

It was amazing how the atmosphere in the house had changed the moment Douglas had arrived home. Only Freddie – and even then, only to a certain extent – managed to keep a level of normality to his demeanour. Hazel and Emily had immediately and quite starkly become withdrawn and quiet.

This was, in Sandy's view, a classic case of coercive and controlling behaviour by Douglas to his whole family. The Wainwright's probably had no idea what coercive and controlling behaviour was, or what Sandy would mean by it if he talked to them about it. Even more worrying was Douglas talking about spying and people listening. Sandy wondered whether he had ever been assessed for mental illness?

'Is it possible please to have consent from each of you to access all of your medical records?' Sandy asked, gesturing to everyone in the house.

He had a gut feeling there was abuse going on here. Even though it was nothing to do with the investigation into the death of Arthur Barrington, he felt that as a police officer he couldn't ignore finding out more about what was going on in this house.

Leaping to his feet, Douglas jumped across the room, grabbed Sandy by the lapels of his jacket and pulled him to his feet.

'Get out! Get out of my house,' he said, shouting in Sandy's face, so much so that he could feel Douglas's spittle landing on him. 'You're a spy, you're out to kill me!'

Grabbing both of Douglas's surprisingly strong hands and wrenching them off his jacket, Sandy took a decisive step to the side of Douglas and walked immediately out of the room, opened the front door, walked straight out through the garden, and went to stand at the front gate.

Scurrying after Sandy came Freddie, then Emily.

'I'm so sorry about our dad. He is not taking his medication regularly at the moment,' Freddie said. He looked acutely embarrassed.

Emily shoved a pile of letters at Sandy, which he could see when he took them were the ones from Arthur to Emily.

'Please don't read them, but can DS Ashton? It'll prove Arthur's love for me was reciprocated.'

Sandy placed them in his backpack as quickly as he could, in case Douglas came out of the house.

'How long has your father been like this?' Sandy asked.

'As long as I can remember, but when he takes his medication, it's a lot better. He's spent some time in specialist hospitals here and there, and he's always more or less normal after that.' Freddie looked around anxiously to see if his dad was there. 'He's not been well for a few weeks, and he keeps disappearing for a couple of days or so at a time. We don't know where he goes, but I don't think it's anywhere good. He's probably afraid that if he goes to court, he'll get locked up.'

The Wainwright children returned into the house and Sandy made his way to the George Hotel, reflecting on what a sad life the family had, in particular the lives of Hazel and Emily.

Poor Emily, Sandy thought. The love of her life, Arthur, was now no more, and she was left to live at home in this toxic environment.

He decided then and there that he would do whatever he could to help them.

Chapter Thirteen

When he got to the George Hotel, Sandy saw his grandfathers waiting for him.

'Are you ready for your lunch?' he asked as he walked towards them.

'It is very nice in there,' John said. 'We've already been in and had a coffee.' John paused before he continued speaking. 'There is a long wait for a table in the Garden Room, though, so I thought we could mix it up a bit. I've booked us in for lunch at the Orangery at Burghley House. It is only ten minutes away.'

'I know where Burghley House is, Grandpa, but why are we not eating in here?' Sandy said, pointing at the George. 'Especially if it is so nice? I'm sure that the wait wouldn't be as long as you say.'

'Well… since we've already had a coffee here, and it really is rather busy, we thought it would be nice to broaden the experience and take in Burghley House too,' Tom said, now getting involved.

'Fair enough,' Sandy said, smiling at Tom, which brought big smiles from both his grandfathers.

Still trying to process what had just happened at the Wainwright's house, Sandy walked with them to John's car, which was parked nearby.

'How has your morning been?' asked Tom as they drove,

seeing how deep in thought Sandy seemed. 'Emotional, isn't it, meeting families that have loved ones who have been killed so tragically.'

'Yes, I know exactly what you mean, but that's not what's troubling me,' Sandy said, looking directly at Tom. 'At the Wainwright's I met the father, Douglas Wainwright, and he was extremely unhinged.'

'What do you mean by unhinged?' John asked, turning around to look at Sandy. 'Like he was suffering from mental health issues?'

'Keep your eyes on the road, Grandpa,' a startled Sandy said, as the car veered towards the right. After the car corrected itself, Sandy continued, 'Yes, exactly that. And apparently, he's on medication that he isn't taking at the moment. He was so coercive and controlling towards the family – that's what's worrying me the most.' Sandy was speaking carefully so that John didn't turn around again while he was driving. 'The mother Hazel and daughter Emily, who you met at Trinity College, were terrified of him.'

'The danger of that kind of coercive controlling behaviour was sadly not in the slightest bit appreciated during almost all the years that I was in policing,' Tom said, shaking his head.

'Well-known by me in the family courts, though,' John told them as they reached the road leading to Burghley House. Making sure he looked where he was going, he turned the car, before darting a glance at Sandy. 'When I presided over cases in the private law court regarding access to and residence of children, this coercive controlling behaviour was evident more often than not.' Finding a spot to park, he pulled his Mercedes in front ways. 'I often thought the children were just used as a ploy to continue the control of the partner involved, mostly women of course, but occasionally men as well. It's awful to witness, and harder still to do anything about.'

Sandy nodded solemnly. *Still,* he decided, *I will do what I can.*

∞

Lunch was delicious and John had done well to get them a table that looked out onto the pleasant and well-kept garden area, where people were strolling around.

Although he loved the company of his grandfathers, Sandy was still feeling distracted, so he sent a text message to Freddie halfway through his main course, just to ask if they were all OK.

Freddie replied:

We're fine. Nothing unusual for us. This is our lives! Dad's gone off anyway. We're more worried about you and hope you weren't disturbed by being in our home. ▯

Putting his phone away in order to continue his meal, Sandy saw that both grandfathers had stopped eating and were waiting for Sandy to tell them about the message he had received. Although he didn't need to tell them anything, he thought it best to.

'I was just checking the Wainwrights were OK. Freddie assured me they're fine,' Sandy said, before putting a large mouthful of food in his mouth, as if to say "topic now closed".

After they had finished lunch and the usual fight with John about who should pay, which Sandy had won for a change, he convinced his grandfathers to have a little walk around to look at the outside of Burghley House. The inside of the house was presently closed to visitors, but they were free to walk around the grounds.

The first thing they noticed was the large herd of deer roaming around. It was, after all, a deer park, John told them, re-designed by Lancelot 'Capability' Brown, like he had done for so many of these types of grand estates in the 18th century, turning the formal gardens into rolling parklands. The 16th century house itself was without doubt one of the most incredible works of Elizabethan architecture, and a testament to the original owner, William Cecil. At the time, he had been one of the most powerful and influential figures of that era, though in Sandy's view, the most interesting thing about him was that he had been an undergraduate at his own beloved St John's College in Cambridge.

They walked a nice distance, albeit at a slow pace, enjoying the sunshine, and made it to the stone bridge, stopping halfway across to look back at the landscape, the house and the grounds. *What a lovely experience after such a hard day*, Sandy thought.

As they headed back to the car, Sandy responded to a text from Juliet. He told her briefly about both visits and the actions of Douglas Wainwright, and that he had the letters that Arthur had sent Emily for her to read to see if there was anything of concern in them.

He sincerely hoped there wasn't.

∞

As soon as he got home to Ely, Sandy made a call to the Lincolnshire Police Safeguarding Hub. He had researched and found their number in a list of his police contacts. A few years ago, when he was a detective sergeant in the Met Police in London, he had needed to work with them on an enquiry.

'Lincolnshire Police, how can I help you?' a male voice answered.

'DCI McFarlane here, former detective for the Met Police, though I currently work for the Foreign Office,' Sandy explained, switching his laptop on while talking on his phone. 'I'm investigating the death of a British citizen in Vienna a few weeks ago.'

'That sounds fancy,' the man replied. 'What's that got to do with Lincolnshire, and more to the point, with me and the Safeguarding Hub?'

This may not be as straightforward as I hoped, Sandy thought.

'The person who died, a man named Arthur Barrington, was a resident in Stamford.'

'Also very fancy, Stamford, but how does that concern the Safeguarding Hub?' the man replied. 'Not to be awkward, but this feels like one of those Friday afternoon phone calls where you just want to dump something on us. Is it?'

'Not in the slightest.' *Well, a bit, but not that I am going to admit to that*, Sandy thought. 'As part of my enquiries, I had cause to visit the home address of a Douglas Wainwright and his family in Stamford. The daughter living at the address, Emily, is the fiancée of the deceased.'

‘Yes, yes, go on,’ the bored voice said, ‘I presume you’re going to get to the point shortly.’

Deciding to get straight to the point, Sandy told the man what had occurred during his interactions with Douglas Wainwright.

‘So, you told him you were a police officer then?’

‘Yes, but he thought I was a spy,’ Sandy said. ‘He was convinced I was MI5 or MI6.’

‘If you thought an offence was being committed, why didn’t you arrest him?’ the man asked.

Starting to get exasperated, Sandy explained, ‘I’m not saying an offence was being committed at the time I was there, but the whole situation was one, in my view, of domestic abuse and coercive and controlling behaviour.’ Sandy shook his head and stood up. ‘If you check your records, you might have more information pertaining to this incident that I am raising, which will help you to build up a picture.’ Now walking about in his room, Sandy added, ‘And our partners, in particular health and mental health services, might be able to help.’

‘But if we haven’t got consent from any of them to share this information further, I can’t even refer it or ask them, can I?’ the man replied.

‘Well, I did ask for consent for their medical records, but this was in essence declined. Look, I felt I needed to raise my concerns and that is what I am doing,’ Sandy said, deciding that this pointless conversation now needed to end.

‘Look, I know you probably haven’t done this for a long time, being a DCI, but you’ll need to fill out a DASH risk assessment form – stands for domestic abuse, stalking and “honour”-based abuse. If you submit one of them to the email address I’ll give you now, then we will have a record of it. If you have no consent, I can’t refer it on, since it doesn’t sound high risk enough.’

After taking a note of the email address, Sandy opened up his Met Police account, found an electronic DASH form, and proceeded to fill it in. The form was made up of a risk checklist designed to help professionals from all agencies identify the risks that victims of domestic abuse were facing. Sandy was sure that all of the Wainwright family were victims of domestic abuse from Douglas.

As he filled the form in, Sandy felt dejected. Most of the risk checklist should really have been filled in alongside the victims themselves. He sighed. Work over the last three weeks really had not been going well for him.

At least his personal life, what with his engagement to Hannah, was a bright spot.

Chapter Fourteen

Sitting at his desk in the FCDO offices in London, Sandy looked around the large open-plan office space. He was surprised at how few civil servants came into the building since COVID-19. He had been climbing the wall working at home, but he did understand for some that the commute was draining and the flexibility that working from home gave them far outweighed being in an office in London. He, on the other hand, was very happy to be there, especially as he had hardly been in the office for weeks due to his work, firstly in Barbados, then Vienna, and then on the enforced period of home confinement.

He had spent the weekend excitedly discussing buying a house with Hannah, and when Hannah saw how much Sandy had saved because of the generosity of his parents allowing him to live with them, both at their flat in London but also in the family home in Ely, she had realised that buying a house in Cambridge was a reality for them, which had only made her more excited.

Sandy did have to admit that he made a hasty retreat whenever wedding arrangements had been mentioned though. He would get involved when he needed to, but talk of dresses and colour themes was not something he needed to engage with.

Their team meeting had been cancelled earlier that

morning, giving Sandy time to catch up on the team's outstanding enquiries and to file those that they could do no further work on. Sandy couldn't help continuously glancing at his email inbox, expecting to see an email from Lincolnshire Police telling him all the things he'd got wrong on the DASH form, but there was nothing. To be fair to them, he had only submitted the form late on Friday and it was only Monday morning. He probably wouldn't get the dubious pleasure of any feedback for a few hours, or even a few days.

When his phone rang, Sandy didn't recognise the number, but answered it anyway.

'DCI McFarlane,' a female voice said. 'I am not sure that you remember me. My name is DC Caroline Grant from the Durham Constabulary.'

Although the name and the voice rang a distant bell in his memory, Sandy couldn't place why, so rather than bluff it, he decided to be honest. 'I remember your name and voice, but I'm sorry, I'm not sure why.'

'No worries,' Caroline said, chuckling softly. 'I'm calling about the case of Tania Miles and John Groves.'

Instantly, Sandy remembered the case. Both of them had been nineteen years old, and while backpacking in Asia, they had been found dead in a hotel room in Singapore. The Singapore Police had concluded that the deaths were from a drug overdose.

'I remember the case. It was written off as an overdose,' Sandy said, while picking up a pen and notebook to make some notes.

'Both families, as you know, have been unable to accept that Tania or John would have taken drugs at all. The theft of their belongings has also troubled them greatly,' Caroline said, then, as if reading something on a computer screen, she added, 'I have an email from a detective in the Singapore Police that says they have agreed to forward the remaining blood samples of both deceased to the families and they've asked whether we, the Durham Police, could arrange it.'

'OK, that makes sense. Sometimes families want every part of their loved ones returned, whether that is nothing more than tissue or blood samples,' Sandy said, not yet having needed to make any notes himself. 'Who is paying for this though? I don't think we at the FCDO' – he looked around to see if Clare Symonds, the custodian of their forensic budget, was about, but couldn't see her – 'will be able to fund it.'

'Paying for it isn't a problem, sir, and that is not why I'm calling,' Caroline said, a little bit flustered now. 'The families have agreed to pay as they have found a toxicology laboratory here in England that is going to examine the blood samples, and before you ask, they are going to pay for this too.'

Sandy felt a little bit annoyed with himself that he had come across as a penny-pinching bureaucrat, but let Caroline keep talking.

'The trouble is, we have no idea how to get the sample from the police laboratory in Singapore to the one we are going to use here. Please can you give me some advice so that I can help the families?'

Knowing what to do in this situation, Sandy brightened up. 'I have a little bit of experience here that may be of use. We have used the services of FedEx in the past to transfer body samples. Let me see if they have offices in Singapore.' He put in an internet search on his laptop while talking to Caroline.

'Yes,' he said when he saw an office in Singapore come up. 'Let me give them a call now – with the time difference, they might be closing soon.'

The call with the person in the FedEx office in Singapore was, as he expected, very straightforward. Sandy relayed the delivery requirements and pricing structure to Caroline, who was pleased to finally offer the families in Durham some help. Sandy hoped that if the toxicology revealed anything of note, he would be able to get involved in this case – it was very interesting indeed.

∞

By mid-morning, there was still nothing from Lincolnshire Police Safeguarding Hub, and there might never be, but Sandy had a missed call and message from Otto Wagner, asking if he was available for a video call with him and Professor Von Tripp that afternoon.

Deciding on a lunchtime walk around St James's Park to clear his head – he wasn't quite up to fitness following his rib injury, so had decided a walk rather than a run was best – Sandy found Juliet waiting for him upon his return, her laptop switched on and the Zoom call live, though no one had joined from the other end yet.

Just as Sandy was getting settled, Otto and Professor Von Tripp joined.

Without waiting for anyone to greet each other, the professor, who could clearly be seen on the screen sitting at a desk with a sheaf of paper and the outline of another screen visible to his left, said, 'I can confirm that the neuropathologist agrees with my findings that Arthur Barrington died from most probably, in their view, strangulation, but with a remote possibility that it was suffocation.'

Before Otto could get his words out – Sandy could see him trying to ask a question – Professor Von Tripp continued, this time picking up a couple of sheets of paper off his desk.

'The fibres on the neck are a dyed blue wool.' He then took his glasses off and scanned the papers he was holding. 'Yes, here it is. Almost certainly it is sheep's wool. They might be able to find a breed, but it looks like a generic type of sheep's wool.'

The minute Professor Von Tripp paused for a moment, Otto jumped in.

'Are you and the other pathologists able to put anything in writing for me?' He turned his hands to show his palms facing upwards. 'I have no reports. I have nothing to say young Mr Barrington was murdered, just your verbal account to me.'

'I have the fibre report here now.' Professor Von Tripp lifted up the papers to show them. 'I have the neuropathology report on my computer screen.' He pointed to the other screen that they could only see the outline of. 'Isn't my word good enough for you, Inspector Wagner?' He shook the papers about at the screen. 'It is good enough for the British detectives, but not you, Otto. You are such a cautious man.'

'Actually,' Sandy said, before Otto could respond, 'Inspector Wagner changed the death classification from a suspicious death to murder based on your verbal account.' He could see Otto threading his hands through his quickly diminishing hair. 'We also arrested the young man's father,

Andrew Barrington, for murder. Your word counts for a lot, professor.'

Before the professor had a chance to respond, Sandy continued. Juliet sat back, letting her boss have the whole screen to himself.

'We do need the findings in writing, though. There are numerous examples of verbal diagnosis given to officers by medical professionals that later turn out to be wrong when the full facts are known. And we, the police, get into trouble from all sides, if the medical professional says to us later that it was only an initial diagnosis and not one on which to base an arrest of somebody.'

'Those medical professionals were obviously not as experienced as me though, DCI McFarlane,' the professor said in a very authoritative voice.

In a quiet and far less confident voice, Otto requested, 'Timescales for written reports,' before quickly adding, 'please.'

The professor looked down at his keyboard, then up at his other screen. 'I have sent you the neuropathology report now.' He looked at the papers and picked up what looked like four sheets. 'I will get these copied for my records and courier them to you. Your CSI, Paulina Steiner, should also have them, as she is copied in.'

'Your report please, professor,' Juliet said, having now moved forward so both her and Sandy could be seen on the screen. 'Also, when can the body of Arthur be released to his family?'

'I have already agreed to the release of the body, as has the medical examiner. It is Inspector Wagner here' – he pointed at the image of Otto on his screen – 'who is being too cautious and has not agreed. What do you say now, Otto?' A mischievous grin spread across the professor's face.

'Yes, of course the body can be released, when I get your report, professor.'

Touché, thought Sandy.

'It is done and will be with you in the morning.' He looked at his watch. 'I need to be in class now.' With that, he had clearly pressed the "leave" button on his screen, for his image disappeared.

'I take it then, Otto, that you will release the body as soon as you get the report from the professor?' Sandy asked.

'Yes, I will contact you as soon as I have it in my hand.'

'I will hold off discussing options with the Barringtons until then,' Sandy said, having known this would be the answer. 'What's the current situation with the two boys who tried to steal my backpack and assaulted me?'

'The only thing I've heard is that something is most definitely bubbling. I have permission for us three to be briefed in person.' Otto looked glum. 'Will you both be able to come at short notice to Vienna?'

'In theory, yes, but you'll have to email our boss to make the request,' Sandy said, before saying goodbye to Otto and terminating the call.

CHAPTER FIFTEEN

The next day, Sandy received a text message from Freddie Wainwright, telling him that he had convinced his father to sign a consent form for all his records, whether police or medical, to be shared with other professionals and only professionals. Freddie went on to say that as soon as his father had signed, his mother had also signed a consent form.

They had agreed to meet the following day in Cambridge outside the Senate House and to go for a drink in The Eagle pub nearby. Emily would not be able to join them, and whilst Juliet had finished reading Arthur's love letters to Emily, she was loathe to hand them over for Sandy to give to Freddie. In her opinion, they were deeply private and only for the eyes of Emily, so Juliet had decided she would return them to Emily herself sometime in the future.

With the letters on his mind, almost as soon as he got back to the flat that evening, Sandy began writing his own love letter to Hannah, something he had considered doing since he had first seen the letters from Emily to Arthur in Vienna. He'd even bought paper and an envelope for that purpose.

As he put pen to paper, his words flowed, and he was glad his father was in Ely and wouldn't be turning up to disturb his writing. He began the letter with the first time he had seen Hannah in his grandfather's office at Fenners Chambers in Cambridge, then mapped out their relationship from there, explaining how his affection had deepened over the years. The letter was no doubt equally as personal and romantic as Emily's; a display of his honest feelings. In this digital age, where technology changed so fast, the writing of a handwritten love letter had a certain specialness to it.

Taking an early train the next morning, Sandy made it into Cambridge in good time to see Freddie. While walking to King's Parade, he resisted the temptation to take a diversion to look at the house where he was due to meet Hannah later. It was just off Hills Road, and as he walked past the side road, he realised it had taken him just short of ten minutes to walk there from the station. *Perfect!*

Freddie was waiting for him once he reached the Senate House, dressed in jeans, a sweatshirt and trainers, looking every part the student he was. They greeted each other warmly, then headed into The Eagle pub, just around the corner. The Eagle was infamous in Cambridge as the location where the discovery of DNA was first announced, and Sandy was a fan of its history. There was even an area at the back of the pub called the RAF bar, where graffiti left by airmen during the Second World War had been preserved for all to admire.

Sandy led Freddie to that same bar, though having both been to The Eagle many times before, neither Sandy nor Freddie took much notice of their surroundings, instead taking a seat opposite each other in the empty room, it being far too early in the morning for even the regulars to be in attendance.

As Freddie reached into his backpack, turning his body to get the consent papers out of it, he visibly winced.

'Have you injured yourself, Freddie?' Sandy asked, concerned, though he was careful to keep his voice soft and sensitive.

'Oh, it's nothing,' Freddie said, his face going bright red. As he placed the papers on the table, he winced again.

The pain was clearly *not* nothing. 'Let me see, please,' Sandy asked gently, looking around to ensure they were still alone. His detective gut feeling was blaring alarms in his head.

Freddie sighed heavily, but complied, lifting his sweatshirt to reveal a very bruised left side, which looked an unnatural blue and yellow colour. It appeared that the bruising, although all in one place, was from three separate and distinctive bruises.

'Your dad did this, didn't he?' Sandy said in a firm voice, at the same time shaking his head with empathy. He realised it was a closed question and that he should have said "tell me how this happened" or "how did you get those awful bruises", but it was obvious given Freddie's brush off earlier and Sandy's knowledge of his family situation. He knew that if he hadn't asked directly, Freddie might not have told him the truth.

'I'm not going to make a complaint,' Freddie said, pulling his sweatshirt down quickly. 'But yes, it was him. Almost as soon as you left the other day. I wasn't going to let him take it out on mum, so I took the hit.'

Before Sandy could say anything, Freddie continued talking very fast.

'He's fine now. After he punched me a few times, I convinced him to go with me to the hospital. We saw a nurse from the crisis mental health team and he's back on his meds now, compliant and doing well.'

He hadn't paused to breathe while blurting this out and wasn't even looking at Sandy, instead gazing at some non-distinct point on the table between them. Freddie picked up his coffee and took a large mouthful, as though he was trying to stop himself from saying more.

Looking at the signed consent forms, Sandy saw they were signed not only by the parents but also Emily and Freddie. He put them in his backpack and took out his laptop. Freddie was still not looking at him. After opening a blank electronic DASH form, Sandy paused and sipped his coffee, which was now going cold. He let the silence hang over them while he finished his cup.

'Freddie,' Sandy said softly. The frightened young man looked up at him and their eyes met. 'I am a police officer, and I have a duty of care. I need to fill in a risk assessment form about the incident and the injuries you have just showed me, and I would be grateful if you could help me as much as you feel able to.'

'What has this got to do with Arthur's death?' Freddie asked, his tone defensive.

'It hasn't got anything to do with his death, but it is about protecting you and your family from domestic abuse.'

Seeing Freddie nod, Sandy went through the form with him. Although unpredictable and still volatile at times when he thought he could hear voices, it was clear that when Douglas Wainwright was on his medication, he was a more even-tempered man.

When Freddie described an incident from a few years ago,

before he went to university, when he had seen his father attempt to strangle his mother, Sandy could picture the petite Hazel Wainwright with Douglas's huge hands around her throat. "Non-fatal strangulation" it was called these days, and was a huge risk factor. Sandy just hoped that all his efforts would help protect Hazel from similar incidents in the future.

Just before Freddie had to rush off for a final revision cramming session before his exams, he allowed Sandy to take a couple of images of the bruising on his phone, though he remained adamant that he was not going to make a statement or a complaint.

After Freddie left, Sandy glanced at his watch. He had plenty of time before he was due to meet Hannah and the estate agent, so decided to chance his luck at Parkside Police Station, to see if they could scan the forms Freddie had brought him. He walked quickly across Parker's Piece, bustling with pedestrians and cyclists, before crossing the road and making his way to the station. On seeing his Met Police warrant card and his FCDO identity pass, the very obliging and helpful man working on the front desk let him into the building.

Unfortunately, the man wasn't so helpful when it came to scanning the consent forms to send to Lincolnshire Police.

'No idea how these things work,' he said, pointing at the machine. He looked like he was in his late sixties – most probably a long-retired police officer.

It was all very straightforward to Sandy, fortunately, and he had soon sent over the documents, though due to the patchy internet connection, it took a lot longer for his laptop to send the DASH form and the images of the bruising on

Freddie. While he was waiting, Sandy glanced over at the noticeboard, and spotted an advert for the recruitment of superintendents to the Cambridgeshire Constabulary. One was for a detective role, as the head of major crime.

After a moment of consideration, he took a photograph of the advert for further thought. Whilst he was happy enough at the FCDO, he'd been there a long time, and he was getting tired. The opportunity for something a little different, here in Cambridge, excited him greatly.

∞

When he reached the road on which the house they were going to view was located, Sandy noticed that as well as the inevitable student accommodation within a university city, a number appeared to still be family homes.

The estate agent was waiting in her car outside and, on seeing Sandy, jumped out to greet him. She had in her hand a bunch of keys. The house had a garage at the side, which, although not the only one in the street, seemed to be quite rare. They went to look at the garage first. The door was an up and over type and was perfectly serviceable, though was in urgent need of a fresh lick of paint. On glancing over at the outside of the house, that too definitely needed painting. The house had just come through probate and had been empty for two years, but by the look of it the place had been neglected for a few years before that.

'I knew that the garage would be a priority for him,' Hannah said, laughing as she came up the drive. Seeing the estate agent looking confused, she added, 'The thing he loves most in the world is not actually me but his Morgan Roadster car, and he wants to ensure it will fit in the garage.' She chuckled again. 'If it doesn't, I am afraid we won't be looking any further.'

Sandy assured her that the Morgan *would* fit in the garage, so they proceeded to look around the house. They spoke about the considerable amount of modernisation they would need to do to it, but the price was in their budget. As the owners wanted it to remain as a family home and not student accommodation, they were in a good position to put in an offer, which they decided to do. The estate agent promised she would get back to them within the next couple of days.

A very excited Hannah and Sandy went to the house she shared with two housemates, which was nearby. The plan was for Sandy to stay over, then head back to London the next day and stay until the weekend.

Sitting in the communal lounge, as she and Sandy sipped their tea, Hannah said, 'I don't know how to say this but…' She paused and looked straight at Sandy. 'I intend to keep my surname and not change it to McFarlane when we get married.'

Sandy was stunned silent for a moment, not because he was against the idea, but because it had never even occurred to him.

Hannah went on. 'I have the development of a good legal practice now and they know me as Hannah Tobias.'

Seeing her obvious nervousness on raising the topic, Sandy reached across and put his arm around her. 'If that is what you want, it's perfectly fine by me.' He smiled widely and kissed her.

Hannah still seemed tense as he pulled away.

'There's one more thing I would like you to consider,' she said.

She's softened me up for the big one then, Sandy thought.

'I know you want to get married in Ely Cathedral and have the reception nearby, but I would really like to get married in your old college, St John's, in the chapel there, and have the reception in the hall.'

Not saying anything at first, and with a pensive look that showed he was thinking about it, Sandy eventually spoke. 'Is it possible? I am not sure how we go about it. I know a couple of friends of mine got married there, but it was while they were still students, or soon after they left.'

'I think it should be still feasible, though you might have to contact the Master, since it's been well over five years since you left. But you're up for it, are you, if we can get it arranged?'

'I'm definitely up for it. I can write to the chaplain or the dean of the chapel, and can also try the Master of John's. It's all monies for them anyway, if we fit in with their schedule and can be flexible,' Sandy said encouragingly.

Both of their phones rang almost simultaneously. It was Otto on the phone for Sandy.

'You and Juliet need to come to Vienna, now.'

'Why? What's happened?' Sandy asked. He could feel his phone buzzing with other calls: one from Juliet, another from Jane Watson. 'What time tonight?' was all he said, before a clearly agitated Otto responded.

'We have a confidential briefing tomorrow at noon that the two of you and myself have been invited to.'

Noon, that sounds more feasible, Sandy thought.

'We will get the first flight out in the morning,' Sandy said, finishing the call, and after glancing at a perplexed-looking Hannah, he rang Juliet. 'They want us to fly to Vienna urgently, are you able to come with me?'

'Yes, Detective Superintendent Watson has us booked on a very early flight tomorrow morning from London Heathrow. Shall I organise an airport hotel for us to stay in? We'll need to check in for the flight at 4:00 a.m.?'

Sandy gave her the go ahead, knowing Juliet was extremely efficient and would organise everything perfectly. This way, Sandy would just need to get to his flat and then to the hotel at Heathrow that evening.

He was sad to miss out on an evening and a night with Hannah, but his adrenaline and excitement were rising by the minute. It was looking like they would finally be getting their hands on his assailants... and presumably Arthur Barrington's murderer.

Chapter Sixteen

The sound of the wheels of their British Airways jet hitting the ground and then the noise of the reverse thrust and braking woke both Juliet and Sandy. They had fallen asleep almost as soon as they had reached altitude on leaving London.

It was a bright day in Vienna that morning, and Sandy still had a warm glow inside and a grin on his face after the phone call Hannah had received yesterday from the estate agent, telling her that their offer had been accepted. All the way to London on the train, Sandy had been emailing, their solicitor, then a company that the solicitor had recommended for a house and environmental survey, and finally the mortgage company, confirming the amount of mortgage they would need. He'd had no time to tell his family, but Hannah had been on the phone to her father, Howard, as he was leaving to catch his train.

The only thing niggling at him was that Hannah had failed to mention the love letter he had given her as he left yesterday, despite them messaging back and forth and calling since then. Perhaps, in all the excitement, she hadn't opened it yet? He hoped that was the case.

Waiting to meet them as they came out of customs was Otto himself. He was wearing his usual suit but had on a trilby-type straw hat. He looked almost smart with this one addition to his clothing attire – a present from his wife, he told them, so he felt obliged to wear it.

They went straight to the Vienna District Police HQ, situated on the ring road around the city centre. They were the first people to arrive in the large lecture theatre. The officer on the door to the room had ticked their names off his list and had given them both inclusion notices and confidentiality notices for them to sign. The officer also showed them to seats towards the back, clearly indicating that they were observers and not participants for this briefing.

It was a good job they had taken an early flight as, unbeknown to them, the briefing had been brought forward and people were already starting to flood into the room. Superintendent Isabella Mahler, Otto's boss, came over and said hello. She told them how she had pushed hard for all of them to be included in the briefing. She was apparently also an observer as she sat with them.

A high-ranking representative of the Federal Minister of the Interior took their place at the front of the room. The room was filled with firearms commanders and Otto pointed out their chief, the Inspector General for Vienna. This was serious business and was clearly not about the simple arrest of two Albanian teenagers.

Felix Bauer, an assistant commissioner from BK – which, Otto told Juliet and Sandy, was the abbreviation for the Central Intelligence Service for Austria – stood at the front and addressed the room, showing on the large screen behind him the images of two Turkish Cypriots who were in prison in Austria. They were serving sixteen years for the importation and distribution of drugs. They'd had complete control and almost total monopoly distributing all sorts of recreational and class A drugs that circulated through the ski resorts every winter in Austria. A very complex, involved and highly successful long-running operation had put these two, plus many others, behind bars.

What has this got to do with our suspects? Sandy wondered, looking at Juliet to find her seeming equally confused. Otto too looked uncertain, but Sandy reasoned that was often his look.

The next image the assistant commissioner showed was of three faces. One of the images, he told them, was of a Polish man, and the other two men were Turkish Cypriots. One of the Turkish Cypriots was a brother to one of the men in prison for the drug offences. He went into a description of the intelligence against each of the men, and it was heavily littered with violence and extreme violence, though sadly this had amounted to very little in the way of convictions, as no one seemed to want to give evidence against them.

The next image he showed them was of Alexander Van der Bellen, the President of Austria. Juliet and Sandy, when they were last in Vienna, had passed by the door to his office when they had visited the Hofburg Palace.

'These three,' the commissioner said, as he went back to the images of the three violent criminals he had just shown on the screen, 'according to our extremely reliable sources, are planning to kidnap Mr Van der Bellen and hold him hostage for an exchange of the two Turkish Cypriot drug dealers.'

'Fascinating,' Sandy whispered to Juliet.

'But where do we come in?' Juliet said quietly in response.

'This evening, when the President leaves his office, he will, as he usually does, walk to his car, which is situated approximately one hundred metres away from his office building, where his driver will be parked in a line of parking spaces waiting for him. These two' – he put up the images of Flamur Hysa and Marin Ismalaj, the two Albanian boys – 'are the lookouts.'

'How did they get involved in such a big operation?' Juliet wondered aloud, more rhetorically than looking for a response from Sandy or Otto, who was putting his hands through his hair again.

Maybe that's why his wife bought him the hat, to stop him pulling out his remaining hair? Sandy mused.

'As lookouts, they will be riding electric cycles, which, as we know, can achieve dangerous speeds and are extremely hard to follow. They will take it in turns to watch for the exact moment the President leaves the building, as they have thirty seconds or so for the van carrying the others to make a move and scoop the President up. The other one will be doing circuits around the block, looking for police.'

The assistant commissioner looked around the room and nodded towards Otto and Superintendent Mahler.

'They are both wanted for a series of hotel room thefts and are the priority suspects for the murder of a British man in one of these hotel rooms. If we can get hold of them, they are going to be arrested, along with the others, for conspiracy to kidnap the President of Austria and an act of terrorism against the country of Austria. The other offences, I am afraid, will have to wait.'

'So this is why we've been trumped in our investigation,' Sandy said, loudly enough that almost everyone could hear.

A number of people sitting in front of them turned around

on hearing his British accent.

The assistant commissioner nodded curtly, then drew the briefing to a close, though a specialist firearms briefing continued in one corner of the room, as did a briefing with the police government communications department. It made sense: they needed to get ready for the worldwide media storm that was about to hit them.

∞

Not wanting to say anything due to the confidentiality agreement they had signed, Sandy, Otto and Juliet walked silently through the HQ building. When they got back into the car, Sandy whistled.

'Wow! What a briefing. If this actually happens, it will be like living through a real-life Hollywood blockbuster.'

'Are you going to take us to the office or to check in at our hotel?' Juliet asked Otto as he started the car and edged out of the parking space.

They had three hours before they needed to be back at HQ – they had been given permission to sit in the control room for the operation, code-named Operation Sparrowhawk. The assistant commissioner, they had learned from Otto, was highly regarded as a top man. *Well, his briefing was first rate*, Sandy conceded.

'I will drop you at your hotel and pick you up in good time for us to get into the control room before Operation Sparrowhawk begins. I suggest you rest and get something to eat. It's going to be a long day.'

'I thought we could say hello to Mia and Johanna,' Juliet

said. 'That's why I suggested the police office.'

'I am not even going into the office myself.' Otto said, putting on a rather dapper pair of sunglasses. His wife's doing, Sandy assumed. 'Those two young women are far too nosey, far too inquisitive, and far too good at wheedling information out of me. I dare not risk it.'

Both Juliet and Sandy chuckled at that, prompting Otto to laugh along with them. *It's nice to see him laughing*, Sandy thought. He was a man who carried all the cares of the world on his shoulders.

Fortunately, they were able to check in at their hotel early – the same hotel they had used last time. Juliet decided a nap was best for her and Sandy decided a visit to the nearby St Stephen's Cathedral was a better use of his time.

The square was as busy if not busier than the last time they were there, and it was dominated by the cathedral in the middle of it. There had been a cathedral there for nearly one thousand years, although Sandy knew the roof was comparatively new, only completed around 1950. The previous roof, of wood construction, had been destroyed in the final remaining days of the Second World War, the embers of the fires caused by bombing alighting St Stephen's Cathedral roof. The new roof was magnificent, and Sandy walked right around, admiring it before entering the cathedral itself. On the south side of the steep roof, the tiles formed a mosaic of the double-headed eagle, symbolic of the Austrian empire, and on the north, the coats of arms of the City of Vienna and of the Republic of Austria.

Whenever he entered a cathedral, Sandy had to stop himself from comparing it with his beloved Ely Cathedral.

St Stephen's was a lot more compact and not as airy, which might have been because the cathedral was as packed with people inside as there were outside in the square.

As he hadn't bought a ticket for a tour, Sandy dodged the tourists, looking along the sides and into the main part of the cathedral and at the altar. The visit took him a lot less time than he had thought it would, and Sandy felt somewhat disappointed, though the vast number of tourists flooding the space had certainly not helped the ambiance.

Looking at his watch when he got back to his hotel room, and seeing he still had plenty of time, Sandy rang the Barringtons. The previous night, Otto had sent him an email telling him that he agreed with the medical examiner and the pathologist for the release of Arthur's body to his family.

'Mr Barrington,' Sandy said as soon as the phone was answered. 'It is DCI McFarlane.'

'I'll just get him for you,' the voice of Faith Barrington said.

A few moments elapsed before Andrew came on the phone.

'Is it possible for you to put your phone on speaker please, so that your wife can hear what I'm about to say, Mr Barrington?' Sandy asked.

'Already happening,' Andrew replied. 'You know Faith by now shc wouldn't want to miss out on any conversation about our son.'

Sandy smiled to himself. 'I have received confirmation that Arthur can be released to you.' There was an audible sigh of relief from the other end of the line. 'I understand Professor Von Tripp, the pathologist, is content to keep Arthur for a few more days, but not for much longer than that.'

'What does all this mean?' Andrew asked. 'It's all a mystery to me. Can you help us to understand?'

Sandy stood up and walked around his hotel room as he talked. This sort of conversation was better done in person, but he needed the Barringtons to know as early as possible about Arthur.

'You will need to get a funeral director here in Vienna to collect Arthur.'

'How do we find one of them?' Andrew asked.

'Normally, the FCDO suggest you do a Google search and look at reviews for funeral directors,' Sandy said. When he heard the exasperated noises from both Faith and Andrew, he added, 'I did say "normally". In this case, I will personally get you recommendations for at least two of them for you to consider.' He would ask Otto, Mia and Johanna if they could recommend anyone, though he was keen not to tell the Barringtons he was in Vienna at the moment.

'I do have details of British-based funeral directors who are experienced and would be able to do the flight part of moving Arthur back to England for you.' Hearing them both say "thank you", Sandy continued, 'I am presuming that Arthur had no insurance that would cover this eventuality? I warn you that the flight part, what we call repatriation of a body, is very expensive. I'm not sure what the cost would be in this case, but in a recent case I worked on in the Caribbean, flying the body back to the UK cost just over £30,000.'

Andrew Barrington whistled.

'There is another option: you fly to Vienna with whoever else you would like to be here with you and have a cremation service, then bring the ashes home with you,' Sandy said, pausing while this piece of information was absorbed. 'You could then have a memorial service or celebration of life service back at home.' He paused to let what he'd said sink in further. This was why it was much better done in person, to be able to judge the reactions. He then added, 'Let me find out some funeral director names from Vienna while you think on what I have just said. I will get back to you in the next day or so.'

Chapter Seventeen

The control room already had a number of people in it as they entered, including the man leading Operation Sparrowhawk, Felix Bauer. They were all milling around and chatting to each other.

The room contained banks of screens with tables, and chairs in front of two screens at a time. On the desks were laid headsets, which had small microphones attached to them. Also on a desk towards the back of the room that had seating around it were a number of handset radios.

Otto, Juliet and Sandy were to be sat at this table. It looked like they would have a good view of all of the screens that were already switched on and showing images of streets. Sandy recognised on two screens, each from a different angle, the building and the door that the President would exit from in a couple of hours' time.

Assistant Commissioner Bauer came over and introduced himself to Otto and the British detectives. He was a very smart man, probably around fifty years of age, dressed in a bright blue three-piece suit and of a slim build, so much so that his waistcoat sat flat with all of the buttons fastened. His bright yellow silk tie and matching handkerchief added to this elegant look.

'Sorry that you will have to wait,' Felix said to them, at the same time taking a seat at the table and gesturing for them all to sit. He clearly wanted to chat. 'As soon as we are finished with the boys, you can have them.'

'Thank you for inviting us to observe, sir,' Otto said.

'It was my decision. You are dealing with a murder enquiry and would expect precedence, but I wanted to show, by you being here, that the death of your young man and his worth has not diminished. Unfortunately, we needed to deal with this scenario first.' Not only did Felix look elegant, he also had a devastating smile.

'This looks like a solid operation, but involves incredibly high risk,' Sandy said, looking at the screens and seeing people and cars, the general public milling about.

There could be a high level of risk to public safety occurring here. The smile on Felix's face had gone and he had shifted into serious mode.

Sandy continued, 'In the UK, I'm not sure we would be able to run an operation like this – the potential for collateral damage would be deemed too high risk.' Pausing while he saw Felix thinking of a response, he added, 'It could be described as an ambush, and I think our commanders of any such firearms operation would be pushed down the disruption route.'

Felix frowned. 'Disruption route… ah, I understand. *Störung*. Yes, it was a strong consideration of mine,' Felix said. 'I can't deny it. But to catch them in the act of moving towards abducting and kidnapping the President of Austria? Anyone, and I mean anyone, trying to think they can commit crimes against the very fabric, the very being, of the Austrian state must be dealt with swiftly and publicly.'

'Where are all these images coming from?' Juliet asked,

pointing at the various screens. 'Are they from city or police CCTV?'

'Those,' he said, pointing to a bank of four screens, 'are streamed from Vienna city CCTV. And those two' – he pointed to one screen showing the door to the President's office and the other one pointing to a line of car parking spaces that had a few empty places – 'are from the helmets of two firearms officers in each place, who took up covert positions just as dawn was breaking this morning. The firearms officers are highly trained marksmen. Four of our best.'

Felix walked over to the screen showing the car parking spaces and pointed to a blue van with the name of a work firm on its side, the name of which was not distinct enough to be made out. The van was parked facing inwards.

'This van also arrived at the same time as the firearm officers, and in the rear are four highly trained, rapid assault firearms officers.'

On one of the screens, aerial footage took over the streaming images being shown.

'That is one of two drones we are going to be using.' Looking from the screen and then back to the detectives, Felix said, 'It's being flown very high and silently, so we are of the opinion it won't scare them off. That's as well as the occasional police helicopter passing by as that is what happens normally.'

The excitement of anticipation, although high, had not yet reached fever pitch, but that would happen very soon, if all went according to plan.

A visibly very excited Sandy, desperately hoping that the operation would happen and be a success, asked, 'Where are the suspects now?' He looked earnestly around the images, but they were all located around the Hofburg Palace and surrounding streets. 'It doesn't look like we have eyes on them.'

'You're right. Their location is quite isolated and we have not been able to get a permanent image. However, the drone has gone over and the white van we believe they are using is at the premises, and our information from the informant is that they are there, so everything is set for it to go ahead as planned.' Felix looked directly at first Otto, then Sandy. 'Your boys, on the other hand, are not at the place they normally stay at. We have the details for the phones they normally use, so I have just asked for GPS phone tracking to be put on them to see if we can locate them.'

A couple of the control room operators left the room then, and Sandy was pleased to see them return a short while later with two trolley loads full of what appeared to be interesting buffet food, accompanied by soft drinks. He realised the operators must have fetched the food themselves because no one was allowed access to the control room aside from those involved. There was already a coffee machine and tea-making facilities in the corner of the control room – the police, like many other organisations, operated best whilst caffeinated and on a full stomach. The firearms officers that had been in place for many hours now had no doubt had double, if not triple, pack-ups to keep them happy. At de-brief sessions, it was always the quality of the food that was commented on, not the operation itself!

While they ate and waited to see if any action would take place, Otto had given Sandy the details of a funeral director that he had used in the past. He had sent a message to Mia and Johanna asking them for any recommendations too. They had both messaged back saying:

Where are you? What are you doing? What are you up to?

'See,' Otto said laughing. 'Those two are far too nosey for their own good!'

They had both recommended the same one that Otto had, and Johanna one other that she had recently had a good experience with. Sandy sent a message with the names and contact details to Andrew Barrington.

'What's going on here?' they heard Felix cry out in a loud and very frustrated voice.

Everyone, including the detectives, immediately swizzled round and looked at the screen that Felix was pointing to. There, clearly to be seen on the screen, was a parking enforcement officer, in full but ill-fitting uniform, with his blue hat, which was far too big for him, sitting on his head at an angle. He was walking around the blue van and was on his radio.

'Boss,' one of the operators said to Felix, 'we've seen him walk around at least three times today and on each occasion he took the van's registration number.'

Before Felix could make a decision on what he wanted doing, a police car turned up and parked in front of the van doors. Two equipment-laden and very burly built officers got out of the vehicle and spoke to the parking enforcement officer. They started to walk around the van and took a note of the firm's name on the side and the registration number themselves. One of them returned to the car and could be seen on the car radio.

'Get rid of them!' Felix shouted at almost a fever pitch. 'Now!'

His staff officer, who was in uniform and was of the same rank as Otto, a senior inspector, stopped typing on his laptop, which he had been doing continually since the detectives arrived, updating a live log that was being shown on a large screen to the side of the room. The operational firearms lead along with others were also inputting into the log, keeping it updated. Sandy had seen this type of IT log system in place at New Scotland Yard in London when they had been managing crimes in action, such as kidnappings, just like they were dealing with here in Vienna.

The staff officer was gone for no longer than ten minutes when, on the screen, they saw the officer who was sitting in the car gesticulate wildly with his arms for the other two to come away from the van. They all got back into the police car and drove off at speed, causing everyone walking near that side of the Hofburg Palace to look at them. Hardly an unobtrusive exit!

When the staff officer returned, he said, 'They had just called for a tow truck to come and collect the van!'

Everyone in the room found this hilarious, and the tense mood lifted.

As the time moved on to almost 4:30 p.m., an excited operator called out, 'The GPS tracking of the phones is telling us that the white Mercedes van is now on the move towards the city.' He looked around to see if everyone was listening to him, in particular Felix. 'The two boys' phones are now switched on as well.'

'Here they are,' another operator called out.

Felix gave a command for the drone to be sent to track the Mercedes van.

He then stood as they saw the two Albanian boys come into view on the screen, which was being streamed from outside the office of the President. The marksmen outside this building could have been no more than ten metres away from them. Hearts were beating fast in the control room. *What must it be like for those two marksmen?* Sandy wondered.

The boys were on identical electric cycles that really did look more like motorcycles. They were also dressed identically in blue jeans and blue hoodies with the hoods pulled over their heads, and both were wearing green chequered scarves across almost all of their faces. Only their eyes were visible. This seemed almost like a uniform for youths that rode these electric cycles all over the world, as certainly Juliet and Sandy had seen their intimidating silhouettes travelling at speed around the streets of London.

The boys could not be told apart. One of them stayed in situ while the other whizzed off, no doubt doing laps to make sure the coast was clear. The one watching the door could be seen speaking into a small handheld radio that he got out of his pocket.

The aerial drone footage followed the Mercedes van along the Vienna streets. It was moving cautiously, not doing anything out of the ordinary, then it turned into the street that led up to the palace building with the President's office and finally into the line of parking spaces. A slight cheer resounded round the control room. This was now real and, it appeared, happening. The boys had changed over and the one now sat watching the door gave a nod of acknowledgement to the occupants of the van as they reversed into the parking place.

'I don't believe this,' shouted Felix. The van had only gone and parked directly next to the blue van containing the rapid assault firearms officers. 'Not a word from them. Tell them to be quiet,' Felix shouted out to the room, not sure who was the person in radio contact with the officers in the van.

Although he had been chewing gum throughout, Felix was now chewing at such a vigorous rate that he was in danger of causing himself permanent jaw injury. Juliet walked over to him and gave him a cup of coffee that she had just made and a fresh packet of gum from her handbag. She gave him a slight smile and a nod, indicating, "you can do this".

Earlier than they had anticipated, the door to the building where the President's office opened.

Out stepped a smiling Mr Van der Bellen into the sunshine of the beautiful late afternoon in Vienna. He had no idea what was about to befall him in the next few moments.

The tension in the control room was off the charts.

Felix Bauer shouted out, 'It's showtime.'

His career was about to be made or ended in the next few moments.

Chapter Eighteen

The signal that the President had appeared in the street from his office was relayed to all the firearms officers, informing them that they now needed to be in a position ready to "strike, strike, strike!". The same message must have been relayed by one of the Albanian boys to the occupants of the white Mercedes van as, coincidently, at that moment, both boys were nearby the entrance and would have seen the President exit.

As the President emerged, however, so did the Chancellor from his office opposite, and all hell broke loose.

One of the boys rode his electric cycle at speed towards the gap between the President and Chancellor – trying to isolate the President, Sandy assumed – but because he had propelled himself from a standing start so vigorously and violently, he lost control of the cycle and came tumbling off it, leaving the cycle to continue moving, heading along the ground at speed. The front wheel struck the President on his ankle and lower leg and knocked him violently to the ground. The blood oozing out of the wound was almost immediate and the President wasn't going to be getting up too quickly or too soon.

The Chancellor's close protection staff reacted almost instantaneously: one jumped and pulled the Chancellor to the ground and spread themselves over him for his protection, albeit no ballistic protection but at least something; the other bodyguard went onto their haunches in front of the Chancellor with their Glock pistol in their hand, pointing it at the Albanian boy. Their special service training had clearly kicked in and they were protecting their principal – the man they had a duty to protect. If the boy had come one step closer, the bodyguard would have no hesitation and would shoot, of that there was no doubt.

During this time, the Mercedes van had lurched out of its parking space at speed and swung right towards where the President had been walking. At that instance, one of the marksmen opposite the car parking space quickly moved out of his hiding place and got ready to throw across the road a contraption called a "stinger" – a long strip of metal that went across the road, full of very sharp steel spikes designed to stop cars, vans or even buses effectively, reliably and safely, by penetrating all makes and models of tyres and deflating them.

The marksman made the required pull on the handle to send it across the road, but because the angle was too acute and too close to the Mercedes, the stinger just struck the side of the van and was rendered useless, meaning the van kept moving forward unhindered.

The four assault firearms officers had leapt out of their vehicle, but only as the middle and then the back of the Mercedes van became level with them as it hurtled along. The officers were equipped with ballistic helmets and body-worn ballistic vests and had holstered at their side a Glock pistol. Each of them were carrying a Heckler & Koch submachine gun, which had been in use since the 1960s and was widely used by law enforcement officers worldwide.

On seeing that the stinger device had not had its desired effect, the man who was leading this team, known as Raid One, gave an urgent directive to the others.

'Tyres!' he shouted.

All four of them moved almost in unison, their hours, weeks and months of training kicking in. They went down on one knee and took aim. The rattle of gunfire for anyone nearby must have been extremely loud and would no doubt have made Sandy startle and jump if he was there.

The shots, or at least some of them, were successful, but in contrast to what the stinger would have achieved to bring the vehicle safely to a stop, this didn't happen with the use of high-velocity bullets and their impact. The explosion of both rear tyres was even louder than the bullet fire.

On the explosion of its tyres and the bullets hitting the metal of the wheels themselves, the Mercedes van, which had begun to build up a reasonable amount of speed, lurched left, then right, colliding with heavy impact into the only other vehicle remaining in the parking spaces. The driver, trying to regain control, must have yanked on the steering wheel, for as it continued to plough through the remaining parked car, it turned one hundred and eighty degrees and then front faced the four assault firearms officers. By this point, the marksmen were standing on either side of the road, their Steyr AUG rifles focused on the doors of the Mercedes van.

From nowhere, the boy who hadn't fallen from his cycle came up the road at extreme speed and, with incredible agility, manoeuvred around the van and the firearms officers and sped off away from them. Because there had been no threat to Raid One's operational plan, he had seemingly decided to ignore the electric cycle, presumably because he needed all of his officers to give their undivided attention to eliminate any threat by the occupants of the van.

Through the windscreen, three people could be seen, all wearing balaclavas. They appeared to be shaken, not surprising after the impact of the rear tyres exploding and the crash with the other car. The windscreen itself didn't appear to be cracked but the occupants not wearing seatbelts must have hit their heads at some stage.

'Armed police!' shouted Raid One. 'Armed police!' He and the other three shuffled around, with two going to the driver's side and the other two to the passenger side. 'Come out of the vehicle with your hands raised and not carrying any weapons.'

The driver roared the still running engine and tried to get the van to move, revving even harder and making a loud screeching noise. The vehicle was not moving anywhere and the driver gave up.

Doors opened on each side and the occupants could now be seen to be three large burly men. They were all wearing dark blue boiler suits and black balaclavas. There was no sign of any weapons in their hands, and with the marksmen now taking position to cover their colleagues, the assault firearms officers grabbed each of the men, with one of the officers having to quickly go round to the driver's side to assist his two colleagues there as the driver was thrown on his front onto the floor and handcuffed with his hands behind his back. The other two were dealt with in equally the same manner.

A marked police van screeched up behind them and

another two armed and ready officers leapt out. The three detained men were bundled into the police van, which then turned around and sped off.

The detained men were clearly injured, the level of which was unknown, but Felix Bauer gave the instruction that the police cell centre was the safest place for them to be taken to and asked for a doctor, nurse and paramedics to be called to attend to them there. Any stay in a hospital for any of them would be a logistical nightmare.

Looking into the front of the van, three handguns and one shotgun could be clearly seen on the floor. No one was to touch the van and forensic officers were already on the scene, with search officers standing by to take over after they had finished.

As the arrests were made, the boy whose cycle had hit the President started to move towards him. He hadn't looked along the road to see what was happening, so he was unaware that the abduction and kidnap was over. He clearly thought he still had a chance and could still isolate the President.

'Armed police!' shouted the two police marksmen who had emerged from the bushes opposite, their Steyr Aug rifles pointed at the boy. 'Go back down on your knees and put your hands up.'

Whether he was simply shaken by the fall off the cycle or was deliberately choosing to ignore the shouted command, the boy moved closer towards the fallen President. The closest marksman's rifle kicked up slightly, the double tap sending two bullets hurtling towards the boy at such velocity and speed that in a micro-second, both of the bullets hit the boy's torso and the force whirled him round and then onto the floor.

The armed officer who had taken the shot moved forward to the lifeless body of the boy while his colleague stood cover for him. The officer placed his weapon to the floor and, slightly lifting up the scarf that was around the boy's neck, chin and mouth, he felt for a pulse on the boy's neck.

'No pulse,' he reported to the control room.

The boy had been shot dead.

Through the camera fixed to the officer's uniform, Sandy could clearly see a tattoo on the neck of the boy featuring three stars, two smaller silver-coloured ones and a larger one in the centre, which was a faded red.

The priority suspect for the murder of Arthur Barrington was now lying dead on a street beside the Hofburg Palace in Vienna.

Chapter Nineteen

It could only be described as carnage and pandemonium on the streets around the Hofburg Palace. There was a body lying prostrate, dead on the floor; other people, including the President and the Chancellor of Austria, were also lying on the floor nearby. Along the street only one hundred metres away were two smashed up vehicles. Police were everywhere. Two drones were flying low overhead. The police helicopter was less than five hundred feet above the carnage. The drones and helicopter were filming everything.

Beside the white Mercedes van, the first uniform police officers that had arrived formed a close cordon, not letting anyone in or out.

A man and woman approached an officer at the cordon, the man shouting, 'That's my car!' He pointed to the car in the parking space with a smashed grill; in fact, the whole of the car was damaged where the Mercedes had crashed into it. 'What happened to it? It wasn't damaged when I parked it there.'

He looked from his car to the four rapid assault officers who were standing inside the cordon and started shaking his head in disbelief and incomprehension at what he was seeing.

After a brief conversation with one of the officers, the man and woman were swiftly placed into a detective car and driven away for their statement to be taken.

CSI officers arrived to carry out a meticulous search of the Mercedes after firstly taking possession of the weapons in the vehicle as exhibits. A number of officers in plain clothes arrived, who, it appeared, were from internal affairs. They took possession of the Heckler & Koch submachine gun from each of the officers in turn. Shots had been fired and as well as the criminal investigation into the kidnappers, or attempted kidnappers, an internal affairs investigation had started into the actions of the firearms officers on the streets of Vienna. The firearms officers were all taken away in one car and their vehicle, the van they had been in, was left in situ to be dealt with later. It was the least of anyone's worries.

The Chancellor, with the help of his close protection staff, got slowly to his feet. To say he looked shaken was an understatement. He stood there looking at the scene in front of him: the police cordon, two police officers armed with rifles standing over a boy, lying presumably dead on the ground. His close protection staff firmly moved the Chancellor away to get him into his waiting chauffeur-driven car. A detective spoke to him briefly as he got into the car and said they would be in contact to take a statement from him and his two members of staff.

More internal affair officers had arrived at the scene and each of the marksmen had their rifles taken from them. Their hands were swabbed, and as much as the internal affairs officers wanted to take the clothing they were wearing, out in the middle of a street was not the right place for this to happen. Shots had been fired and a life had been taken. It would need to be proved that this was a lawful killing and each of the officers were taken away separately. Their nightmare that only commenced a few moments ago was now starting to get much worse.

Two paramedics and two detectives were with the President. The paramedics' initial assessment was that the ankle was probably shattered and, by the angle the foot was now positioned in, one or both of the President's tibia or fibula bones were also broken.

He was placed onto a stretcher and moved into a nearby ambulance, which was positioned just outside the police cordon. A detective and paramedic got into the back with the President, and with blue lights flashing and sirens going off loudly, the ambulance made its way off to the hospital followed by a police car, also with blue lights flashing and sirens sounding. This police car contained firearms officers that would be on guard for the President at the hospital.

This left an electric cycle lying on the floor and the dead boy, Flamur Hysa, all alone lying there. No one was going to touch him until the forensic medical examiner got there, and a forensic pathologist might turn up as well. *What a sad end to what was no doubt a sad life*, Sandy thought morosely. This life of crime that he had been criminally exploited into really shouldn't have ended like this.

Photographs had been taken before the President had been moved, and markings had been placed on the ground where he had been lying. A 360-degree imaging had also taken place. Once this had been completed, three CSIs in full barrier clothing, double gloved and with their hoods up and masks on – no one was going to be making any mistakes here – were on their hands and knees making their way methodically and systematically forwards to where the President had been and then to the electric cycle. After Flamur had been seen to by the medical examiner, they continued up to him.

By this point, the control room had descended from a cacophony of noise to almost silence, just punctuated with officers giving almost whispered instructions or responses on their microphones attached to their headsets.

They were all watching, when they could, the drone and helicopter footage of the aftermath of the live stage of the operation, other than Felix Bauer, who was sat slumped in his seat with his head in his hands. No doubt he was struggling to come to terms with what had happened, and how it had all gone so wrong in just a split second. Sandy had been informed that the Chancellor only occasionally worked from that office, so it was a terrible coincidence that he had appeared at the same time as the President did.

Sandy wasn't sure what the outcome would be. After all, they had achieved the objective of Operation Sparrowhawk, which was to ensure the President wasn't kidnapped and the country wasn't held to ransom, and they had arrested three major criminals. However, the President had sustained a serious injury to his ankle and leg, the Chancellor had also been involved, one of the boys involved in Sandy's assault and Arthur's murder was dead, and the other, Marin Ismalaj, had disappeared. He reasoned that the objective now was to prove the case. At least they were well on the way with the weapons found in the van.

Sandy saw Felix lift his head as his staff officer approached.

'You are to stand down, sir,' the officer said to Felix. 'The operation has now been taken over by a detective superintendent who will lead on the criminal investigation into the kidnap attempt.'

Felix nodded in acceptance.

'There is a superintendent from internal affairs who is going to work parallel to this criminal investigation to examine the shots fired at the Mercedes van, but in particular, examine the death of Flamur Hysa,' the officer continued. 'They want to speak to you, not tonight but first thing tomorrow.'

'What is that saying, "it is not the critic's opinion that counts"?' Felix said out loud.

Sandy took out his phone. 'It is indeed – President Theodore Roosevelt.' Sandy found what he was looking for and read it out loud so everyone, especially Felix, could hear. '"It is not the critic who counts: not the man who points out how the strong man stumbles or where the doer of deeds could have done better. The credit belongs to the man who is actually in the arena, whose face is marred by dust and sweat and blood, who strives valiantly, who errs and comes up short again and again, because there is no effort without error or shortcoming, but who knows the great enthusiasms, the great devotions, who spends himself in a worthy cause; who, at the best, knows, in the end, the triumph of high achievement, and who, at the worst, if he fails, at least he fails while daring greatly, so that his place shall never be with those cold and timid souls who knew neither victory nor defeat".'

The smile on Felix's face was much brighter now. He was, and had been, the man in the arena.

'Sir,' Sandy said, gesturing for Otto to join them. 'Before you do stand down, can you as a last decision action Inspector Wagner to find and arrest Marin Ismalaj and then hand him over to the Operation Sparrowhawk crime investigation team?'

'Yes, great idea.' Felix looked at Otto. 'Is this something you can do?'

Having now perked up considerably, Otto smiled and nodded. 'Absolutely, sir. As long as he has gone to the address we know for him or the GPS is still running, we will have him in custody within the hour.'

Felix nodded at the staff officer, who was busy typing the direction on the command log.

The staff officer then said to Felix, holding up Felix's phone that he was looking after, 'Sir, almost every police commissioner we have in Austria has called you at least twice. The President's office, the Chancellor's office, the Federal Minister of the Interior themselves.' Seeing Felix turn a pale colour again, the staff officer said, 'Plus your wife, your children and your mother.'

The detectives left the room quickly, but just before they left, Sandy turned and smiled at Felix and gave him a nod and a mock salute, as if to say, "well done, Assistant Commissioner. No one would have, could have, done better, and in fact most would have turned and run from leading this operation".

Otto was on his phone even before the door had shut behind them.

'Johanna, don't ask any questions, just do what I say.'

'Have you seen what's going on at the Hofburg Palace?' they overheard Johanna reply. 'We all have our phones on watching the scenes. They are calling staff in to help.'

'Which bit of don't ask questions was not clear, Johanna?' an exasperated Otto said, and before Johanna could say anything else, he continued, 'Get hold of Mia Eckhart and at least four uniform officers if you can find them not out on cordon duty. Meet me at Headquarters as soon as you can.' Then, as an afterthought before he finished the call, he said, 'No, change that, we will come to you. Also get hold of a CSI. Paulina Steiner would be best.'

They didn't wait for a response from Johanna as Otto began running down the stairs and out of the HQ's rear doors towards his car, so they had no choice but to follow him. Yes, even Juliet was running!

CHAPTER TWENTY

Waiting in the meeting room at the police office situated just off St Stephen's square was Johanna and Mia. There was no sign of anyone else.

Before Otto could ask, Johanna said, 'There are no spare uniform officers. It could be three hours they reckon before they can spare anyone.'

'What about a CSI?' Otto asked, his face set in a frown, clearly working out if the five of them were going to be enough staff to carry out the arrest, bearing in mind that Sandy and Juliet didn't have any jurisdiction in Austria.

'Yes, Paulina will be with us shortly,' Johanna said. 'She's just had to take some spare boxes to the officers carrying out forensics on the kidnappers' van.' Johanna looked at Otto. 'Are you going to tell us what's going on or do we, like everyone else in Vienna, have to get our information from what we are seeing and reading on our screens?' Johanna sounded very aggrieved as she said it.

'I have signed an inclusion and confidentiality notice,' Otto said. 'So, I am not sure how much I can tell you both.'

'I think you can tell them almost everything,' Sandy said, sitting down and indicating to the others to do so. 'The operation first phase has finished, and I am sure the investigation, search and forensic teams are being briefed on what they are investigating.'

Johanna and Mia flashed smiles at Sandy as they too sat down at the meeting table.

'Very well,' Otto said, still standing as Paulina rushed in and took a seat. 'The two Albanian boys, Flamur Hysa and Marin Ismalaj, that we have as suspects for the city centre hotel thefts and the possible suspect for the murder of Arthur Barrington…' There was complete silence in the room as everyone listened. '… were the lookouts today for the attempted kidnapping of the President of Austria.'

The silence ended and there were cries from both Johanna and Mia of "never!" and "you're joking!". Otto passed around his phone and showed them an image of the two boys together on their electric cycles outside the President's office. One of the control room officers had sent it to him a few moments ago.

'Sadly, and I do mean sadly, Flamur is dead. He was shot by a firearms officer to protect the President.' Otto didn't, quite rightly at this time, have a photo to show them of Flamur lying on the floor. 'Although three others who are the main offenders have been arrested, our job is to arrest Marin, who made good his escape from the scene.'

'Do we need firearms officers with us?' asked Paulina.

'No intelligence to suggest that he has a firearm,' Sandy added. 'Nor was there ever one mentioned in any of the hotel thefts or used in our murder investigation.'

There were nods all around.

Looking at his phone again, Otto said, 'I have just been sent the coordinates of where his phone is currently sending off a GPS signal.' He looked again at the message he had been sent. 'It has been at this location for thirty minutes and not moved.' Otto read the address out to them. 'Does anyone know it or have any information on it?'

'It's in a run-down area on an outer suburb of Vienna,' Johanna said, while Mia looked up more information on her laptop.

'Nothing on that address, but others in the area have various reports of anti-social behaviour, criminal, drugs and alcohol issues,' Mia added.

'I accept we should have uniform back-up,' Otto said, looking at the others in the room, 'but is everyone happy to go with me to effect this arrest? I feel I must do it and understand if you want to wait, but I can't.'

There were nods all around, and they got up to join Otto as he made a move out of the meeting room to his office to get his stab-resistant vest and his handcuffs. Unfortunately, he had no spare equipment for Juliet and Sandy and resolved to keep them in the background.

∞

The two cars didn't take long to get to the address that Otto had given them. As they got closer, the affluent streets of central Vienna became more run-down, and more rubbish could be seen in the streets and the occasional shop boarded up.

The address was in a rectangular block of apartments, all three storeys and made up of ten single-level homes, making thirty in total on one side and an identical thirty on the opposite side. There was a covered walkway that completely encircled the first and second floors, to give access to both sides of the apartments. The building looked like a post-Second World War build, no doubt on a former bomb site. There was a stairwell on each side that went to the top floor, with an entrance/exit for the middle floor.

Looking round at the scene before him, Sandy didn't really know how they were going to cover this block of apartments, with the limited amount of staff at Otto's disposal. Surprisingly, there were very few people milling around or going about their daily activities that evening. Possibly a number of the flats were not occupied or not fit for habitation.

Turning to face them, Otto asked Sandy and Juliet to take up a position at the bottom of each stairwell, leaving himself, Mia and Johanna to carry out the arrest. They all had on their stab-resistant vests, carried pepper spray, and had their Glock pistols holstered to their sides. Juliet and Sandy had never seen them carrying guns before, but this shouldn't have been a surprise – it was typical for the Austrian police, like many other law enforcement agencies throughout the world.

When Sandy went to the stairwell that he was allocated, he was pleased to see the electric cycle, or one identical to it, lying around the back at the bottom of the stairs. He had been excited about the arrest finally taking place, but that was nothing to how he felt now – the adrenaline was flowing, the butterflies of anticipation were going wild in his stomach and he was desperate to be the one knocking on the door of the apartment. Sandy indicated to Mia, who looked down from the middle floor as they got in position, gesturing to her that the cycle was there. Her thumbs up and smile told Sandy everything: how he felt was how they all felt.

Having sent a message to firstly Hannah, then his mother

Katherine, to tell the family that he was not involved in whatever they were seeing on their screens in relation to the chaos in Vienna, he also messaged Detective Superintendent Watson, telling her that Juliet and he were observers and nowhere near the action in Vienna. What he was doing now though… what would the British ambassador to Austria, Dame Lillian O'Brian, have to say if she knew? He would be on the next plane out of there, of that there was no doubt.

They hadn't brought any door openers with them, the type that uniform officers carried for these sorts of method of entry operations. In the UK, and no doubt around the world, they were called an Enforcer door ram, a tool made of hardened steel that was normally red in colour – with its easy-to-use handle, most doors gave way instantaneously. This meant that Mia had to knock on the door, which she did loudly, so loudly that the noise in the quiet, breezeless Vienna evening reverberated around. Everyone outside of the block of apartments or the homes either side at the very least would have heard it.

The door opened to reveal an older couple. They let the three of them into the apartment, soon to be followed by Paulina, who had been waiting along the corridor. Sandy and Juliet shifted from their positions to look up at the doorway. On seeing each other doing the same thing, they smiled and nodded at each other in excited anticipation. *This was it!*

After what seemed an inordinate amount of time, the other three all appeared out of the apartment, empty handed, and came downstairs. The odd door had opened up nearby, with occupants wanting to see what was going on, but they had quickly gone back inside – a culture of not wanting to get too involved was obviously the order of the day for the apartment block.

'I can't understand it,' a very dejected Otto said, his shoulders slumped. 'He was definitely not in that apartment and never has been.' He looked again at the message on his phone. 'They are telling me that the offender's phone is still pinging, as they call it, at this very location.' He indicated up to the apartment.

'The electric cycle is here that he was using as well,' Juliet said, then added, 'Could it be that he is in the exact apartment, but the floor above or below?'

'I had a case,' Sandy said, but unlike when his Grandad Tom said this and the family rolled their eyes, the other detectives all looked at him in earnest anticipation. 'Well it wasn't actually my case,' he corrected, seeing them all look at him. 'When I was the staff officer to the homicide commander in London, I was asked by them to observe an international kidnapping case in the control room at New Scotland Yard.' Sandy took his hands out of his pockets – the memory was making him excited and he needed to gesticulate with his hands to tell all the details. 'It was in a similar European capital city to this one. They went in armed with a rapid firearms response team, used smoke bombs and everything.' Pausing for effect, Sandy then said, 'They got the wrong apartment. The actual apartment was the one that abutted directly to it on the other side. A situation just like here.'

They all looked up at the apartment block and realised what he was saying: they may have just gone to the wrong apartment – they should try the identical one on the exact opposite side of the block. Otto was running his hands through his hair again. He hadn't brought his hat with him; that was safely in the boot of his car.

Nodding at one another, they all ran up the stairwell again, this time going right around to the opposite door.

'There have been a couple of calls from neighbours about this address with concerns for the occupant, a man with a learning disability, being exploited by teenagers,' Mia said, having completed a rapid search on her phone. She started shaking her head. 'We did nothing, didn't attend, just passed the information on to social services to deal with.'

Mia knocked on the door while the others stood a little distance away. After a short while and before Mia felt the need to knock again or contemplate whether the door needed to be forced open to gain entry, the door opened. Stood there was a man in his early fifties in a blue leisure shell suit.

'Hello, who are you?' he asked, so quietly that the others waiting along the corridor struggled to hear.

'I am Detective Eckhart from the Vienna District Police,' Mia explained gently, walking past the man and into the apartment.

To the left was a kitchen area that was in an awful mess; dirty cups, plates and liquid spills were everywhere on every surface. There were discarded takeaway packages all over the tops and floor. The rubbish bin was overflowing with as much on the floor around it as in it. Social services, it would appear, hadn't visited either.

The man followed Mia to turn left after the kitchen into the living room. This was no tidier – there were bits of electrical equipment strewn across the floor and on the sofa beside the rear wall. The man had gone to sit on a solitary chair positioned in front of an already switched on television. He paid no more attention to what was happening in his home.

The others had entered through the open door, and Otto and Johanna went into the one bedroom that was on the right and commenced a search. Sandy and Juliet went after Mia, looking at the man watching the TV, who didn't even glance up at them. This seemed to be a classic case of what would be called by police and social services in the UK "cuckooing", a method of criminal exploitation where criminals used or took over a person's home for criminal purposes.

Unfortunately, there was no sign of Marin in the apartment, although one place they hadn't looked was behind the sofa, which wasn't quite straight against the wall. Johanna, after she had finished in the bedroom, knelt on the sofa and looked over the top, and there he was. They had found Marin Ismalaj.

With the help of Mia and then Sandy, they pulled him over the top of the sofa and in a swift movement placed him on his front and handcuffed him. Otto poised himself ready for a struggle and Juliet made her way and stood in the door. Marin made no attempt whatsoever to resist the arrest. He looked like what he was: a child. A young boy who was missing Flamur, his partner in crime, his best friend; who had no idea where said best friend was, or what had happened to him.

'I am arresting you for the murder of Arthur—'

Mia's words were cut off by Otto. 'No, not yet,' he said, quickly taking over. 'You are under arrest for the attempted kidnapping of the President of Austria.'

As they took Marin out, he looked at Sandy with a confused frown. 'What are you doing here with the police?'

Sandy had to hold back a laugh. The boy clearly remembered their close encounter a few weeks ago on the hotel corridor floor.

Chapter Twenty-One

They had been told by Otto that there was no need for Juliet or Sandy to go to the Vienna District Police Headquarters until later in the afternoon, as the Operation Sparrowhawk team would have priority to interview Marin. They had the other three prisoners to interview again first before they got to him, so it might be a bit ambitious to think they would be allowed to interview Marin until much later.

It had been a very long day the previous day. From the time they had arrived at London Heathrow to getting to bed in the early hours of this morning, over twenty hours had elapsed, so the lie-in was very much welcomed. The previous evening, after Otto and Mia had gone off with Marin, a search of the apartment was made by Paulina, with help from Johanna and Juliet. There was clear evidence in the apartment of the hotel thefts, with the remnants of the unsaleable items strewn about the apartment. Sandy had stood guard over the electric cycle until a police van was available to collect it. Johanna ran down when they arrived and took possession of it as her exhibit. Johanna had also called social services about the male occupant of the home that she was, as they all were, really worried about. She had been told they would get a social worker out to see him in the next few days.

While waiting there, Sandy marvelled at how exciting the day had been, albeit his part for almost all of the time was only as an observer. He also pondered the application that he had downloaded for the Cambridgeshire detective superintendent post – would he or wouldn't he apply? That was the question that he was wrestling with.

After a very late breakfast, the British detectives wandered down the main shopping street, and at the end on Opernring, they found themselves near the Vienna State Opera, a beautiful building built in the Renaissance style. Sandy was desperate to go inside, and after much wrangling, managed to convince Juliet to join him on a tour. He had discovered so many things, including that an allied World War Two bomb had demolished most of the building aside from the main front, and they had been forced to rebuild much of it.

While the tour guide described the stage and orchestra pit that they were looking at, Sandy pictured in his mind a concert in full flow and the magnificent Vienna state orchestra playing. There was Arthur Barrington, sat in the orchestra pit, playing his violin and having the time of his young life doing what he clearly loved and did the best. Sandy sincerely hoped Marin Ismalaj would tell them everything they needed to know in order to finally put Arthur's case to rest.

After their tour, they went for a leisurely coffee and cake at the famous Café Mozart. As they sat there, Sandy mused that they could have been in an earlier century, for nothing in the well-maintained decor of the building or the dress of the waiters had changed since then.

Since they couldn't really discuss the case, not that there was much more to discuss until they had Marin's testimony, Sandy talked through his dilemma regarding the Cambridgeshire Police superintendent position. Juliet was surprisingly supportive, and she talked of going back to her old force to be nearer to her children in the run up to their exams and then her retirement.

They decided not to take a taxi, instead walking around the ring road to the Vienna District Police Headquarters. Once they got there, they had no idea where to go inside the building. They couldn't get hold of Otto, so they were not allowed in, forcing them to sit in the foyer, looking lost. This constant sitting, waiting and observing was starting to trouble the all-action Sandy.

To occupy the time and to feel like he was doing something, Sandy called the Barringtons. He asked them if they had made a decision as to what they intended to do about Arthur's body.

'We are holding a service in Vienna next week,' Andrew told him. 'It is just Faith, my younger son and myself who are going to be there. Emily is too distraught.'

Assuming it was going to be a cremation service, Sandy said, 'I presume you will take the ashes back to Stamford afterwards with you?'

He had presumed right.

'Yes. We are going to have a celebration of life service. Well, of his twenty-two years of life,' a mournful Andrew confirmed. 'It will be in two weeks or so time and everyone is invited, including you and your colleague Juliet, and Mia and her colleagues if they can come from Vienna for the service. Mia has been very kind to us.'

The automatic glass reception doors opened and in walked Mia and Johanna, walking at speed.

'We have an interview slot in half an hour,' Mia called out

to them as she passed and let them into the building, taking them out of the reception area.

'Was that Detective Eckhart?' Andrew asked. 'Are you in Vienna? Do you know anything about this attempted assassination of the Austrian President?'

'Sorry, got to go,' Sandy said, not responding to Andrew in any way.

He knew he was being abrupt, but he had no choice but to end the call as he walked through the door.

∞

The small office that they were crammed into had been taken over by Otto earlier in the day. He told the previous occupant that he needed it to act as his team's base while working from the Headquarters building. Otto was sat behind the desk, and as there were only two other chairs in the office, they all ended up standing as it seemed the fairest thing to do, even if it did look a bit odd. It felt pointless to go and look for a bigger office now.

Seeing them all standing, Otto stood up too. Surprisingly, he looked bright and alert, and was wearing a new – though still grey-coloured – suit, looking *almost* smart. *Another gift from Mrs Wagner, no doubt*, Sandy thought.

Once he had everyone's attention, Otto launched into a briefing without any preliminary discussion.

'The situation with the three arrested kidnappers,' he said, 'is that the two Turkish Cypriots have asked for extradition back to Northern Cyprus. They are not making "no comment" in the interviews, but all they keep saying is that they are political prisoners.'

'Northern Cyprus?' Sandy interjected. 'That isn't recognised as a country in its own right though, is it?' He paused, recalling a case his Grandad Tom had told him about. 'I was told' – he didn't mention *who* had told him, as he often got funny looks if he mentioned his grandad telling him things like this – 'about a murder case where the offender was a Turkish Cypriot national and he had escaped from the UK and made it back to his home country, Northern Cyprus. They refused to extradite him back to the UK to stand trial as no extradition treaty existed.'

'What happened then?' Mia asked, fascinated.

'They tried him for murder there,' Sandy said. 'By there, I mean in Northern Cyprus, and he was convicted and jailed for manslaughter.'

'Is he still in jail?' asked Mia.

'Who knows, and who knows if he ever went to jail in the first place. He did receive a sentence of 14 years though.' Sandy now looked at Otto. 'So, what I am saying to you, Inspector Wagner, is don't let them go anywhere. Ensure they face justice here in Austria.'

'Don't worry, that is not going to happen,' Otto replied. 'They found plastic tie clips, a thick adhesive roll to no doubt apply across his mouth and a black woollen hood in the back of the Mercedes van.'

'Convicted, home and dry,' Johanna said.

'Even more evidence than that,' Otto continued, smiling. He looked years younger when he smiled. 'At the safe house are numerous pictures of the Hofburg Palace and maps with routes in and out.'

'Did the Polish man talk?' Johanna asked.

'Yes…' Otto paused. '"No comment" is all he kept saying.'

'What about Felix?' Sandy asked – he was a man Sandy had great admiration for.

'I think he's going to be OK,' Otto said, no longer smiling, concerned for the assistant commissioner. 'He has taken full responsibility for the operational part of Operation Sparrowhawk and has said that the officers that took a shot, including the fatal ones, are in his view absolved from responsibility – that sits with him and him alone.'

'How is the President?' Johanna asked.

'He is doing fine – as the paramedic stated at the scene, he has a shattered ankle, which is now pinned, and a broken tibia, now also pinned and set in plaster.' Otto smiled again. 'The President is saying that Felix Bauer is an Austrian hero and saved his life!'

'That should mean that Felix will be OK, shouldn't it?' Sandy enquired.

'Not necessarily. Of course, Flamur was unarmed and only a child, so that complicates matters. In addition, the lead investigator from internal affairs is a nasty piece of work. Him and Felix went for the same job once many years ago, which Felix got ahead of him.' Otto looked round, then added, 'And the Chancellor is still furious, but he is slowly calming down, especially when he found out his Minister of the Interior did know in advance and that the threat was against the President and not him.'

Sandy did a little punch in the air of relief. He was, as were the others, pleased for Felix that things looked to be working out well.

'Has the autopsy happened for Flamur yet?' Juliet asked.

'Professor Von Tripp did it this morning. Very straightforward. Died as a result of two bullet shots causing major internal trauma. One of the bullets was a direct hit through the rib cage into the heart.'

'Does Marin know his friend has died?'

'Not yet. He thinks he is also in custody,' Otto told Juliet. 'Marin, when interviewed by the Operation Sparrowhawk team, told them he thought he was acting in a movie.'

'What!' almost everyone in the room exclaimed at once, but Mia's voice was the loudest.

'I know. Unbelievable,' Otto said. 'But he says that two incredible new electric cycles turned up and they were told what their part was, and he says he played it well.'

'Did someone actually tell him he was going to be in a movie?' Sandy asked.

'Not exactly. They said, this is your part, and he thought that he had a part in a movie,' Otto said. 'And of course he had long gone as he'd sped away on his cycle when his friend was shot. He may just get away with his part in it.'

'Why was he hiding when we went to arrest him?' Sandy asked.

'He told the interviewers that he and Flamur always did this whenever anyone knocked at the door, until they knew who it was.'

'His story is all so implausible, isn't it?' Sandy said, shaking his head.

Otto agreed. 'The interviewers from Operation Sparrowhawk did say wait until you have spoken to him before you decide.'

CHAPTER TWENTY-TWO

There was a knock at the door and a uniform officer told them that Marin was ready for interview. Mia and Johanna went off to the interview room and the others found the room that they could monitor the interview from. Otto placed the headset on so he would be able to communicate with Mia, who was going to wear the earpiece.

Sat in the room waiting for the interviewers were already a roomful of people. Marin looked even younger than he had yesterday. He was dressed in jeans and a grey sweatshirt that was at least two sizes too big for him. Sandy stated the obvious, that the clothes were too big for him.

'His now appointed social worker,' Otto explained, gesturing to one of the women in the interview room, 'felt that it was demeaning for a child to wear a white paper boiler suit after they took his clothes off him for forensic testing, so brought in those clothes.'

Inside the room were another two adults. Otto told them that the other woman was Marin's solicitor, and the man was an Albanian interpreter.

Mia with Johanna entered then, bringing in an extra chair. The interview room was packed full. None of them had ever seen this many people in an interview room before and it made the smallest person, Marin, seem even less important, though, of course, he was the most important.

After positioning Marin opposite them, and the other adults to almost the corners of the room, Mia switched the recording equipment on. She got everyone to introduce themselves.

After Mia and Johanna had said who they were, Marin smiled.

'Detectives. How cool.' His German was really good and he certainly didn't need the interpreter, but everything needed to be done correctly. 'I want to be a detective when I grow up.'

Everyone smiled sadly at his innocence and naivety.

'I think you're going to struggle,' said Mia, 'after all you've have been up to here in Vienna.'

'I'm getting some tablets for that, to calm me down,' Marin said in reply.

'Well, let's hope they work,' Mia said, prompting a chuckle from the others in the room, aside from the social worker.

'The ones I used to get just made me want to do crazy things all the time.'

Johanna nodded sadly. 'You were taking Speed, weren't you? We call them amphetamines.'

Marin nodded. 'They're great sellers.'

His solicitor leaned across and put his hand on Marin's arm and shook his head.

Marin looked at his solicitor, saying quietly, 'Flamur and I always keep a few back for ourselves.'

'We can talk about that another day,' Mia said, taking pity on him, 'but I want you to answer the next question truthfully. Tell us about you and Flamur entering hotel rooms and stealing from them.'

Looking at Mia, confused for a moment, Marin asked, 'Truthfully?'

'Yes, truthfully,' Mia re-emphasised.

'Truthfully,' Marin said again, smiling broadly that he had got it right.

They looked at each other and Sandy realised then, just as Mia and Johanna likely did, that Marin's intellectual age of understanding may be much younger than his fifteen years. He certainly didn't have the guarded demeanour most fifteen-year-olds had who were dragged into these kinds of formal situations.

'Marin, can you tell me what the difference is between a truth and a lie,' Mia asked. 'Am I blonde or do I have dark hair?'

Marin looked her up and down and then did the same to Johanna.

'You were brown and are now trying to say you are blonde.'

Mia, with her heavily-dyed blonde hair, chuckled at that, as did Sandy. The boy was funny, he'd give him that.

'Do you know how many hotel rooms you broke into?'

'No. Do you?' Marin replied.

'We know of' – Mia looked at her notes – 'at least twenty-four.'

'Is that all? I would have thought a lot more than that.' Marin's solicitor put her hand on his arm again. 'Will you stop that?' Marin told her. 'The detectives want to know.'

'How did you get in the rooms?'

'We were given this awesome card thing – it lets you into

any hotel room,' Marin said, smiling.

They had recovered this from the apartment the previous night, and Johanna showed a picture of it to Marin, who nodded.

'Who gave it to you?' Mia asked.

Otto furiously spoke into Mia's earpiece, making Sandy and Juliet look at each other in surprise.

Before Mia could take back the question, Marin said, 'Flamur and I call him Darth Vader.' He was smiling again.

Moving on, Mia asked, 'In one hotel room, did you come across a young man?'

'Yes. We got into a fight.'

Suddenly, everyone in the interview room and in the observation room went on high alert. This was it. They were going to find out what happened to Arthur.

'Go on,' Mia coaxed gently.

'We had gone into the room and pulled the curtains across. We always do that.' There was a hush in both rooms, everyone hanging on to every word that Marin was saying. 'I picked up a bag. Didn't know what was in it. Flamur shook his head at me to say nothing else in there.' Marin shook his head to emphasise the point.

Mia nodded encouragingly, barely able to contain her excitement.

'We both felt like someone else was in the room with us,' Marin said, looking straight at Mia as if it was just the two of them in the interview room. 'I ran for the door and brushed past the man and was gone in a flash.'

'So, you left the hotel room?' Mia said, a little confused. 'You left Flamur in there to deal with the man?'

'Yeah, but not with the man. I think he was American. He came after me and tripped me up, hitting me hard on my ankle. I fell on the floor. He was on me in a flash and grabbed the backpack off me and pinned me to the floor.'

The disappointment was palpable, not only from those observing but from Mia and Johanna, whose shoulders were seen to visibly slump on camera. It was the incident with Sandy that Marin was talking about.

'OK, what happened then?' Mia said almost dejectedly.

'Flamur came and saved me. He tried to throttle the man and then started booting him so hard he rolled off me and then we ran before the big lady came out of her room and came after us.'

'Have you ever seen Flamur throttle, as you say, anyone before?' Johanna asked, taking over the questioning.

'Yeah, he was good at it. He puts his arm around the throat from behind. It is really effective – they almost pass out.' Marin looked at his social worker. 'When can I see him, please. I miss him. He's my best friend, my only friend.'

'I want to ask you about a hotel in the Neuer Markt,' Johanna said.

'Where is that?' Marin asked, looking very unsure of names of places.

'Off the main shopping street. It has a statue and a fountain almost in the middle of it, where another hotel is,' Johanna said, trying to give something for Marin to picture.

'We did go in a hotel there, but there were too many cameras everywhere.'

'Did you and Flamur throttle a young man in a hotel room there?'

‘No, never even stole from there,’ Marin replied adamantly.

‘Did Flamur ever go off and steal without you?’ Johanna asked.

‘No, we were a team.’ Marin then paused, thinking. He spoke to his interpreter in Albanian and then said laughingly, ‘I can’t pronounce what he said.’

The interpreter explained, ‘He was in hospital for a couple of days with appendicitis.’

‘They told me it was rumbling,’ Marin said, smiling. He had such a naivety to him, which contrasted with the trail of crimes he was involved in. ‘He must have stolen without me – he brought an iPod into hospital for me.’

‘We recovered one yesterday from your address,’ Johanna said. ‘When was this and which hospital?’

‘The big one near the centre of the city. No idea when,’ Marin said.

‘Can he have a break? He’s been questioned for long enough,’ Marin’s social worker said, looking at Marin and then the detectives.

The solicitor nodded. ‘I think my client has had more than enough for one day. He’s only fifteen.’

Nodding in assent, Mia closed the interview and smiled at Marin to tell him he had done well.

Otto was already onto the hospital to confirm if Marin was telling the truth.

Moments later, he said, ‘He was in hospital for two and a half days. One of those days was when Arthur was killed.’

∞

The team assembled back in the small office. Otto had received a message that he was required in a debrief meeting in twenty minutes with the Operation Sparrowhawk team and the prosecutors.

'Right,' he said, getting straight on to business. 'Where are we now with our investigation?' He didn't wait for a reply. 'In terms of the hotel thefts, we have enough evidence to charge Marin with all of them bar the days he was in hospital. Yes?'

The first to respond was Johanna.

'We have recovered property from his apartment that we can presume is from the hotel thefts.'

'Have we any complainant statements that we can use that correspond with anything that we have recovered?' Otto said. 'I need probably just one, or two would be great to have a basis for a first charge.'

'We also have his admission,' Mia said as she was opening up her laptop, having placed it on the desk as she was speaking.

Otto moved out of the way to allow her to sit behind the desk. They had a major job on their hands, putting together a full file of all the complainants' statements and then getting the bits of property they had recovered identified. By the nature of the thefts being in hotel rooms in a major European city, the victims no doubt lived all over the world.

'We,' she nodded to Johanna, 'have put together eighteen thefts from hotel rooms, and we have statements on file from ten of them.' She looked again, having tried another search. 'We have one that had an iPod stolen and has the owner's son's name engraved on the back of it.'

'We have that,' Juliet said. 'I found that yesterday.'

Was it only yesterday that we searched the apartment? Sandy thought.

'Great,' Otto said. 'What about the murder? It looks like Marin has a valid alibi. Johanna, can you go and get a statement off any hospital administrator that can evidence him being in hospital at that time?' Looking at Mia, he added, 'You go and get that victim statement printed off and take a photo of the iPod with the name on the back of it.'

'Hang on,' Sandy interjected. 'The iPod was stolen by Flamur when Marin was in hospital.'

'Damn!' Otto frowned. 'Mia, can you go and have a sift through what we recovered back at the station? We must have something we can charge Marin with tonight in case they don't charge him with the attempted kidnapping.'

Otto went off to his debrief, Mia and Juliet went off to the police station, and Johanna and Sandy went to the hospital.

'I think we also need to make sure that Marin stayed in hospital the whole time that he was there,' Sandy said as they drove there.

One and a half hours later, they were all back in the cramped office where the desk was now covered with takeaway pizza boxes and soft drinks.

Having finished a big mouthful of pizza, Otto began, 'Pretty straightforward in terms of the adults. They are going to charge them with conspiracy to abduct the President of Austria rather than an attempt.'

'Court hearing in the morning, sir?' Mia asked, also eating while she spoke. The team were ravenous.

'Yes, a special court hearing. They're organising armed

escorts and protection in the court and everything.' While he grabbed another slice of pizza, he added, 'They don't know what to do about Marin, though. Too close to the informant.'

So Sandy's suspicions were correct – though it would likely never be confirmed, "Darth Vader", as the boys called him, was the informant. No doubt he was going to be paid handsomely for his information.

It frustrated Sandy greatly that the man who had exploited these two young, vulnerable boys was not just getting away with it, he was getting away with it and being paid a fortune.

As if second guessing what Sandy was thinking, Otto said, 'If Mia has got at least one statement' – Mia nodded, pointing to two victims' statements she had with her – 'they are going to charge Marin with those thefts as a holding charge.' Looking at Sandy, he added, 'Before you say anything, his social worker and solicitor have raised the prospect that they will argue he was a child victim who was exploited, and not an offender.'

Sandy nodded. 'We have a similar scheme in the UK – the National Referral Scheme – for just this sort of case of child criminal exploitation. You submit the paperwork and a member of their team looks at the case and responds to the court if they believe the child is a victim or not.' He nodded again. 'It works. Well, I think it does. I just hope it works here too.'

CHAPTER TWENTY-THREE

As their flight to London Heathrow wasn't until the afternoon, Juliet and Sandy visited Schönbrunn Palace, situated just outside the city centre. They hadn't wanted to be alone; the enormity of what they had witnessed a couple of days ago had hit them both, and lingered strongly that morning. They were used to pushing through, given their jobs as detectives, and the adrenaline and hectic nature of the investigation had helped while it lasted. Now though, their human emotions had taken over.

Even though they had only witnessed the events, in particular the shooting of Flamur, on a screen, the experience was nothing like watching a TV drama or a movie. It was absolutely real life. Watching the bullets hit Flamur and his jerking movement as he fell to the ground, almost lifeless before he hit it, would be an enduring image that would play out in their minds strongly. This was happening now, but they both knew the image would forever trouble them from time to time, almost out of nowhere.

When the police marksman had lifted off the scarf and pulled the hood down and they had seen who it was, that had been an incredibly impactive image. The star shaped tattoos on Flamur's neck, so at odds with his youthful face, would linger in Sandy's mind's eye for years to come.

Walking through the beautiful gardens of Schönbrunn

Palace, the summer residence of the Habsburg royal family, made for a pleasant distraction from all that had happened. Both the interior and exterior were truly something, and Sandy and Juliet brightened up a bit, appreciating the bright sunshine. That was, until they realised a daily concert was being set up, the violinists already tuning up. Reminders of Arthur Barrington were seemingly around every corner in this city.

They decided to end their sightseeing after that, grab a taxi, collect their bags, and head to the airport. They were paying lip service, pretending to have normality to their lives.

At the airport, after they had checked in and were waiting for their flights, Sandy received a message from Otto.

'The three kidnappers have all been remanded in custody,' he told Juliet.

'No bail application for the Turkish Cypriots?'

'Yes, apparently the judge' – Sandy looked at the message again – 'was having none of this political asylum and political prisoner application and told their lawyer to sit down every time he wanted to mention it.'

'What about Marin?' Juliet asked, moving her bag from in front of her to the side to make herself more comfortable.

'That's in the next message from Otto.' Sandy looked at his phone screen again. 'He has been remanded to the care of Vienna's Child and Youth Welfare Service, to be placed in a secure facility, and the judge is passing on the case to juvenile court to deal with.'

'I think he'll get a positive outcome from his application to be regarded as a victim of child exploitation and not an offender. Don't you, Sandy?' said Juliet, looking at Sandy for reassurance. ‘In terms of our case, he couldn’t have killed Arthur, could he? He was in a hospital bed.’

‘I agree,’ Sandy said. ‘But only if he’s not going to be prosecuted for the conspiracy to kidnap the Austrian President.’

‘I don’t think that’s going to happen to protect the informant,’ Juliet said, looking up at the departure board. ‘Damn!’ she exclaimed. ‘Our flight has been delayed.’

‘Only thirty minutes.’ Sandy smiled. He wanted to get home as much as Juliet did. He got his notebook out of his backpack. ‘We have collected the fibres from a number of jumpers and tops from the apartment,’ he said, as he wrote in his book.

‘Including the fibres from the top Flamur was wearing when he was shot,’ Juliet said. ‘The CSI Paulina Steiner went and collected the sample and also took his fingerprints and a DNA swab after the post-mortem examination had finished.’

‘That is all we’ve got then,’ Sandy said, as he put his notebook away and they picked up their bags in order to make their way to wait nearer to their departure gate.

‘Remember, we have an unidentified fingerprint and unidentified DNA, both on the coffee cup. Then the fibres from Arthur’s neck.’

‘If any of it matches Flamur that will be plenty of evidence, especially as there will be no trial.’

∞

When he placed his bags in his bedroom at his home in Ely, Sandy saw that on his desk were three envelopes. The envelopes were pink in colour and his name was written on the front in blue fountain pen. The writing was Hannah's. She hadn't not read his love letter to her; she had, and had replied. He couldn't wait to read them, but a supper with his parents was needed first.

While he was eating and enjoying his parents' company, Sandy's mind strayed to thinking about Marin and Flamur. They hadn't had this privileged upbringing of being in a loving family. How fortunate he was – he must never abuse that privilege.

Before going to bed and settling down to read his letters, Sandy received a call from Otto, who told him that they had identified almost all of the stolen property recovered from Marin and Flamur's apartment where they were acting as cuckoos. There was a businessman and a couple from the London area that they hadn't been able to contact and Otto asked if Sandy could get their statements early next week. An email with the photos of the property arrived shortly afterwards. Another fifteen- to sixteen-hour day for Otto, this time on his day off. Sandy doubted Mrs Wagner was the slightest bit happy!

The thought gave him pause. Once he and Hannah were married, he wanted to be around more – to be able to spend more quality time with her than he could at the moment, with his current job. It was another point in favour of considering this Cambridgeshire position.

Opening the first of her letters, Sandy began to read.

∞

The next day, as soon as Hannah arrived at the house – they were all due to go out for Sunday lunch, where his Grandpa John apparently had some announcements to make – Sandy couldn't kiss his fiancé fast enough. Her letters had been wonderful and Sandy had even felt a little bit embarrassed to have not realised some of the little things he did that Hannah liked. Mostly, he was filled with an enduring feeling of an outpouring of love.

This had been a good idea that he had got from Arthur Barrington and Emily Wainwright.

Since Hannah had arrived in plenty of time, they managed to sneak away to Sandy's bedroom for a while before they were expected downstairs, and both of them vowed to write to each other again, especially during those times when they were apart for a week or so and when Sandy was working abroad.

A short while later, the family had all assembled at the Poets House in Ely for lunch, including Grandad Tom, Sandy's sister Aileen, and her family. Grandpa John had also brought along a woman in her mid-sixties who he introduced as Karen, whom Sandy had heard of before, though never met. She was a former court clerk and someone that John had enjoyed the occasional dinner with over the last couple of years.

This was the first announcement from John, who had been a widower for a number of years. Apparently, he and Karen, who had also been a widow now for five years, were actually going to be a couple. Sandy's mum and dad had known about this for a little while, and though they had initially struggled with it, they were happy for John. Sandy didn't know what to think, and his sister Aileen, on looking at her, might need some convincing. Though he supposed, at the end of the day, it was John's life, and as long as he and Karen were happy, it didn't matter what the rest of them thought!

The next announcement, after the starters had been taken away, was that John was retiring completely from any university work, but he would still carry out research into his academic field of medico-legal studies. John then passed a letter around, asking them all not to comment until everyone had read it. This became complicated as the roast dinners had started to arrive and Aileen's children were keen to get started eating, not being sure what all the adult talk was about anyway. The letter, as it turned out, was the conferring of an emeritus professorship on John, so he was now Professor John McFarlane.

There was still more news to come.

A final letter was passed around after the main course was cleared away, but not before some ice cream arrived for the children. Something was afoot as two waitresses arrived with champagne. There were gasps as the family read this letter. King Charles' Birthday Honours that following Saturday would include Grandpa John, who had already received an OBE a few years ago, was now going to be knighted for his work in the medico-legal field, advocating for children who had been denied expensive treatments by the NHS.

'What are you to be called now then?' Aileen asked.

'Grandpa to you,' John said, and everyone laughed as the champagne was being poured. 'The Knighthood is a secret until Friday night though,' he said, squeezing Karen's hand. 'I presume others though will call me Sir John or Professor

Sir John McFarlane.'

'Not me,' called out Tom from the other end of the table, grinning broadly. 'You'll always be just John.'

They shared three grandchildren and two great-grandchildren, but more than that, over the last forty years, and since their children started courting, they had become good friends.

'Oh no, you in particular will be using all my titles, at all times.'

Everyone laughed at that, and Sandy felt comforted, seeing his family so happy. It had been a rough few months, but his family were safe, well and content. That was all that mattered.

∞

The early morning commute into the centre of London was hard for Sandy, especially the getting up before 5:30 a.m. and leaving Hannah sleeping as she was working from home in Cambridge or at Fenners Chambers most of that week. John McFarlane had also resigned from his occasional work for the barristers' chambers, which he had been part of for over forty years.

Juliet was in the office even before Sandy, and was talking to Clare Symonds, the lead crime scene investigator from the FCDO investigation team. They were best friends and if Juliet ever did leave the team, Sandy was sure Clare would find it difficult to lose her.

There was no team meeting that morning, so he briefed Detective Superintendent Watson, who luckily hadn't heard from Dame Lillian O'Brien, the ambassador to Austria. There had been a request from another team that dealt with Foreign Office advice to British citizens travelling abroad as to whether Austria, and Vienna in particular, was a safe place to travel following the incident near Hofberg Palace.

Sandy asked Juliet to brief them and he made a call to Andrew Barrington.

'I'm sorry, Mr Barrington, that I cut you off and couldn't speak to you the other day,' Sandy said as soon as the phone was answered.

'I realised you were in Vienna and tied up,' Andrew replied. 'I knew it as soon as I heard Mia talking.' After a slight pause, he asked, 'Can we meet this morning, please?'

'I'm sorry but I'm in London.'

'In London? I thought you were here in Vienna.'

'Obviously you are in Vienna then,' Sandy said. 'What do they say about ships that pass in the night? I was just going to let you know that we are working on a couple of forensic leads and should have an answer to them by the end of this week.'

'We will be back in England either on Friday or Saturday,' Andrew replied, and he could be heard whispering to his wife, 'It's DCI McFarlane, sweetheart.' Talking to Sandy again, he said, 'We have the cremation service on Wednesday morning – it will just be me, Faith and Henry present. Mia and Johanna told us they wanted to be there, but sadly they are unable to.'

'Juliet and I would be there if we were in Vienna,' Sandy told him.

'Would all of you be able to attend the service to celebrate

Arthur's life in a couple of weeks or so?' Andrew asked. 'We have to let Henry finish his exams first as he has already had two extensions, and there are no more allowed before having to re-take the year.'

'Of course, we will try to be there. Just keep us posted.'

After hanging up the phone, Sandy got to work on filling in his Cambridgeshire detective superintendent application. Juliet had volunteered for her and Clare to go take the statements of the London victims of the Vienna hotel thefts, giving Sandy the time to complete the form. He had already let his boss know he was doing this, and why he was doing it at this time.

Sandy also had time to ponder another announcement that John McFarlane had made. Apparently, he and Tom had set up a business called Plato Solutions, and they were offering investigative and legal services. Sandy hoped that these two old codgers, who were well into their seventies, were not going to get themselves into trouble that he no doubt would have to get them out of.

Detective Superintendent Watson had also body swerved a meeting with Support After Murder and Manslaughter (SAMM) Abroad, now called Murdered Abroad, and had passed it to Sandy to attend on her behalf later in the week. They were, quite rightly, after someone like a senior investigating officer and/or a family liaison officer to be allocated to each of their cases when a loved one was murdered abroad. Sandy totally agreed with them, but there was a totally inconsistent service across the UK.

He stopped his application form and set his mind to how to improve the situation for these bereaved families. The service he was giving the Barringtons was on the whole unachievable, and better support was required. He just needed to work out how this could happen.

CHAPTER TWENTY-FOUR

The news the next weekend had not only focused on John McFarlane, albeit he had been flooded with literally hundreds of congratulation messages when the media made the King's Birthday Honours list announcement. The weekend news was all about Hannah and Sandy. They had got an indication from their solicitor and estate agent that the 1st of August was a reasonable date for them to aim for to take possession of their new home. The chaplain and dean of St John's College Chapel had also responded to them, delighted at their nuptials, and had agreed to arrange for them to get married in the chapel. The Master of the college, however, had needed a bit more persuading, which Hannah dutifully did.

The wedding reception was going to be held in the college. They were told that they would have to get married outside of term time. After a bit of negotiating, bearing in mind that students would be arriving at the college for Michaelmas term, the last Friday in September was set as the wedding date for Hannah and Sandy. They liked the look of the Wordsworth Room, a 450-year-old room where the poet William Wordsworth lived when he was an undergraduate at St John's College in the late 1700s, but the room was too small for the number of people that they hoped to invite. In the end, they went for the Great Hall.

There had been no update received from Otto that previous

week, and it wasn't until early the next week that he sent a message to Sandy asking him to be available for a Zoom meeting later that day.

Juliet and Sandy squeezed into the only available private room that afternoon, which was meant for one person. They waited until Otto joined them on Zoom, and when he appeared on the laptop screen, they looked at a glum-faced man, then looked at each other.

'Bad news.' Otto launched into the meeting without even saying hello and the usual pleasantries. They could see how much he was giving the impression of being down and out. 'The fingerprint and DNA is not Flamur Hysa's.'

'Let's be honest, Otto,' Sandy said, trying to lift the mood. 'I never thought he would be one to sit down and have a drink with Arthur Barrington. He was fifteen. To be honest, I've always been shocked that the fingerprint wasn't his father's.'

'What about the fibres then?' Juliet asked. 'That would be good evidence.'

'That is what's taking the time.' Otto glanced down at his paperwork. 'They have compared fibres from five different tops, including the one Hysa was wearing when he was shot, and there is no match.'

'Is that all of them tested then?' asked Sandy.

'Two more to go but those tops are Marin's so we are not hopeful.'

'They could have interchanged clothing, couldn't they?' Sandy said, trying to nod encouragingly.

'I know, DCI McFarlane, you are an optimist and I am a pessimist, but I think we need to let this go. Flamur is not our murderer.' Otto was shaking his head.

'There are three possibilities that we need to consider,' Sandy interjected.

Before he could list them, Juliet said, 'Flamur could have got rid of the top. The murder was some weeks ago, wasn't it?'

'Yes,' Sandy said, looking at Juliet. 'Option one, Flamur is the murderer, but disposed of the top. Option two, Professor Von Tripp got his cause of death wrong – it could still be an infection or sudden adult death syndrome.'

'*You* ask him to confirm his diagnosis. If you do, you are braver than me,' Otto said, smiling at last.

'Highly unlikely,' Juliet said. 'The other pathologists assisted in confirming Von Tripp's diagnosis.'

'I agree,' Sandy said. 'The final option is that someone else, someone unknown, is our murderer.'

Now, Otto was very much unsmiling. 'But who could that be? We have no idea whatsoever.'

The investigation had ground to a halt with no investigative leads whatsoever for them to action. Juliet and Sandy now looked as glum as Otto, and this was made worse by neither of them ever having been in this position before.

How could someone get away with murder like this?

∞

Determined not to give up and not to let Arthur and his family down, Sandy couldn't stop thinking about what other investigative activity they could do. Later in the week, he sent Otto an email, outlining some suggested further enquiries that he had thought of. He was conscious it was

Otto's investigation and not his, and he was doing his best to tread carefully.

The email suggested that Otto make a request for a crime analyst to search maybe the last five years of reports of violence in hotel rooms, then to narrow that search down to those where a theft had taken place or had been attempted. This database search should be firstly for the city of Vienna, then widened to all of Austria. The search could also look across Europe. There was easy border access throughout Europe so the murderer could have been operating in and from another country.

Then, as an afterthought, Sandy sent a further email, wondering if a search could be made again for that five year time period, of any murder, or even violence that involved a chokehold.

Surprisingly to Sandy, Otto didn't call to discuss. He just sent an email in response, which said: "Good ideas, DCI McFarlane. We are going to start the search with Vienna and then look further if the time to do this isn't prohibitive."

The next call Sandy received that week surprised him, but at the same time made him feel slightly anxious. The call was from the Lincolnshire Police Safeguarding Hub. The lady calling him said her name was Detective Sergeant Linda Palmer.

'I am calling about the Wainwright family,' she said.

'I am so sorry,' Sandy said quietly. 'I am not used to filling out the domestic abuse stalking and harassment risk assessments.'

'You did a great job,' Linda assured him. 'Far better than many of my DCIs could do.'

Sandy immediately felt his chest puff out and a smile travel across his face.

'Especially as you got those consent forms signed,' Linda continued. 'I have been to visit the Wainwrights. I waited until I saw Douglas go out, but they won't make a complaint against him.'

'Yes,' Sandy said. 'That was their position with me as well. I don't know what to think, whether it is loyalty or they are afraid of him, or a combination of both.'

'I am sure they are afraid of him. He is totally and completely coercively controlling them and gets violent if he doesn't get his way,' Linda responded with passion.

'When you add in his mental illness, it makes him an extremely dangerous man to his wife, Emily and Freddie. You obviously agree.'

'I have been building a file and his mental health record says he is diagnosed with paranoid schizophrenia,' Linda said, reading from a report on her computer. 'I spoke to his psychiatric nurse, who told me that this diagnosis is treatable if the person keeps to their medication, which Mr Wainwright does not.' The passion was coming out again from Linda. 'Coupled with him being a persistent domestic abuse perpetrator, he is one dangerous man.'

Looking at his watch, Sandy realised that he had a meeting to attend. 'DS Palmer, I am happy to do whatever I can to help, but I sadly have to go just now. I could ring you back in a couple of hours?'

'No need,' Linda said. 'I know you don't know this, but I am a cousin of the Barringtons and I am going to the celebration of life service for Arthur at the end of this week.

Are you going, sir?'

'Yes,' Sandy said, surprised by the connection. 'I will be there. Myself and a colleague, DS Ashton, plus two detectives from Vienna as well.'

'Please can you help facilitate a discussion with Emily and Freddie? They both seem to trust you greatly,' Linda implored. 'If we can both get them to come forward, that would convince their mum to do so as well. Douglas has been arrested four times for domestic abuse and three times for mental health issues, always sectioned to a mental health institution. I need something to stick. He can't go on terrorising this family.'

Wow, thought Sandy, as he ran up the stairs to his meeting. *DS Palmer is in the right job!*

∞

The arrival of Johanna and Mia for the celebration of life service was like the welcoming of old friends to London. Juliet met them at Paddington railway station after they had taken the Heathrow Express there straight from the airport. Superintendent Isabella Mahler had given them permission to attend and allowed them a few days for the visit. Only that morning, Otto had embarked on a two-week holiday with his wife, Mrs Wagner, and under no circumstances was he to be disturbed. It was unknown if that direction was from the superintendent or Mrs Wagner – probably Mrs Wagner!

After Juliet had got them settled into the hotel not far from the FCDO buildings, they had done a little bit of sightseeing and a lot of shopping. They then met up with Sandy for a meal that evening at the Cinnamon Club, a fantastic Indian restaurant on Great Smith Street, just down the street from Westminster Cathedral.

Also able to join them was Hannah, who had a case at the Old Bailey law courts running for a couple of days.

After they had ordered the food, and the four women had extensively discussed their wedding, Sandy redirected the conversation. 'Have you had any result yet on the last two pieces of clothing to check if the fibres are a match?'

'Are we OK to talk in front of Hannah?' Johanna asked, not just looking for permission from Sandy but more so from Hannah herself, who nodded.

'Hannah is a lawyer so she understands what we're talking about,' Sandy said, smiling.

'Not only beautiful but also intelligent!' Johanna replied, prompting laughter from around the table as the starters arrived for them to eat. 'Negative result, I am afraid,' she continued. 'We also got the digital forensic investigator to look through the CCTV in the area for the day and, again, negative. He also checked the hotel internet wireless router and no trace, not that our suspect would have logged onto the hotel wi-fi anyway. Plus, we understand the phone we have is a new one specifically for the attempted kidnapping.'

After the empty plates had been taken away and wine glasses had been topped up, Mia piped up. 'Our analyst has only looked at our Vienna district databases and we have, would you believe' – she took a sip of her wine – 'literally into the hundreds of reports of violence in hotel rooms over the last five years.'

Getting in on the conversation, Johanna added, 'We

have looked into only a few so far, and they are all cases of domestic abuse.'

'The other search you instructed us to do,' Mia said.

'Suggested,' said Sandy.

'Well, it felt like an instruction, sir.' They all laughed again. 'There were no reports of cases where a chokehold was used. Strangulation, yes, but not reported as a chokehold. We will again need to look at each report.'

Detective work looks exciting from the outside, Sandy mused, *but with it comes a lot of painstakingly boring, detailed hard work.*

∞

The following morning, Sandy showed Mia and Johanna around the FCDO building, which was a far cry from their tiny police station in Vienna. The building was built during the Victorian period, and included various impressive suites of rooms and a rather magnificent staircase.

The Churchill War Rooms, almost next door to the FCDO, were next on the agenda, as Mia in particular wanted to see them – her grandfather was a huge fan of Winston Churchill. They had been transformed into an underground museum, preserving the place where Churchill had run a lot of his operations during World War Two.

When they went with Johanna to walk through St James's Park to visit Buckingham Palace, Sandy left them so he could finish off some outstanding work. He was then heading home to Ely, ready for the trip the following morning to Stamford for the church service for Arthur.

CHAPTER TWENTY-FIVE

The music from the string quartet positioned at the front of the church just to one side of the altar struck Sandy emotionally as he walked into St George's Church. It was impactful not only because the two violinists, a cellist and a viola player were so incredibly talented, but because they were playing music that was not soulful or sad but instead joyful and uplifting. They were Arthur's peers from all his years at the Royal College of Music, and had clearly been told by Faith Barrington that this was not a funeral service nor a remembrance service, but a celebration of life service.

Having driven to Stamford in his Morgan Roadster, Sandy himself felt uplifted – he'd had his car's top down and at times felt the power of the car's engine and, as always, he had enjoyed the admiring glances of motorists that he passed or who passed him.

Juliet and the Austrian detectives had travelled from London by train, and Sandy, having parked in the Cattlemarket car park near the Meadows, had walked up and met them at Stamford train station. They had all then walked together in the summer sunshine in amiable company to the church.

There was no sign of the Barrington family in the church as the detectives arrived, but there were pictures in frames of them with Arthur almost everywhere. Also included were a number of photographs of Arthur and Emily Wainwright together. Neither Emily nor her brother Freddie could be seen in the church yet either. Juliet had Emily's letters in her bag ready to return them to her today.

The people in the church were a mixture of older people, families and a number of young adults, and all were dressed in bright colours. Sandy himself, although wearing a dark blue suit, had on a bright pink tie. Juliet was all in red in a two-piece skirt suit and looking "mighty fine", as she would say when putting on her best Bajan drawl.

By good power of deduction on her part, Detective Sergeant Linda Palmer from the Lincolnshire Police Safeguarding Hub came up to them and introduced herself. She was much younger than Sandy had originally thought – possibly not even thirty. Although she was going to sit with her mother, she told Sandy she would seek him out afterwards for the promised introduction to Freddie and Emily.

The Barrington family arrived in a party that contained maybe twelve or fifteen people, including probably grandparents of Arthur's and aunts, uncles and cousins. They mingled slowly, talking to people as they made their way to the front of the church.

Just as they sat down and the vicar was about to begin the service with a hymn, Freddie and Emily hastily walked in. They were about to position themselves at the back of the church but Faith walked towards them and gestured for them to come and sit alongside them at the front.

The tributes alongside musical pieces and hymns were from many people: Andrew Barrington, who was in tears while he spoke, the headmaster from Stamford School, the violin tutor from the Royal College of Music Junior department, and others.

Although the celebration of life that Faith was trying to achieve for the service was happening, the sadness of the brutal loss of such a young life couldn't be taken away and the emotion, melancholy and tears around the whole church was evident. Emily Wainwright was in bits and never stopped crying once throughout.

When Freddie got up to speak almost at the end of the service, he was visibly shaking and his bottom lip was trembling. He told them he had written a poem, alongside a longer-form prose about his friendship with Arthur and Arthur's love of his sister. He had, however, decided to keep those private, though had printed out copies for his sister and Faith for them to keep.

Instead of reading his own work, he wanted to read to them a poem, In Memoriam, which the Victorian poet Alfred, Lord Tennyson had written following the death of a friend he knew from his student days at Cambridge. Tennyson had attended the same college in Cambridge that Freddie and Arthur had both been students at, so his works had an added significance for them, and he was also from Lincolnshire, which added further to the connection.

The key words from the poem that, although well-known, emotionally struck everybody at Arthur Barrington's service, and surprisingly lifted the mood, were: "It is better to have loved and lost than never to have loved at all."

The memory of knowing Arthur during his short life was all the better for everyone there than never having known him.

This uplift in mood soon crashed again though, when a

montage of video clips from Arthur's musical career played on the screen, culminating with him playing at the Vienna opera house only a few days before his death. *What a splendid young man and what a talent*, Sandy thought solemnly.

The reception after the service was to be held at The George Hotel, but before people set off there, they mingled outside the church, talking in the sunshine. Juliet, Mia and Johanna could be seen talking to Faith and Emily, and Sandy managed to say hello to Andrew Barrington and Freddie.

Linda Palmer soon slid up beside them, waiting for Sandy to support her in talking to and gaining the confidence of Freddie.

'Do you know who that man is with the grey straggly beard?' Andrew asked all of them before this could happen. 'I recognise him, I think, but not sure why or from where.'

They all turned around and looked at the person he was talking about. He was stood opposite and just down the road from the church.

'That's my dad,' Freddie said. 'He's been following Em everywhere. He's obsessed with this idea that she's going to go off and leave the family.'

'That's your father?' Andrew asked. 'He looks so different now. Strange, I've seen him recently, not sure where though. I certainly didn't realise he was your father!'

Gut instinct kicked in for Sandy – detective gut instinct.

'Could he have been on your first flight to Vienna after all?' he asked.

Andrew peered at the man again. 'Why would he be on the plane? I told you he didn't turn up, didn't I. It must have been around Stamford that I've seen him.'

‘The person you thought looked like the Douglas Wainwright of old didn’t turn up, but this man might of,’ Sandy said, indicating to Douglas but trying not to look at him to scare him off.

Extricating himself and moving subtly away from Andrew so he couldn’t hear, and whispering to DS Palmer while indicating for Juliet, Mia and Johanna to come over, Sandy said, ‘Can you go to the Wainwright house with Juliet and get ready in case he runs off from me now? I am going to try and speak to him.’ He looked at Linda. ‘It might be worth calling for a uniform car as back-up.’

He got Johanna to take a photo of Douglas on her phone camera.

‘Can you send that picture to the manager of the Neuer Markt hotel and see if anyone recognises him?’ he asked.

‘What are you thinking, Sandy?’ Juliet said as she and Linda began to move off to the home as instructed.

‘Just a hunch, but what if he did turn up in Vienna after all? Can you phone someone in our office and get them to check the British Airways flights manifesto for all of the morning flights on the day Arthur died?’

As Juliet nodded and headed off, Sandy said to Mia and Johanna, ‘Stay with Emily and keep her safe. Go to the reception at The George and we will meet you there.’ Then, as an afterthought, he said, ‘Can you get your CSI Paulina Steiner to organise the outstanding fingerprint mark and DNA sample to be sent to Juliet, who will get our CSI, Clare Symonds, to search the UK databases?’ He turned back to Andrew and Freddie. ‘Freddie, come with me.’

Sandy subtly looked across at Douglas, who was walking

up and down the street opposite. Back and forth, back and forth, a bit like a metronome. He didn't seem to be even glancing at the church entrance.

'Let's go and talk to your dad,' he said to Freddie, but as he did so, Douglas was off and away, not quite running but moving at speed.

Sandy and Freddie went after him, causing everyone waiting and congregating outside the church to look around and wonder what the commotion was about. A foot chase was now on.

As they followed as quickly as they could without running themselves, Sandy realised this was not the route he'd walked to the Wainwright house before. Douglas must be trying to lose them and then double back to the house. Sandy hoped that Linda and Juliet got there before Douglas did.

They just about kept him in sight as they made their way onto Broad Street. As it was Friday, the market was on, with its numerous stalls running all the way along. They could see that Douglas, when he looked around to see where they were, had smashed into what looked like an old lady, knocking her over and the eggs that she had just been handed by a market stall holder.

Shouts were now being levelled at Douglas, not just from other shoppers but also from the stall holders. This didn't bother him and he just went on moving forward.

When they reached the lady being helped to her feet by other shoppers, Freddie hesitated and went to see if she was all right, but Sandy thrust his hand out and gesticulated, pointing at Douglas, who they needed to follow immediately. Douglas could be seen turning right and then left onto Ironmonger

Street, which had more market stalls along it.

'He is heading along there to the Meadows and then through the Cattlemarket car park to the George Hotel,' Freddie said, panting a little bit. 'He must have heard us mention we were going there after the church.'

Due to the volume of people out in Stamford enjoying market day in the sunshine and with the cafés overflowing with people, they were starting to lose sight of Douglas. As much as Sandy was desperate to, he didn't want to run with Freddie with him. Freddie was alarmed enough without adding to the tension any further.

Having now completely lost sight of him when they got to the car park, Sandy felt that he had his other bases covered, albeit they were Austrian detectives. Mia and Johanna were by now hopefully at the George, but whatever happened, they were looking after Emily. Juliet and Linda were at the home address. Yes, Douglas had nowhere to go.

CHAPTER TWENTY-SIX

Linda Palmer led Juliet swiftly to the Wainwright house, having been there before. On arrival, they could both see how run-down and neglected it looked. No work had been done to it for years, if not decades. The door was closed and there was no sign anywhere of Douglas. Maybe Sandy had caught up with him or he had gone off somewhere else? They were pretty certain that Douglas hadn't beaten them to the house.

Looking around, they were not sure where they could stand and wait. It needed to be where they could not be seen by Douglas should he approach. Juliet glanced up and down the road, spotting a medium-sized white van that they could hide behind, but it was probably too far away. There was a garden opposite with a wall that they could almost crouch behind, but the very thought made Juliet shudder. She was getting too old for that.

As she turned back to the house, a thought struck her. Why hadn't she considered this before? She suggested to Linda that they could wait in the house. Where better to ambush Douglas than within the safety of his own home? The ladies stepped up the short pathway and Linda knocked loudly on the door. The sound of the knocking would have definitely been heard in the house, but even so, when there was no reply, she knocked again, harder. Still no reply.

Frustrated, they walked the few steps back to the road and

Juliet made a call to her office, asking Clare Symonds, the CSI, to get someone to look at the BA flight manifesto and to await fingerprints and DNA for verification.

Linda had rung her local police station in Stamford for back-up, and it wasn't long before a marked police patrol car turned up with sirens wailing and blue lights flashing. To add to this cacophony of light and sound, the car was being driven at speed and the very noise of the engine would have alerted the whole neighbourhood.

A few choice words were being shared with the officers by Linda. The officers were not taking the blindest bit of notice, but at least the lights were now switched off and they were out of the car.

"Urgent assistance was what the call was," they kept saying.

Knowing that both Freddie and Emily were safe, as they were with other officers, Juliet wondered where Hazel had gone off to. Once more, she walked up the path to the house. Juliet thought there was no point in knocking again and peered into the front room through the dirty window. The white net curtains that hung there were no longer white, but had a dark grey tint to them, hampering her getting a clear view into the room. She could just about see – lying half on, half off a chair – a body, though she had no idea whether it was male or female.

'There's a person in here,' Juliet shouted back to Linda. 'But looks like she's unconscious.'

Before Linda could make a move to walk up the path or Juliet could make her way the few steps to the door, the uniform officers charged up the path. One of them eyed the door up for a moment, then charged at it. The ancient lock made a cracking and splintering noise, then just split away from the door frame.

They were into the house.

Following them into the front room, Juliet pushed the officers out of the way, telling them to give her space. She could now see the person was a middle-aged woman in a blue dress, presumably Hazel Wainwright. Juliet shouted for Linda and the uniform officers to immediately call an ambulance.

As far as Juliet could see, there was no visible blood or any trauma showing, but the woman, Hazel, was not moving.

Linda came alongside Juliet with her phone on speaker, talking to the emergency services operator. Linda had given her own details as the caller, along with the address.

'I have someone on their way to you now. I will stay on the line until they arrive,' the call taker advised. 'Is the patient breathing?'

Juliet listened close. 'Yes. Very faint.'

'Has the patient a pulse?'

Juliet placed her fingers on Hazel's wrist. 'Yes, again very faint. She is currently unconscious.'

'Lay the patient on the floor and be ready to give CPR if the breathing stops,' the operator said calmly, in contrast to how Juliet and Linda were feeling.

Juliet thought her own heart was going to burst, it was beating so hard, and her legs were trembling.

Hazel was no weight at all as they laid her on the floor, the tension in the room not helped by one of the uniform officers asking repeatedly whether she was going to be all right.

Juliet alternated between listening closely for a change in Hazel's breathing to seeking out the reassuring noise of an ambulance siren.

'Is the patient feeling clammy?' the operator asked.

Feeling Hazel's forehead, then placing her fingers down the back of her dress, Juliet replied, 'No.'

In that moment, Hazel began to stir, her legs and fingers twitching a little, though her eyes remained closed.

'Keep the patient still please. Make sure they make no jerking movements,' the operator said, but this turned out to be unnecessary, as Hazel suddenly and worryingly went still again.

Suddenly, a paramedic burst in through the door, followed by the uniform officers and a couple more paramedics. For some reason, they hadn't used their siren, just the vehicle's blue lights.

'Please can all of you give me space to work,' the first paramedic said. 'Have we a name?'

Juliet had never been so pleased to see anyone in her life before, and after telling him that the lady lying lifeless on the floor was Hazel Wainwright, she sat back to let the paramedics do their job. She just hoped they were in time to save this poor woman's life.

∞

On reaching the George Hotel, Sandy and Freddie did a quick scan through the hotel's car parks. They were full of cars, a number not even in parking spaces, obscuring them from having an unobstructed view, if Douglas was trying to hide from them. Freddie and Sandy stuck together as they worked through the car parks methodically. Sandy wanted to keep Freddie close to avoid the possibility of Freddie coming across his father alone and of a confrontation taking place without him being close by.

They moved to the outdoor seating area for eating and drinking and then up to the Garden Room restaurant, then back down to the bars. No sign of Douglas.

Standing in the bar situated at the front of the hotel, leading out onto the main road into the centre of Stamford, Freddie told Sandy his father used to regularly drink in that bar years ago, as the family had a business premises on the opposite side of the road. Although the business was still just about functioning, his father did nothing anymore, and had done nothing that could be described as work there for the past ten years.

When they got into the room where the reception was being held, they could see that Emily and the Austrian detectives had arrived. Just at that moment, Sandy had received a message from Juliet:

Don't let Emily or Freddie come back to the house.

Pulling Mia to one side, Sandy conveyed this message to her and told her not to let Emily out of her sight, and to message him if her father was seen.

Going outside again, to the main road this time, and glancing across at the business premises that the Wainwright family owned, Sandy saw Douglas suddenly appear out of the front door. He was carrying what appeared to be a firearm inside a case – probably a shotgun, based on the shape.

Douglas crossed the road and ran along the side road by the George Hotel, carrying the gun easily. Amazed that he hadn't seen them, Sandy and Freddie followed Douglas at a safe distance, at the same time making progress to get closer and closer. To ensure that Freddie didn't alert his father that they were following, Sandy put a solitary finger in front of his lips, as if to say: "keep quiet".

When they got into the Cattlemarket car park, Douglas jumped into an old beaten-up silver Ford Fiesta.

'That's my car!' shouted Freddie. 'I wondered where the spare keys had got to.'

As he said this, the car, after a couple of attempts, spluttered to life.

'He's not meant to be driving,' Freddie said, panicked. 'He had his licence taken off him. He's going to get in trouble for this, isn't he?'

'I think that's the least of his problems,' Sandy replied.

The car darted by them and into the road, where there was a long line up of cars waiting to turn right or left at the junction onto the main road. This gave them time to be able to follow and the two of them ran to Sandy's red Morgan Roadster. On seeing it, Freddie gave a very appreciative whistle.

'Maybe I should join the police,' he said.

Sandy didn't have time to go into it being a gift from a rich grandfather, so he jumped into the car, key in hand, and incredibly swiftly started the car. He had it turned around and out of the car park before they had even settled into their seats or been able to put their seatbelts on.

Luckily for them, the traffic had slowed Douglas down and the Ford Fiesta could be seen only four or five cars in front of them. Although pleased with this, Sandy shook his head as they all edged forward slowly. Being in a bright red Morgan car was hardly going to be inconspicuous, and it surely wouldn't be long before Douglas clocked them behind him.

When they moved onto the main road leading out of Stamford, Sandy was now only three cars behind.

'Does this count as a police car chase?' asked Freddie, teetering between excitement for what was happening and concern for his father.

Sandy immediately slowed down at that, deciding to hang back. 'No, it is not a police chase.' The last thing he wanted was for Douglas to do anything foolish and smash into an innocent person in another car. 'I am safely following at a distance,' he said to Freddie, but also reminding himself.

When his phone rang, Sandy could see it was Juliet.

'Juliet,' he said, answering the call, 'I have Freddie with me.' He didn't want her to blurt out anything that might upset him.

'OK… just let me know when you're free to talk then,' Juliet said, almost caught off guard. 'Wait, are you in your car? What are you doing? Where are you going?'

'We're following Douglas Wainwright. He's driving a silver Ford Fiesta,' Sandy said.

Freddie then reeled off its registration number.

'He's armed with what we believe is a shotgun,' Sandy added.

‘What!’ Juliet exclaimed. ‘Be careful, Sandy. He’s dangerous.’

‘Can you get DS Palmer to ring the Lincolnshire Police control room and get them to mobilise some staff to come towards us? We need urgent back-up.’

‘We’re on the A606,’ Freddie interjected. ‘That means we are now in Rutland. Leicestershire Police cover this area.’

‘Leave the response police to us,’ Juliet said. ‘And keep your phone line open so we can monitor what’s happening and where you’re going.’

‘I think I know where he’s going,’ Freddie said, as Sandy drove slowly behind Douglas. There were no more cars between them and the Fiesta. ‘Normanton Church. No more than a ten-minute drive away.’

At the junction of the A606 and Normanton Park Road, the Fiesta turned. Sandy followed, only to see the Fiesta lose control slightly when a vehicle came the other way towards them and it mounted the grass verge. Then, from nowhere, a vehicle with a long trailer carrying single-seater canoes appeared. Douglas didn’t have the ability to manoeuvre around it, and after missing the car itself, ploughed into the trailer, almost knocking it over and at the same time spilling loose one of the canoes onto the road.

Douglas abandoned the Fiesta that was embedded into the trailer and Sandy saw him grab the shotgun off the rear seat before sprinting off down towards a car park that had a pathway to the church.

Damn, thought Sandy. Now they *did* have a chase on their hands.

Chapter Twenty-Seven

After parking his Morgan car on the grass verge, well before the scene of the crash, Sandy leapt out of the car and ran down the road after Douglas. He paused momentarily as he passed the scene of the crash, just to make sure the driver of the vehicle was going to be OK. Freddie had joined him in running after Douglas, who was already turning right into the car park and heading to the church.

All Sandy could hear was the voice of Juliet coming from his trouser pocket where he had shoved his mobile phone.

'Sandy, where are you? What's happening?'

Taking the phone out of his pocket whilst still moving forward and into the car park, Sandy responded, 'At Normanton Church, Rutland. I repeat, Douglas Wainwright is armed and dangerous. Get help fast.'

Leaving the phone line open, Sandy put his phone back into his pocket. Juliet could now be heard talking to presumably Linda. She was using a loud and authoritative tone, but clearly with a bit of panic in her voice.

'Tell them to stop faffing about trying to get you to talk to some mental health specialist. Whatever this policy "Right Care, Right Person" is, it's not the case here. This man is armed with a firearm and could kill, and if he kills my friend, I am going to personally destroy them!'

As they reached the small roadway up to the church, they

saw the gun case lying on the floor. The shotgun was now ready and available for Douglas to use.

'Does he know how to use a shotgun?' Sandy asked.

Freddie nodded. 'He was a pretty good shot years ago. Took part in all of the Burghley House shoots.'

'How is he allowed to have a shotgun with his criminal record and mental health issues?' Sandy said, more to himself than Freddie, shaking his head in disbelief as they made their way towards the church. There was no sign of Douglas as they scanned the area.

'The police confiscated the two shotguns he had. I didn't think he had another one, but I must admit, I was surprised when I found he still had his shotgun certificate. They hadn't confiscated this, just the guns.'

'Unbelievable,' was all that Sandy could say in response.

Although he had seen it before, he gazed at Normanton Church, standing proud on the promenade out into Rutland Water. It gave the appearance that it was actually floating. After listening carefully, to no avail, then telling Freddie to keep back, Sandy looked around the left hand side of the church, using the stonework as a sort of ballistic shield. No sign of Douglas.

Damn. He just hoped the man hadn't taken himself to the very front of the church – that would mean exposing himself to the risk of a confrontation with an armed and unhinged suspect.

Shuffling along the wall to look down the right hand side, Sandy's shoulders slumped in relief.

He had spotted him.

Douglas was sitting on a wooden bench, almost leaning

over his shotgun, trying to position the barrel up under his chin by slumping his body down. He was struggling to do this and reach his finger to the trigger.

'Dad, don't do it,' Freddie shouted from behind Sandy.

Sandy twisted around and grabbed Freddie, pulling them both into perceived safety, keeping close to the wall.

'Keep quiet,' Sandy hissed, relieved that he could now hear the sound of sirens coming towards them.

∞

They barely dared breathe as the sirens drew closer, accompanied by shouting. Suddenly, a police car could been seen driving at extreme speed towards them, but with no siren or lights flashing on it. Before they knew it, with tyres squealing, it came to an abrupt halt just in front of Sandy and Freddie, who now moved away from the church itself.

Back-up had arrived.

Out of the front seats jumped two uniform officers wearing black clothing and body armour. Within seconds, they had got into the boot and armed themselves with Heckler & Koch MP5 submachine guns. They also had holstered Glock pistols on their sides and what appeared to be Tasers on the other side of their bodies.

Walking swiftly up to Sandy and assuming correctly that he was their contact, one of the officers said, 'We have been given the authority to deploy our weapons by our tactical firearms commander. Where is the suspect?'

'He's around that side of the church,' Sandy said pointing behind him and towards the right side. 'It looks like he is trying to get in position to take his own life.'

'So he probably killed his missus and now wants to kill himself. Typical coward.'

'What!' Freddie's cry was anguished as he looked directly at Sandy. 'What's happened to my mum? Where is she?'

Sandy genuinely had no idea, but presumed this was the meaning behind Juliet's message earlier in the afternoon, about not letting Emily and Freddie go home.

Before he could say anything, the same officer pointed at Freddie. 'Take him back to behind the police car, now!'

Quite rightly, there was no rank structure in play here, and Sandy simply led Freddie to the car, as the officer had instructed.

While they moved with the firearms officer, back behind the police car, another car turned up. One officer was instructed to go one way and stop pedestrians and the other one to go the other way and do the same thing, but to go to the water's edge where they could have an unobstructed view of the side of the church that Douglas was on.

Sandy was a little concerned about this last order the firearms officer had given, as the officer instructed to go to the water's edge would surely be in line of sight for Douglas to take a shot at. He didn't argue with it though, and presumed that if Douglas took aim, avoiding action could be taken.

While all of this was happening and Sandy got Freddie to sit in the rear of the first police car, the other firearm officer with his machine gun in his hands and at the ready walked up to the church wall. Douglas was slumped on the bench, and although he was still holding the shotgun, it was lying towards one side of him, part on, part off the bench.

The officer decided it would be too risky to try and rush him, as surely one of them would get shot, yet he was too far away to use his Taser.

The officer came back to the police car, pulling his colleague and Sandy away from the range of Freddie's hearing.

'I've been on to the tactical adviser and he's now got hold of the senior firearm commander. Her view is that unless Mr Wainwright is making an actual threat to the public with the shotgun at the ready, we are not to engage and consider taking a shot. A potentially non-lethal shot, though, is not ruled out. I told them I'm too far away to use my Taser. Enroute to us is an officer with a baton gun and another officer with a dog.'

As he said this, a dog section van pulled up, joining what was now a long line of police cars.

Just as all of this was happening, there was a loud crack of a shotgun going off from around the side of the church.

∞

No one seemed to move.

'Dad,' Sandy heard Freddie whimper from the back seat, 'what have you done?'

The firearms officers moved at speed, heading to the church. As much as Sandy wanted to go with them, he fought the urge – he knew his place was to be here with Freddie.

As they got nearer to the church, the police radio on the channel that was dedicated for this operation crackled into life.

The officer watching from the bank said, 'He's taken a

shot at himself and missed totally – hit the stonework five feet above his head.'

Everyone breathed a sigh of relief.

One of the firearms officers came back to the car. 'Has he got any more shotgun cartridges?' he asked Freddie, who had lifted his head out of his hands.

'I didn't even know he had the shotgun. He shouldn't have had a shotgun. Your lot should have taken his ability to buy one away by taking his certificate off him.'

The officer shook his head and frowned at Sandy, then walked away to talk to the dog handler, who already had his dog out with him. The number of police cars that had arrived were now stretching back in a long single line. Two negotiators dressed in suits had turned up and went to talk to Freddie. They had with them a clinical psychiatric nurse. Another two firearms officers had their weapons on show. One of them had a gun that must have been the baton round gun.

There seemed to be no coordination of what was going on and just a throng of people standing or wandering about.

'Keep that dog away from my dad,' Freddie warned. 'He hates dogs.'

Although he didn't say anything, Sandy thought, *not as much as he would hate blowing his own head off or being shot by one of the firearms officers*.

Sandy's instincts were to take charge, as they were all greatly exposed to danger if Douglas came back round and down from the side of the church and took a shot into the crowd.

Another car turned up, but couldn't even get into the lane.

Out of the passenger seat walked a woman in her early forties in a blue calf-length dress with a matching short jacket. The operations firearms commander.

She instantly took control, sending everyone but the original firearms officers and the dog handler back behind her car. She told the negotiators she would come and talk to them in a minute, and she said the same to Freddie and Sandy, deciding to keep them where they were and where she could get hold of them. She needed a private word with the firearms officers first and they strode off out of earshot.

Although he had been muttering to himself, Douglas had hardly spoken. He was just sitting slumped on the same bench. His attempted suicide hadn't worked and his shot had missed by miles.

One of the officers walked up to the side of the church, his gun clearly visible.

'Mr Wainwright, I have a couple of people here to see you. One of them is a nurse. She can help to make you better.'

Seeing another opportunity to end his life, Douglas stood up, making the officer prepare his gun in readiness by the sudden movement.

'Shoot me. Kill me. I deserve it,' his staccato speech rang out. 'Kill me. Come on, you know you want to do it.'

Realising he was antagonising the situation and also realising that they should probably have gone to the negotiator interaction first, the officer slowly walked backwards out of the way, keeping his gun at the ready.

The operation commander called on her radio to the man watching from the water's edge, at the same time waving to the negotiators to come forward to talk to her.

‘What is he doing now?’ she asked, as they were too far away to see clearly what Douglas was doing.

‘He has sat down on the wooden bench again and put his head in his hands. He’s saying something to himself but I can’t hear what it is,’ the officer at the water’s edge replied.

‘Where is the shotgun?’ she asked.

‘Under the bench where it fell after he took the shot that missed.’

‘So, he hasn’t got his hands on the shotgun? He hasn’t got control of the shotgun?’

‘No.’

Turning around at lightning speed and seeing the dog handler, she shouted loudly and in an even more authoritative tone, ‘Set the dog on him, now.’

At pace, the dog handler moved up the path and unhooked his dog, who went bounding around the side of the church, barking loudly as she did.

The next thing they heard was some shouting from Douglas, then a loud splash as something heavy hit the water.

CHAPTER TWENTY-EIGHT

Even though they were on high alert, the noise of the splash surprised everyone. Two firearms officers had gone forward following the dog and his handler, one with the baton gun.

In an instant, Sandy was off and running; he no longer could contain himself. He was past the firearms officers before they realised and could do anything to stop him.

As soon as he rounded the side of the church, the police dog started snarling and barking at him, then looking back into the water and barking at what was in the water. Luckily, the dog handler was also there and quickly put the dog on his lead before he attempted to bite Sandy.

There was no sign of Douglas, and his shotgun could be seen lying on the floor under the bench. There was something in the water, frantically splashing around trying to get back to the rocks on the bank beside the church.

Douglas.

'He can hardly swim,' shouted Freddie, who had also made an appearance, now making the area along the side of the church very crowded.

The firearms commander was instructing a firearms officer to make the shotgun safe and for everyone else to go back to beyond the first car. Sandy ignored her, and in just a few seconds, he had his jacket and tie off. Kicking his shoes off as well, dived into the water, nicking the side of his head on the rocks just before he entered and catching his right ankle as his feet followed him in.

Buoyed by adrenaline, he didn't feel a thing, and was at Douglas almost instantly. What he did feel was the shock of how cold the water was, and he must have had his mouth open on entering the water as he seemed to have swallowed a whole load of it, causing him to splutter terribly as he surfaced, and the water had gotten up his nose as well, making breathing difficult.

Getting ready for a struggle and while treading water, Sandy positioned himself behind Douglas to keep out of the way of his fists and feet. He needn't have worried – Douglas was passive and was just moving his arms and legs, to try and keep himself afloat.

'Let me die,' Douglas murmured in a small voice. 'Let me die,' he kept saying as Sandy, desperately trying to remember his life-saving classes from twenty years ago, manoeuvred them round to be on their backs and then propelled them to the muddy bank rather than trying to scramble up the rocks.

He concentrated on moving them backwards. Sandy was telling himself it was less than a length of the pool at Ely that he had used in the past. He could do this. Douglas was not helping at all, but at the same time was not fighting Sandy either. He was just a dead weight to try to keep moving.

As soon as he got near the bank, two police officers and a paramedic were in the water and pushing Sandy out of the way. They grabbed Douglas and manhandled him up onto the grass. Another paramedic entered the water and helped Sandy to get himself up onto the grass bank. He was not sure when the paramedics had arrived, but Sandy was grateful to see them and also the two ambulances that were now nearby.

Lying flat on his back trying to recover from the extreme burst of exertion and breathing heavily gasping for breath, Sandy heard one of the officers say, 'Douglas Wainwright, I am arresting you for the attempted murder of your wife Hazel.' He then cautioned him.

Glancing up, Sandy saw the officer and paramedics take Douglas off to one of the ambulances. Freddie was also with them.

Pulling Sandy up to be half sitting, a paramedic set about examining the wound that was oozing blood on the right-hand side of his head, just below his hairline.

'Has Mrs Wainwright survived then?' Sandy asked an officer who had brought his jacket, tie and shoes to him.

'Not sure,' he said. 'The only information we were told was that she was critical.'

'You need to go to hospital, young man,' the paramedic, a woman in her fifties, said. 'You need an X-ray to make sure you haven't got a skull fracture and the same for your right ankle.' She looked at Sandy and smiled to reassure him. 'And you are going to need stitches too.'

'Which hospital is Mrs Wainwright in?' Sandy asked to whoever might know from the number of officers that were milling around.

Lots of shakes of heads, but one of them said, 'Peterborough City.'

Before he could ask, one of the paramedics said, 'We'll take you to that hospital.'

As they got Sandy to his feet, he yelped out in pain – his ankle was extremely sore.

‘Can Douglas be taken to this hospital as well?’ Sandy asked, only to be told “no”.

As he was under arrest and needed an urgent mental health assessment, he was being taken to the Leicester Royal Infirmary, the nearest hospital that could deal with him without going into another police area.

∞

While this was all happening, back in Stamford, Linda and Juliet followed the ambulance transporting Hazel from her home address. They were in a marked police car. The ambulance this time had its siren and lights on, as did the police car, so they were able to follow it through red lights and past cars that pulled over to let them through. The journey took less than fifteen minutes.

They arrived at the hospital just as the paramedics were pulling Hazel out on a trolley at the hospital emergency department entrance. The sergeants were able to see lots of medical equipment was being used and could see the endotracheal tube they had inserted into Hazel’s windpipe through her mouth to assist with her breathing. One of the paramedics was continually doing manual ventilation to help Hazel’s breathing at that time.

Unable to follow through the private doors at the side of the emergency department, the sergeants went back outside and into the main hospital entrance and followed the directions to head to where they were now. The only conversation they’d had with a medic was that Hazel was doing better but not out of the woods yet, and a consultant was weighing up whether to carry out surgery to release some pressure on the swelling of her brain.

Linda and Juliet were now sat on hard plastic chairs, waiting in the corridor outside the locked doors into the intensive care and high dependency unit. They both felt at a loss. There was no way that they would be allowed into the unit while a number of highly qualified medics were working on Hazel Wainwright.

Juliet's thoughts shifted to Emily. She needed to be at Peterborough City Hospital, as did Freddie, but he was otherwise engaged. Hazel needed her family and they needed her.

Juliet called Mia. 'Hazel Wainwright is critical in hospital at Peterborough. It's not known if she is going to survive or not. We need to get Emily here.'

A clearly shocked Mia didn't know what to say. Things were starting to wind up at The George and they were a bit lost as to what to do with Emily or whether they should go to the train station and head back to London.

'We can bring her,' Mia said after a short pause, 'but we have no transport. I could order a taxi, I suppose.'

Linda piped up then, rising to her feet instantly. 'I will go and get them. Ring me if there's any change to the condition of Hazel. I'll be back in thirty minutes or so.'

She left before Juliet could comment.

Looking at her phone, she saw there was a message from Sandy, telling her he was on his way to Peterborough City Hospital in an ambulance. Juliet, who hadn't been able to get hold of him for some considerable time, was shocked that something had clearly happened. Her initial thoughts were that he must have been shot, though she managed to calm herself when she realised he couldn't possibly be that bad if he had been able to send a message. Gosh, what a day it had been!

∞

On the way to the hospital, Sandy had an overriding concern, and it had nothing to do with his injuries. No, Sandy had left his beloved Morgan car at the side of the road in the middle of nowhere, and it was causing him not a small amount of distress.

His only answer was to get his two grandfathers involved. If it didn't hurt so much, he would have shook his head vigorously at the thought. He called his Grandad Tom, telling him he was in hospital at Peterborough and that he needed to get hold of John and either get the spare keys from Sandy's room in Ely or, better still, so as not to worry his mother, come to the hospital and get them from him. Neither of them were to tell Hannah anything, Sandy insisted.

On arrival at the hospital, a very harassed and clearly very busy doctor gave Sandy's two cuts a cursory look and told him that he would live and was gone.

Not long afterwards, a nurse came in with a healthcare assistant. They helped Sandy to get out of his still wet clothes, shoving them into a big clear plastic bag and placing his jacket over the top of them. Painkillers had been prescribed and given, then they too went off, telling him that he would have an inordinate wait until the X-ray for any broken bones and a CT scan for any brain injury. He was to try not to sleep, to sit up on the trolley bed, and to call if he felt drowsy or was sick.

Looking at his phone and answering and sending emails was not something that Sandy particularly wanted to do, but what else could he do with his time?

Before he could start though, Juliet burst into the room.

'The nurse says you should be OK, so I should thump you for the stress you've caused me,' Juliet said. 'I don't care for one minute that you are my boss and a senior officer. You deserve it for worrying me like this. I had visions of you having been shot! Sending me a message with no details, I can't believe you.'

Before Sandy could apologise, in came four more women.

Emily was the first to speak, tears in her eyes and running down her cheeks. 'I'm not sure why I still care about him, but thank you for saving my dad's life.'

'Have you had an update how he is then?' Sandy asked, pulling a sheet over himself to cover his legs. The gown didn't hide much.

'Freddie is with him. They are at a hospital in Leicester. My dad isn't talking to anyone, not even Freddie. He's blanking them apparently, but is constantly swatting imaginary flies.'

A nurse arrived and told the ladies that only one of them could remain. Linda took Emily off to see what they could find out about her mum, and Juliet offered to organise a taxi to the station for the Austrian detectives so they could get back to London.

Suddenly, Sandy was left with no one. Maybe he should call Hannah, he thought, but before he could do this, a porter arrived and told him that the technicians at CT were ready for him and then it would be straight on to X-ray. Apparently, rumours were circulating around the hospital that Sandy was the hero of the siege at Rutland Water.

By the time the doctor arrived to give him the results of the scans, Juliet had returned. He had no fractures and no brain injury, but both of his cuts needed stitching, and she told him she would do the one on his forehead as she was apparently neater at stitching than the other doctor in the emergency department.

There was no update as to how Hazel was doing, so the two of them remained in the dark regarding what had actually happened to her, other than their assumption that her husband had tried to strangle her. But Juliet did have some news about Arthur's case, though it wasn't good. The contact at British Airways had sent an email to say that Douglas Wainwright had *not* been on Andrew Barrington's flight from London to Vienna, or indeed on any other flight around that time.

But if Douglas Wainwright hadn't killed Arthur Barrington, then who had?

CHAPTER TWENTY-NINE

On Sunday morning, Sandy was sat opposite his two grandfathers in Peacocks Tearoom, a short walk from his home on Waterside in Ely. Sandy must have been to the tearoom hundreds of times over the twenty years or so it had been in business, but this was the first time he'd been for breakfast – a new venture for them, and as a result of the promise to his grandfathers to treat them to breakfast for bringing his Morgan car safely home.

The previous day had been a quiet one for Sandy, with strict instructions from the doctor to take it easy and to remain off his ankle as much as possible. The crutches that he had been given were taking some getting used to, especially getting up and down the steep stairs to his bedroom. Hannah had turned up early on Saturday morning, and after seeing that he was going to be fine, had headed off back to Cambridge late that evening to get on with her preparation for a court case next week.

'What is happening in Vienna then Sandy?' Tom asked him, after they had ordered their food.

'Nothing, as far as I am aware,' Sandy said, trying to position his right leg in a more comfortable position. 'I asked them to send across the outstanding DNA and fingerprints found in the Barringtons' hotel room. I've also asked them to check with immigration to see if Douglas Wainwright had somehow arrived in Vienna on the day in question.' He looked at his grandfathers, who were staring intently and with concern at the stitched cut on his forehead. He gave them both a frown, causing them to look away. 'British Airways has not got him on any of their flights that day.'

'Lots of other airlines and lots of other airports are used to fly to Vienna every day,' John said. 'Your grandma and I went from London Stanstead on one occasion.'

'You're stating the obvious,' Sandy said as their teas, coffee and cutlery were brought to the table by the waitress. 'Hence, I asked for Austrian immigration to check. Everything seems to have stopped while they wait for Otto Wagner to return from holiday at the end of this week.'

'What about that dear lady in hospital, is she going to be OK?' John asked.

There was a pause while their breakfasts were placed in front of them. Sandy, who was very hungry, had to eat at least two mouthfuls before he replied.

'Apparently, she's going to be OK. No surgery was needed, but we still don't know what happened to her.' Another mouthful delayed him talking further. 'DS Palmer in Lincolnshire has told me that Hazel has both Emily and Freddie with her, and they and the doctors are hopeful that she will be able to talk to the police in a couple of days or so.'

Putting on his judge's voice and his poshest Scottish accent, presumably because he was talking about the law, John said, 'What about the husband, the man whose life you saved? I presume he was sectioned under Section 2 of the Mental Health Act 1983.'

Sandy smiled. His Grandpa John was slightly wrong on

that count. 'Actually, it was under Section 3 of that Act. He wasn't consenting to anything; in fact, he wasn't talking at all, so two doctors and Freddie – as the eldest able family member – agreed to it.'

Never one to not have the last word, and needing to show he knew what he was talking about, John added, 'If my memory serves me right, under Section 3, they must have an appropriate course of treatment for him then, and it can be for up to six months.'

Sandy actually didn't know some of this detail, but he hoped that in this six-month period they would know whether Douglas was likely to be the murderer of Arthur and whether he had actually tried to murder his wife.

No more talking, he decided. He needed to order some more toast and finish his breakfast. Once finished, he would find out more about the investigations of the firm Plato Solutions, which his grandfathers had set up, and their two new cases – their only cases – which were unsurprisingly to do with possible hospital neglect in two cases of child death.

Though he didn't want his grandfathers to get themselves in any trouble, he knew they were the right men for these sorts of jobs.

∞

By lunchtime on Monday, Sandy was feeling jittery and frustrated. Stuck at home, he was already up to date with his emails and was making progress on reading the team's files that were ready for filing. He felt he had hardly been in the FCDO offices in London for weeks and weeks, due to working away and being injured, twice, but his boss had been quite clear with him: she didn't want to see him for two weeks, and due to summer leave, didn't want him injured any more as she needed him in the office.

An equal cause of the reason for the frustration was that Sandy had truly believed that Douglas Wainwright could be Arthur's murderer, but nothing, absolutely nothing, was helping to confirm that belief.

Breaking the monotony was a call from DS Linda Palmer.

'How are you, sir?' she asked.

'A bit frustrated – I've had worse injuries playing rugby. Being confined to home is not helping me to get on and find out who killed Arthur Barrington.'

'Well, I have some good news for you,' she said. 'The chief constable of Leicestershire has put you forward for a Royal Humane Society award and after everything is sorted with Douglas Wainwright, he intends to give you, the dog, and his handler a commendation from him as well.'

Sandy didn't really know what he thought about all of this praise. His initial thoughts were that he was embarrassed by it all.

'I also took a statement from Freddie this morning at his home,' Linda continued in response to Sandy's awkward silence. 'It was a long one. He went right back to childhood. I now have a great case for coercive and controlling behaviour against Douglas.'

'Excellent,' Sandy said, very pleased with this outcome. 'I can give you a statement as well for the small interaction I witnessed when I first saw him in the house with them.'

'I'm taking Emily's statement tomorrow morning as they

both wanted to go off to the hospital to be with their mum.'

'How is Hazel?'

'Doing much better. I'm going to see her later in the week and she will, well, according to Freddie, make a statement. I'm going to visually record this, so I've secured a room in the hospital. I think this will protect her, if we ever get to court, from the control of Douglas,' Linda said.

She was as impressive as Sandy's first impression had been of her. This was a young lady who was going to go places in the police service, if that was what she wanted.

'Do we know what happened to her?'

'I only have this from Freddie, so it might not be what actually happened, but from what his mum has said, he thinks Douglas tried to strangle her because she wouldn't tell him where Em was going off to.'

'Strangle her? How?' Sandy asked in anticipation.

'How? What do you mean by that?'

'With his hands around her throat or a choke-type hold from behind her?' Sandy clarified.

'Likely a chokehold. Freddie has seen him do that to his mum before,' Linda replied.

Sandy didn't know what to do with himself – he was too excited by how well this aligned with Arthur's case. Of course, this didn't mean that Douglas had been to Vienna, but it was the same method that was used to murder Arthur.

'Have you searched the house at all?' Sandy asked.

'Yes, with Freddie's consent this morning. I found a lot of his medication, which should have been used, as well as alcohol. He is also taking cannabis as I found some traces in one of his clothing drawers.'

'Did you see a blue woollen jumper at all?'

'Umm, yes as it happens,' a confused Linda answered. 'Why?'

'Is it possible to seize it? It might be important to the case of Arthur Barrington's death.'

'Oh, of course. I'll get it tomorrow morning when I'm taking Emily's statement.'

∞

It wasn't until the end of the week that Sandy got a message from Inspector Otto Wagner, agreeing to a video call with Juliet and himself.

The only news that Sandy had was that Hazel Wainwright had so much to say that another session was needed with Linda, which was going to take place early the following week. Sandy had also had some good news – well, he wasn't quite sure as yet whether it was good news or not. He had been shortlisted for the Cambridgeshire detective superintendent role, and interviews would be in September.

The first person on the call that Sandy saw was Juliet. He had spoken to her numerous times already that week.

'Show us your scar, then,' was the first thing she said.

Ignoring her, Sandy was pleased to see Otto come onto to his screen. He looked suntanned but as anxious and harassed as always. Maybe the holiday hadn't worked for him.

'How are you?' Sandy offered as a question, but suspected he knew what the answer would be.

'Well, I had a great holiday, but have come back to eight hundred and ninety-three outstanding emails.' He put his hands through his hair. 'I told my wife I should keep on top of them, but no, complete rest, she said.'

It was a good job Juliet was on mute – Sandy could see her sniggering away.

'All morning I have been in catch-up meetings and briefings,' he went on. 'I am the only inspector actually on duty all weekend too, and we have three events on in Vienna city centre.'

Sandy's world was an absolute picnic in comparison to this. Did he really want to go back to full on policing like the Cambridgeshire job?

'Have you seen our requests to get immigration to check if Douglas Wainwright came to Vienna on the day of Arthur's murder or a day or so before?' he asked Otto.

'No, sorry. I did see something from Mia, but I haven't read it as yet.' Otto looked distracted now. 'Why are you obsessed with him? We have no evidence.'

'What about the chokehold he used on his wife?' Juliet said.

'What about the chokehold that Flamur Hysa used on DCI McFarlane? He is our best bet, DS Ashton, isn't he?' Otto was nodding more to himself than the other two. 'I was working out while walking how I could write up and close the investigation nicely, now that Flamur has died.'

'I am not sure,' Sandy said. 'The family of Arthur will agree that that works. But they, Juliet, myself, and I am sure you, Otto, want proper justice for him.' He lowered his voice to an almost pleading tone. 'Just make this request please and either you or we can check the outstanding DNA and fingerprints if Paulina sends it to our CSI.'

Otto signed heavily. 'All right. Not sure we would ever get justice though – I understand from Mia that he is in a secure mental health hospital.' Otto wrote a note in his book before he spoke again. 'Now, I need to update you on the case of Marin Ismalaj. This is me talking to you,' Otto said, looking at Sandy, 'as a victim of his.'

Not knowing whether to speak or listen, Sandy just said, 'Go on.'

'He, as you know, or I think you know, is not being included in the prosecution of the attempted kidnappers of the Austrian President. They are on remand and will plead not guilty with a trial date sometime late next year.'

'What about the investigation against Felix Bauer into the shooting of Flamur? Is he in the clear?' Sandy asked.

'Not sure on that,' Otto said, flicking through his notebook to see if he had written anything down. 'Nothing further. I think someone said it will take a long time, but he is looking to be OK.'

Reverting back to the note that he did have, Otto said, 'Ismalaj pleaded guilty at juvenile court yesterday to all charges, including the attempted theft from you. The judge accepted the submission that he was a child victim of criminal exploitation and gave him a thirty-month rehabilitation order.' Otto paused as he looked up and directly at Sandy again. 'I know this is not what you may have wanted to hear, but that is what happened.'

'On the contrary,' Sandy said, a smile on his face, 'I agree. He was a victim too and I sincerely hope that rehabilitation works for him.'

CHAPTER THIRTY

Sandy had enjoyed a quiet weekend at home with Hannah and was getting on well walking with his crutch, though his mind was scrambled by all the decisions Hannah was expecting him to help her with in relation to the house, in particular the new kitchen. He was quite happy to let Hannah decide; he trusted her judgement totally. Well, almost totally – there were the odd few things that he really didn't like or agree with. But, for the most part, he didn't mind, yet Hannah was insistent that he be involved in every decision, even down to whether they should buy an air fryer.

There was a lot of electrical and plumbing work needed throughout, and they had confirmed with the tradesman they were going to be using that they should start on the 1st of August, which was the completion date for the house purchase. The whole house would need painting following this, and although they had a romantic notion of doing the painting themselves, due to work commitments away from Cambridge, this was going to be impossible – only the odd room maybe. Sandy had wondered, with everything going on, whether the wedding was coming up too soon. The problem was, he desperately wanted to marry Hannah, and would marry her that day and happily live in a house that needed doing up, but at the same time, he understood why Hannah wanted it all just right. Perhaps he should talk to her about delaying the wedding until things had calmed down? Something to consider.

His Grandad Tom had arrived too early on Monday morning to collect Sandy to take him to the minor injuries clinic at the Princess of Wales Hospital. Sandy could have gone back to Peterborough or to his GP, but this seemed to him the easiest option for the removal of his stitches.

What this meant was that they got there before the clinic was even open. While waiting, sitting on the plastic seats, Tom asked Sandy how the case in Vienna was going. He had brought a paper with him in case they had a long wait, but he would clearly much rather talk to his grandson.

'The next few days will be crucial in finding out if Douglas has been to Vienna and whether we can place him in the hotel room.' Sandy hesitated. 'If it *is* him, they are not keen to think about trying for extradition, what with all of his mental health issues, so that might be as far as we get.'

'I have always been of the view that you as a detective do all that you can, and the best that you can, then if the criminal justice system comes to a different conclusion, that is something you have to accept,' Tom said, trying to reassure him.

Before Sandy could answer, he was called in by the nurse.

Unfortunately for him, she had the roughest and strongest fingers Sandy had ever come across.

'Ouch! Gosh that hurts,' was all he kept saying.

The nurse commented, 'They put a lot of stitches in your forehead, didn't they?'

'Ouch! Yes, to try and reduce the scarring. Ahh! Just stop for a moment so I can draw breath.'

If Sandy thought taking out the stitches from his head was bad, his ankle gave him even more pain as there was the possibility of an infection in the wound. This involved the overworked doctor coming to examine it and prescribing an antibiotic cream. He was to use the crutch for a couple of days longer and then back to walking and driving too.

In the car for the short journey home, Tom commented, 'I was surprised with you being a rugby player how low a pain threshold you seem to have.'

Biting his tongue and not rising to the bait, Sandy resumed their conversation about the case. 'I don't believe for one minute you were the sort of detective that accepted anything other than justice for your investigations and victims.'

'No. You are right. I was just trying to soften the blow for you if this might end up being the end of the road for you on this investigation. You are my grandson. I remember a case from thirty years ago like it was yesterday, the sickness in the pit of my stomach when a jury found the defendant not guilty of a rape offence. It's rough when it doesn't go the way you want. I'm just trying to prepare you, whatever the outcome.'

Once they had arrived home, and Sandy had said goodbye to his grandfather, he took a seat in the lounge. *Why* do *I get so emotionally involved in my cases*, he pondered. Why did he have such a passion to find out what happened, and why did he care so deeply for his victims? Was this a good or a bad trait? Probably not bad for the case itself, but no doubt bad for him personally – at some time in the future, that emotion would ultimately need to go somewhere.

Was his gut feeling correct that it was Douglas Wainwright who had killed Arthur? There was not a scrap of evidence that he had been in Vienna – well, not as yet. Sandy had been right though, about Douglas being a domestic abuser to his family, his wife in particular. Otto thought Flamur Hysa could be their killer, and yes, he was breaking into hotel rooms and yes, he did use a chokehold on Sandy, but was that just an easy way out as he was already dead? Could it have been someone else? Yes. But who? Sandy was as sure as he could that Andrew Barrington hadn't killed his son, and Douglas seemed to have motive, far more motive than Flamur.

He decided to make a cup of tea and focus on his other work before his mum came home from her part-time teaching job and disturbed his peace, although she did go and volunteer in Ely Cathedral on a Monday afternoon, so maybe he would still have the house to himself.

That evening, settling himself on the settee with a drink to watch Monday night football, Sandy was surprised, in fact very surprised, to receive a call from Otto.

'DCI McFarlane, is that you?' Otto sounded far too excited.

Shaking his head and thinking, *who else would it be answering my phone*, while at the same time hunting round for the television remote to switch the sound to mute, Sandy replied, 'Yes, it's Sandy.'

'Sandy, Sandy,' he repeated. Gosh, he was excited. 'You will not believe what we've found.'

Not knowing whether he should make a guess or not, Sandy decided to keep quiet.

'Douglas Wainwright arrived in Vienna one hour after Andrew Barrington. He arrived on a Ryanair flight from London Stansted and left on their last flight on the same day.'

Sandy jumped up off the sofa. 'I knew it! I just knew it.'

'There's more. His fingerprints and DNA are on the coffee mug too.'

'So, we can place Douglas in Vienna. We can place Douglas in the hotel room with Arthur. We now just need to place Douglas's arm around Arthur's throat. You know an officer from Lincolnshire Police, DS Palmer, has recovered a blue woollen jumper that Douglas owns?'

'I didn't know that… or did I?' said Otto, sounding less confident now. 'Is it possible to somehow take a sample or, even better, get the jumper to us here in Vienna?'

'I'm very sure that something could be arranged,' Sandy said. 'Leave it with me.'

'The next problem we have, and it's a big problem, is Mr Wainwright's mental health. The examining magistrate told me to get all the statements to him. If Wainwright is fit at any time for interview, he wants someone in my team to carry out the interview in England and then he will take medical advice on the best way forward.'

Only that afternoon, Linda had told Sandy that she had finished her video statement with Hazel Wainright. During her conversation with a psychiatrist, she had been told that Douglas was fit for an interview in the secure premises that he was in. This would not harm and would maybe even help their assessment and treatment programme.

'We might be in luck there for the interview too,' Sandy said as they finished the call.

Glancing at the television screen, he realised that he had missed two goals in the match, but rather than watching the football again, he knew that he must now make a call to Juliet.

She was more than delighted with this latest update and told Sandy she would sort the blue jumper out as a priority. She also asked, if she was able to, whether she could carry out the interview.

The next call was to Linda, who was equally delighted, and said she could help interview Douglas on behalf of the Austrian police, when she talked to him about the domestic abuse and the attempted murder of Hazel.

Sandy smiled to himself. Everything was coming together.

∞

The interview room at Rampton Hospital – a secure unit where Douglas had been taken following his discharge from Leicester Hospital – was not like a traditional police interview room, but more like a lounge in a home. Sitting in the room was DS Linda Palmer and DC Mia Eckhart. Linda had set up mobile recording equipment that she had brought with her and had used before. There was no facility to downstream monitor or to view the interview in another room, so this meant that Sandy and Otto would be briefed following the interview. Juliet would need to be briefed too, but Sandy would do that. As much as Juliet had wanted to be one of the interviewers, the two detectives who were going to be carrying out the interview were the right ones.

Rampton Hospital was one of three high-security hospitals in England and Wales, the other two being Broadmoor, the most notorious, and Ashton. The infamous Ian Huntley, who had killed Holly Wells and Jessica Chapman, two ten-year-old girls, had been resident at Rampton before he was interviewed and charged with their murders. Although it was a hospital, the inpatients rooms were more like a cell, especially if the patient needed to be on suicide watch.

Also in the room was a clinical psychiatric nurse, who was part of a team that had been working with Douglas. When Douglas walked into the room, he looked like a changed man. His beard was gone and although not quite clean shaven, he looked years younger. His hair too had been cut, not short, but it now looked much smarter. Douglas smiled at the three women as he took the seat they had allotted to him to ensure he was in the main frame of the camera. With him was his solicitor, a man who was plump and overweight, dressed in a suit with a slight bulge to his shirt buttons, but the blue tie he was wearing covered up the worst of the strain. He wore round-rim glasses and had a smiling face that suggested he could be trusted. Not normally the look of a defence solicitor.

After the necessary preamble of introductions and caution, Linda asked, 'Tell us about your marriage, Mr Wainwright. What is it like?'

'Happy,' he smiled again. 'Next year would make thirty years. Hazel and I have two children. My boy Freddie is at Cambridge University, you know. We are very proud of him.'

Who is he trying to kid? thought Linda. The marriage was anything but happy.

'Our daughter Em looks after us as Hazel and I are not well. We are not well at all. We would be lost without her.'

Deciding to go straight for the jugular, and because the nurse had said Douglas was not able to hold conversations for too long, Linda interjected, 'Your wife Hazel would not agree that your marriage is a happy one.' She looked Douglas directly in the eye, and he stared back intently, not letting his gaze drop. It was almost threatening. 'She has made a statement to me that for years you were physically and verbally violent to her and the children. You are coercive and controlling of everything, including her and Emily's finances. You have used a choke-type hold and tried to strangle her on more than one occasion, and only a couple of weeks ago, she almost died.'

Unable to keep quiet any longer, Douglas replied, 'I have no idea what you're talking about. That's not me you are describing.'

'But it is you.'

Douglas shrugged. 'Only when I'm unwell and the spies are trying to get to me or I'm being threatened by others. I am not myself, then. That is someone else. They listen to everything in my house and Hazel lets them in, you know. She lets them try to get me.'

Realising that Douglas was starting to lose control, Mia stepped in to ask her questions.

'Tell us about when you went to Vienna.'

Douglas looked at his solicitor, who nodded and smiled at him.

'I don't remember ever going to Vienna.'

'We can confirm that you did go to Vienna. We can confirm that you were in a hotel room there with Arthur Barrington.'

On the mention of Arthur's name, Douglas was on his feet, only to be pulled gently back down by his nurse.

'He's a spy.' He looked around at everybody in the room. 'Do you know,' he said, as he put his arms out wide, 'that boy tried to infiltrate my family, my home, brainwash my daughter, the only person who looks after me. Not a nice boy at all. He was trying to get me and kill me.' Douglas nodded knowingly.

'You killed him, though,' Mia said, keeping very calm and talking softly. 'You used the same chokehold on him that you did on your wife Hazel.'

'I don't remember. I have never been to Vienna.' Looking round at his solicitor again, he said, 'Well, I don't remember if I have or not.'

Douglas started to look around and stood up, then looked behind his chair, tapped the wall behind him and sat down again.

Looking at each other and nodding, Linda and Mia decided that it was an opportune time to stop the interview.

Chapter Thirty-One

Sandy had seen Hannah upset before; he had seen her being a strong woman and fighting for justice for her victims. But had never seen her *angry* before.

Their solicitor had not even rung Sandy, he had simply sent an email to say completion on the house was being put off by a week and could – not definitely, but could – take place a week later. Hannah had organised plumbers, electricians and a kitchen fitter who was also going to fit the bathroom. It would appear that slow movement, allegedly by the seller's solicitor, had caused the delay.

The spreadsheet Hannah had put together was now well and truly off track and the tradespeople apparently had holidays that they could not put off. Hannah was trying to get Sandy to postpone them taking the week they had planned to spend in North Norfolk. Sandy had quickly realised that the last thing Hannah needed was for him to join in being angry and cross, or begin to suggest solutions. Instead, she needed him to just support and agree with her about how wrong it all was and to show empathy to her, which he duly did, but maintaining a calm façade amidst all the chaos was exhausting.

Getting back to work in London on Monday felt like a bit of respite, though the office was quiet. Juliet and Clare had somehow convinced Detective Superintendent Watson that they should personally take Douglas Wainwright's blue woollen jumper to Vienna, along with some tapings that Clare had taken from it when they had collected it late last week. They were also going to copy the full investigation file and bring it back with them. A dinner with Mia and Johanna and an overnight stay had also been planned.

The report that Sandy had been working on for Detective Superintendent Watson to present to the next meeting of the UK Homicide Working Group was almost complete, but he decided to take the time to go through it again. He had always been a great supporter of what was now called the Murdered Abroad group (previously called SAMM). He felt passionately that the work they were doing to fight for support for people who had lost loved ones to murder and manslaughter abroad was important and necessary. The report was asking for agreement for police forces to appoint a local senior investigating officer and a family liaison officer in all cases where the death abroad of one of their residents was being investigated as a homicide. He had put together three examples where it worked well. Sandy and his boss both had high hopes that this request would succeed.

Just as he pushed the "send" button for the final report to go to Jane, he received a call from an excited Linda Palmer.

'I've got permission from the Crown Prosecution Service special case work lawyer to charge Douglas Wainwright with the attempted murder of his wife,' Linda said without pausing for breath.

'I presume you will be getting him out of Rampton Hospital to do this, will you?'

'I have no idea at the moment,' Linda said, still talking

quickly. 'I have just come off the phone to the lawyer and wanted you to know, so I've not thought any of that through yet.'

'I am sure there are other ways to do it, but it's typically arrest at the secure premises, take to a police station custody block, then charge and send him to firstly Magistrates' then to Crown Court,' Sandy said, thinking from memory of previous cases, albeit they were from prison rather than a high-security hospital.

He had read the interview transcript that Linda had forwarded him and knew that they would not need to interview Douglas again, as all of the points had been covered in the first interview.

'I don't suppose you will be able to come with me to see the Wainwrights later this week, will you?' Linda asked.

'Not really. I would wait to see how you are organising the charging and have more details of court dates, etcetera,' Sandy said, before promptly ending the call as he saw he had a call from Juliet coming in.

'How soon can you come to Austria?' Juliet said, even before Sandy could say hello.

'What do you mean?' Sandy asked.

'Inspector Wagner has had a discussion with their state prosecutor and they want to discuss if extraditing and prosecuting Douglas Wainwright is even feasible.'

Things were now moving so quickly it was difficult to keep up, especially since they had gone from merely hoping for some kind of prosecution regarding the domestic abuse of his family to him now being charged as the main suspect in an international murder investigation.

Needing a moment to think things through, Sandy went for a walk around St James's Park. Had his ankle been stronger, he would have run around the park – he did his best thinking while running. A plan had formulated in his mind by the time he got back in the office. A quick call to DS Linda Palmer revealed the CPS lawyer's name and the contact details for her.

'Hello, is that Meera Goswami?' Sandy asked when his call was answered by a woman with a thick Brummie accent.

'Yes, what can I do for you?'

After explaining who he was and why he was calling, Meera replied, 'I understand what you are thinking, but I need to clear it with my boss in London.' Meera could be heard tapping on her computer, hopefully checking her boss's calendar for availability. 'But I do think you should only go to Vienna with myself and the officer on our case here to discuss this, as we intend to have criminal proceedings happening soon against Douglas Wainwright and I don't want to confuse things.'

It took another day to organise the meeting, but early that following day, Sandy, a very excited Linda, and Meera Goswami were on a British Airways morning flight to Vienna.

Meera was a barrister by training, but had joined the CPS almost twenty years earlier. She knew Hannah well and they'd had two trials together in the past – complex rape trials. Although born in Birmingham, both her paternal and maternal family came from Vadodara in India, where Sandy had worked on a case a couple of years ago. They spent the whole flight discussing India and Hannah, and did not once mention Douglas Wainwright.

Present in the meeting room once they had arrived was Otto Wagner and a man who introduced himself as the state prosecutor. This man was in his late fifties, or maybe early sixties. He had round-rimmed glasses and wore the most splendid yellow bow tie. They were outnumbered two to one by the British contingent. Juliet, who was present, had somehow – Sandy knew not how – wrangled staying an extra night in Vienna, not only for her but also Clare, who had gone off shopping or sightseeing, or both.

'As you know,' Otto began, gesturing to Sandy and Juliet, 'we have strong evidence that Douglas Wainwright murdered Arthur Barrington.' Otto looked down at his notes out of habit. 'We have him on our immigration system as being in Vienna at the time and also on CCTV at the airport. We have him in the hotel room as we have his fingerprint and DNA. We also have a verbal update that the fibres on a blue jersey that he owns match those found on Arthur's neck.'

Sandy glanced at Juliet on hearing this new information, and they both smiled and nodded to each other.

The state prosecutor took over the talking.

'So you see, we have enough to comfortably prosecute. We definitely have enough to make an application for what we believe would be a successful extradition from the UK to Austria. We have interviewed him – DC Eckhart came to the UK and did this.' He was looking straight at Meera Goswami while he spoke. 'The problem is his mental health issues and that he is in a high-security hospital in the UK. We would not want to try and extradite as the process of him getting well enough to travel could take years.'

Meera answered his question, despite it having been

spoken as a statement. 'DCI McFarlane has a proposal to ensure that justice is done sooner rather than later.' She looked at Sandy, realising she hadn't told him this. 'I have permission from the Director of Public Prosecutions to go ahead with the proposal if the Austrian team agree.' She looked again at the state prosecutor.

All eyes now focused on Sandy. 'We will be charging Mr Wainwright with the attempted murder of his wife Hazel next week.' He looked at Linda. 'We have a rarely used law contained in the Offences Against the Person Act of 1861 to prosecute an offence in the UK that was committed by a British citizen while abroad on another British citizen, as in this case. There is also Article 44 of the Istanbul Convention that I know the Austrian government also support. This means that we can prosecute one of our citizens in the UK for certain crimes they commit abroad, and murder is one of those crimes.'

'So, your suggestion,' the state prosecutor said, 'is that you prosecute him for both offences as a joint trial in the UK?' He looked at Otto, who was nodding vigorously. 'Not sure how our concerns about him ever facing justice due to his mental health issues are any different there than here.'

'We won't have the fitness to travel, or the stress of a foreign jail or court, etcetera, to impact on his mental health. He will have the continuity of medical treatment,' Meera explained.

'We are all in agreement then,' the state prosecutor said, smiling for the first time. 'I will draw up the charge for murder from Austria and we will insist that Inspector Wagner is involved in all conversations and any trial that should take place.'

Chapter Thirty-Two

The charging and first appearance of Douglas Wainwright in court happened without any dramas, though Linda Palmer, when she had rung Sandy, told him that Douglas seemed spaced out and oblivious to what was going on around him. She worried his lawyers would say that, due to his medication and illness, he was unaware of what was being done to him. Only time would tell.

She had also tearfully let Sandy know that the East Midlands Special Operations Unit wanted to take over the investigation, and replace her with a senior investigating officer. Of course, he had immediately leapt into action, making a call to a friend and colleague, Temporary Detective Superintendent Rishabh (Rich) Singh, who was working on the unit carrying out maternity cover. Rich had worked with Sandy before on a couple of investigations, and as he was coming to Sandy's wedding, Sandy used that as an excuse for the call and got agreement that Linda would remain the officer on the case. In addition, as long as Sandy kept involved, he would oversee it. Linda had been understandably relieved.

DC Mia Eckhart had travelled from Austria to be part of the charging of Douglas Wainwright, and had subsequently visited Andrew and Faith Barrington with Linda to explain what evidence they had and what was likely to happen. The two of them had also visited Hazel Wainwright and her children, to explain what had occurred.

As to Sandy's personal life, the completion of the house purchase in Cambridge had gone through without any more hitches, and between the tradespeople they had come up with a plan to complete all of their involvement by early to mid-September. Although Hannah felt this was too close to their wedding, she seemed happy to accept this as the best possible scenario. They would move into the house following the wedding, despite all the decorating that would still need to be done.

Thus far, the only input Sandy had given with regards to their wedding had been agreeing on the food and wine menus for the wedding reception, though he was currently in a heated debate with his paternal grandfather, who was insisting that Sandy wore a kilt. Professor Sir John McFarlane was a formidable force when he had made his mind up about something, and even brought pictures to show Sandy of him in a kilt at his own wedding, and of Sandy's father, Gregor, wearing a kilt at his wedding to Sandy's mother Katherine.

After that, Sandy gave in, not because of the power of the argument but because of his love for the old man. Besides, Hannah had been in agreement, telling him it would be rather sexy.

Speaking of grandfathers, their investigation business had moved on to another couple of cases, both for a large insurance company based in Cambridge. Apparently, they needed to purchase a camera for this particular investigation, so Sandy had taken them to Campkins Cameras on Kings Parade in Cambridge – a beautiful location for a shop. They had wonderful assistance buying two small Panasonic Lumix digital cameras with long-range inbuilt telephoto lenses that they could put in their pockets. As well as the two cameras, they left with two equally powerful pocket-sized binoculars. All of their profit from their first two cases had now been spent.

Unfortunately, Sandy's personal life was soon to be disrupted yet again, this time with a call from Meera Goswami while Sandy and Hannah were on holiday in Norfolk. The call had pulled him straight back to thinking about Arthur Barrington. A judge and counsel had been appointed, and the judge was someone Sandy had worked with in the past, Justice Francis Kane KC. For the prosecution was another barrister he had worked with once before, and who, in Sandy's view, was excellent – Christopher Coke KC. But it was the name of the defence barrister that stopped Sandy in his tracks. Charles Holloway KC, a most undesirable character in Sandy's view, and his nemesis for many years. Sandy just hoped Christopher was prepared.

According to Meera, the diary of proceedings had been agreed, with a fluidity to it that was driving the listings officer crazy at Lincoln Crown Court, where the case was going to be heard. A schedule in September had been agreed: legal discussion between prosecution and defence for one day, one day of legal argument in front of the judge, then up to four days the following week if matters could be moved forward.

Sandy didn't know whether to tell Hannah or not – if the hearing ran to the fourth day, it would be the day before their wedding. He started researching how long it took to get from Lincoln to Cambridge, if by any stroke of bad luck he was required there on the Friday itself. Sandy sighed heavily. This could turn out to be a nightmare.

∞

The courthouse in Lincoln was housed in the grounds of Lincoln Castle, which Sandy was determined to look around if he got the chance. After all, there was currently a 1215 Magna Carta on display there – a real treat for a history buff like him. There had been a court held within its grounds for centuries, but the current court house had been built in 1823. *What a place to have a Crown Court*, thought Sandy, as he walked through the doors to find the room where they were going to be holding their meeting.

He had travelled up that morning, but Otto had arrived the previous evening and was staying in a hotel nearby, where Sandy would join him that night. The weekend had been hectic – a stag party for him had taken place, which started at The Cutter Inn and then carried on in various pubs in Ely, finishing with a late evening curry. They had all been well behaved other than some silly T-shirts someone had made for them all to wear. Ely was hardly Newcastle or Prague, as a place to have a stag night, but it suited him, and with his dad and Hannah's father Howard keeping an eye on things, it had gone without a hitch.

A couple of his friends from the Metropolitan Police had stayed over and they had organised, or tried to organise, a foot surveillance course for the two grandfathers. Tom had never been formally trained when he was in the police so this was a new experience. They were – and there was no other way to describe it – hopeless. John couldn't keep up with his dodgy knee and everyone in Ely seemed to know Tom and wanted to stop and talk to him, so he lost the target time after time.

Sunday had been taken up with painting, and looking at the white gloss paint still on his hands, Sandy was reminded that he was not very good at it.

As he walked into the room, he discovered there was only one other person there. Of course, it just had to be Charles Holloway.

'Oh, it's you,' Holloway said with a scowl, pairing it with a look of disdain. 'I saw that you were involved from the papers. None of your clever tricks this time, Chief Inspector, if you don't mind. My client is a man with a serious mental illness.'

When Charles looked back down at his papers, as if dismissing Sandy's presence, Sandy couldn't resist saying in his most sarcastic voice, 'What a pleasure to see you again, Mr Holloway.'

With that, he walked away, ensuring he sat as far away as possible.

The others arrived almost at the same time. In fact, Linda and Douglas Wainwright's solicitor had travelled together from Stamford, something Charles Holloway found unacceptable – he could be heard telling him not to fraternise with the prosecution. Mr Coke was looking as suave and sophisticated as ever, wearing a blue-striped three-piece suit with a light blue tie and matching handkerchief in his top pocket. Meera smiled at everyone as she walked in, and when Otto arrived, the room felt full but not overly cramped.

Before they could start, it was felt that everyone needed coffee, so off they went to get a cup. Holloway wanted a word with his instructing solicitor in private, so they were the last to return.

Charles Holloway started the meeting off.

'We are looking to pursue an argument that Douglas Wainwright is not guilty by reason of insanity.'

Sandy wanted to butt in, but in this environment, he was far down the pecking order.

Smiling, Mr Coke looked around and replied, 'So, you are after a M'Naghten rules hearing, are you? Predictable, if you don't mind me saying, Charles.' By the look on his face, Holloway really did mind him saying. 'You are going to argue, are you, that Wainwright was under such a defect of reason, from disease of his mind, as not to know the nature and quality of the act he was committing – or, if he did know it, that he did not know what he was doing was wrong?'

Sandy was familiar with the M'Naghten rules, and their history. They stemmed from a case in 1843, when Daniel M'Naghten had shot and killed the wrong man while trying to assassinate the then British Prime Minister, Robert Peel. He was found not guilty by reason of insanity, which had caused an uproar in Britain at the time.

When there was no response from Holloway, Christopher Coke continued, 'I am not sure the judge is going to wear it as an argument. This is a man who bought a ticket, flew to Vienna, and found the right hotel room and murdered his daughter's fiancée there. Come on. I get that he has serious mental health issues, but he is not so insane as to not know what he is doing.' He looked at Meera. 'Myself and the Crown will not accept this. Be prepared for a fight, my friend.'

'All right, will step away from a M'Naghten hearing.' So,

he *was* just trying it on then. 'What about loss of control?'

All of them on the prosecution side of the table knew that this was coming. Sandy and Hannah had spent the afternoon a few weeks ago going through the law created by Section 54 of the Coroners and Justice Act 2009 to replace a defence of provocation. Sandy had passed their written notes over to Christopher Coke, as had Meera Goswami, who had completed her own research.

Christopher held his hand up to Charles Holloway to show he needed time and was reading both his own notes on the subject and the ones that had just been handed over to him.

'I agree, you have a strong argument that Wainwright did lose control at the point of him carrying out the violent strangulation of the victims,' Christopher said.

Sandy, unable to keep quiet any longer, added, 'This defence only applies to a defence of murder and not to attempted murder.' He glanced at Linda. 'So, where will it leave the case of the attempted murder of Hazel Wainwright?'

Charles Holloway totally ignored Sandy, as if he was an irrelevance, but everyone else felt he had made a good point. Holloway let the silence hang in the air; he was not going to fill it.

Christopher, looking back at his notes and the ones he had been given, spoke instead. 'You, Charles, know only too well that there are criteria to be satisfied. If you watch or read the transcript of Hazel Wainwright's video interview, it becomes abundantly clear that Wainwright's so called "loss of control" was an almost, at times, daily occurrence for her.'

Leaning to his side, Holloway had a word with his instructing solicitor, before addressing the room. 'We are not talking about Mrs Wainwright; we are talking about the incident in the hotel room in Vienna.'

Incident, thought Sandy. It wasn't an incident – it was a murder.

Holloway went on to say, 'Arthur Barrington was young and fit. He made Wainwright lose control, get angry and strangle him.'

'What is the trigger you are claiming for this loss of control?' Christopher asked.

'The young man was taking Wainwright's daughter away from him and his wife, a daughter they totally relied upon,' came the swift response from Holloway.

'But he wasn't,' Sandy interjected. 'If you read the statements, Emily Wainwright is quite clear that after her marriage to Arthur, they were going to remain in Stamford so that she could still look after her parents.'

'I am not used to being spoken to in such a manner by a police officer.' Holloway was looking at Christopher, instead of acknowledging Sandy. 'Can you have a word with DCI McFarlane and ask him to desist putting in his two pennies' worth? This is a discussion between the lawyers involved.'

Christopher smiled. It was clear he had no intention of telling Sandy to stop helpfully intervening.

'Well, I am one of the lawyers involved,' said Meera Goswami. 'This defence of loss of control is rarely, if ever, used these days. Previous cases often involved men killing partners or ex-partners. It was just a cop out.' Meera saw that Holloway was listening to her. 'I am not sure you would get any support from Justice Kane. If you look at two of the cases that no doubt your junior printed out for you, you will find that Justice Kane was the judge on one of them.'

After having another chat with his instructing solicitor, Holloway conceded. 'Fine, but I am not going to listen to any more of this. Tomorrow, in front of the judge, I am going to argue diminished responsibility.' With that, he picked up all his papers, shoved them untidily into his briefcase, and stormed out, followed swiftly by his instructing solicitor, who was clearly not getting a lift back to Stamford with DS Palmer.

Although Christopher headed off, the others went for a coffee just around the corner from the castle. Sandy encouraged Otto that this was a positive step in Arthur's case, but he didn't look convinced. Sandy could understand why: Holloway was a formidable opponent and should not for one second be underestimated. Sandy just hoped he hadn't provoked things too badly by poking the bear – the grizzly bear that was Charles Holloway.

CHAPTER THIRTY-THREE

The window in Sandy's room at the White Hart Hotel looked out and up to the towering cathedral behind it. The bells seemed to ring at least every half an hour and Sandy began to wonder if he should have brought some ear plugs. Fortunately, they stopped at a reasonable hour, allowing him to get some sleep.

Otto had not been keen on Thai or Indian the previous night, which had meant a short walk for them to the Duke William along Bailgate and a real ale drink and meal in an old traditional English pub. Sandy supposed it was the perfect choice for the visiting Austrian detective.

Although Sandy should probably have returned to his hotel room to revise for his interview that coming Friday, for the Cambridgeshire detective superintendent post, he kept putting it off. Instead, after dinner, he left Otto at the entrance to the hotel and walked down Steppe Hill, an incredible old cobblestone shopping street, then did a loop around and back up beside the cathedral, to which a definite visit was required.

The next morning, the first people Sandy saw as he and Otto approached the court were Mia and Arthur Barrington's parents, and a younger boy whom Sandy now knew was Henry Barrington, Arthur's brother. Mia had booked herself into a hotel in Stamford to facilitate bringing them to court whenever they needed to attend. Linda Palmer was going to support her in the family liaison role.

Linda was the next to arrive with Freddie and Emily Wainwright. She whispered to Sandy that Hazel felt physically, emotionally and psychologically unable to attend that day.

When they walked into the courtroom, Christopher Coke was present with a junior barrister, as was Charles Holloway with his junior. All of the barristers had on their black gowns and wigs. They looked totally at home in the centuries-old courtroom – it could have been the scene of a trial from another era.

After Justice Kane entered and they had all sat down again, Charles Holloway rose to his feet.

'My Lord, is it possible to make a ruling' – he twisted round to look at the side and rear of the court and looked at both the Wainwright and Barrington family – 'that you make an order asking Andrew Barrington and…' He looked at the names on a note in front of him. '… Freddie and Emily Wainwright leave the court, as they are proposed prosecution witnesses?'

Justice Kane scowled.

'Firstly, Mr Holloway, where is the defendant? I am presuming he is on his way and delayed for some reason. If so, I am happy to adjourn until he arrives.'

'He, My Lord, is deemed not fit to attend today,' Holloway replied.

'Very well. I presume we could go on forever adjourning this case if we are looking for when he might be well enough to attend.' He looked again at Holloway. 'Have you sufficient instructions from him to proceed?'

‘Yes.’ He paused. ‘My request to exclude those names I have asked to be excluded…?’

The judge sighed. ‘Yes, I suppose I have to agree to it, but they are the family of the deceased and the children of the defendant, also linked to the deceased.’

The court usher and Mia took all of the family, including Faith and Henry Barrington, outside while Linda Palmer remained sitting next to Otto and Sandy. The family, who had never been involved in any court proceedings before, let alone a Crown Court hearing at a murder trial – a murder trial where their son was the victim – looked understandably confused, distraught and frightened.

‘The prosecution and defence failed to agree a way forward yesterday, and I would like the court today to consider diminished responsibility,’ Holloway said, still in the standing position, twiddling his glasses in his hand. ‘If you agree with this, I would like to call two psychiatrists to give evidence.’

The judge looked at Christopher Coke, who simply nodded, so he went on to say, ‘Proceed.’

The first psychiatrist, who had been employed by the defence, had an incredible range of qualifications that he reeled out. He told the court that he was approved under the Mental Health Act 1983 as having special experience in the diagnosis and management of mental disorders and that his area of specialty was that of mentally disordered offenders, known as “forensic psychiatry” – a perfect fit and undoubtably an expert who could assist the court. He outlined his examinations of extensive medical records and interviews with Douglas Wainwright.

'In your professional opinion, doctor, is the defendant entitled to the defence of diminished responsibility against the charge he is facing of murder?'

'Yes, based on what I have found out.'

Christopher Coke had no questions and the psychiatrist was released from court.

Christopher rose from his seat, fiddled with his wig and pulled on the lapels of his gown. 'I see no requirement to call the other psychiatrist on behalf of the prosecution as he is going to say the same thing. My concern is whether this is appropriate to the circumstances of this particular case.'

The judge nodded, then looked at Charles Holloway. 'What is it you are actually proposing? It is clear that Mr Wainwright has been suffering from a severe mental illness that has been diagnosed in the past as paranoid schizophrenia, a view supported by the two psychiatric reports we have before us today.'

Rising to his feet, Holloway answered in a low voice that others in the courtroom strained to hear, 'Not guilty to murder due to diminished responsibility as stated in Section 52 of the Coroners and Justice Act 2009. This, as you know, replaces the definition of diminished responsibility contained in the 1957 Homicide Act and states that abnormality of mental functioning means a state of mind so different from that of ordinary human beings that the reasonable person would term it abnormal and therefore guilty of manslaughter rather than murder.'

'Is this something that you find acceptable, Mr Coke? Has the Crown Prosecution Service spoken to the Barrington family of this proposal, and what is their view?' the judge asked, looking disapproving.

When Christopher turned around to Meera, who was sitting directly behind him, she shook her head at him and the judge, to indicate that this hadn't happened.

Christopher continued. 'Can we have an adjournment please, to do this?'

'Return in one hour,' the judge said, rising abruptly to his feet, initiating everyone in the court to unexpectedly rise to their feet as well.

They went into the same room that the legal conference had been held in the previous day. Sandy, Otto and Meera were present, and Christopher had said he would come in and talk to them if necessary, but his view was that he was deeply unhappy about the proposal as laid out by the defence and was working out how best to combat the compelling medical opinion.

Mia and Linda had taken off for a walk with the equally confused Freddie and Emily. They were so young and in such conflict: the defendant was their father, who they loved despite everything, yet it was them and their mother who were the victims of their father, and the person they had both loved, Arthur Barrington, was their father's murder victim. *They'll need some intensive counselling in the future to process all this*, Sandy thought sadly.

After Meera explained what had just happened in court, Faith spoke up. 'He is admitting to murdering my son, is that what you're saying?' She looked from Meera to Sandy. 'Is that what she is saying? Has he said why he killed my beloved boy?'

'It's not as simple as that,' Meera said. 'The evidence is

such that he is trying to get the best result for himself, or at least his barrister is, and that is to accept manslaughter and not be convicted of murder.'

Andrew put his arm around his wife, who was close to tears. 'So he would be, in essence, getting away with murdering Arthur. Manslaughter suggests it was unintentional or an accident, doesn't it?' Before Meera could answer, Andrew looked at Sandy. 'What would you do, DCI McFarlane? You know we trust your opinion.

'It is not my decision, or yours to a certain extent – that sits with the Crown Prosecution Service following advice from counsel,' Sandy said. 'But I would fight for murder as and when he is fit to stand trial, if that is in a year or two years' time – however long, I would fight him for justice.'

They all nodded and headed back into court, including the family this time.

Once they had all trooped in and Meera had advised Christopher and the family of the decision of the CPS, the judge took his place.

'I must admit, Mr Holloway, I am uneasy about plea discussions when the defendant is not here for me to ask what his thoughts are. I am not doubting you have taken adequate instructions.' He looked over his half-moon glasses at Holloway. 'What is the defendant's position in relation to the charge of the attempted murder of Hazel Wainwright?'

Almost sheepishly, Holloway muttered, 'To lie on file.'

The snort from Sandy was so loud that Justice Kane heard it and looked over at him, but did not admonish him, unlike Holloway, who met Sandy's gaze with a furious scowl.

'That is, of course, unacceptable to the Crown, My Lord,'

Christopher said. 'After taking instruction both from those who instruct me and the family, we would not agree to accept the lesser charge of manslaughter.' After the judge nodded at him, showing he agreed with this position, Christopher added, 'I have managed to find during the break a couple of pieces of case law that may help us. In my view, if Mr Wainwright can plead not guilty to murder, he has an understanding of the meaning of guilt and innocence, so passes the "basic" aspects of the test in terms of his cognitive understanding.'

Christopher paused until the judge's pen showed signs that he had caught up with his notetaking.

'The other case I would like to highlight is that Wainwright can clearly instruct solicitors and counsel, which is being evidenced by Mr Holloway himself, but I am not sure he could follow proceedings or give evidence in his defence. If we view his interview in Rampton Hospital, we can see he was unable to keep it under control for the whole length of time – most of it, but not all of it.'

The judge interjected, 'I was a contributor a few years ago to the Law Commission report titled: "Murder, Manslaughter and Infanticide". It recommended, among other things, that instead of the current two-tier structure of general homicide offences, namely murder and manslaughter, there should be a three-tier structure.' The judge looked around to ensure everyone was following him. 'The proposal was to have first-degree murder and second-degree murder. The potential use of this second-degree murder would be used to describe the verdict a jury must reach when a plea of diminished responsibility is successful as a defence to first-degree murder. This recommendation was strongly supported by me but more importantly by groups representing victims' families.'

Sandy watched him look over at the Barrington family and seemingly notice that Freddie and Emily were also present.

Justice Kane continued. 'I am glad the family are in court to hear this legal argument. Sadly, it never became law, but we can live in hope.' Turning his attention back to the barristers sitting in front of him, he said, 'Tell me, Mr Holloway, what has Douglas Wainwright actually said about the two counts on the indictment that we are concerned with today?'

Getting very slowly to his feet after whispering firstly to his junior, then turning around to his instructing solicitor, Charles Holloway said, 'My Lord, Douglas Wainwright has no recollection of either of the specific incidents at all.'

There was a loud gasp and sigh of anguish from the Barrington family. Faith's cry of distress could be heard above everyone else.

Of course, Holloway ignored the interruption and carried on speaking. 'As I have been trying to say for two days, he is a diagnosed paranoid schizophrenic who hears voices and is under the impression that people are always trying to kill him.'

Under his breath, but loud enough for the judge to hear, Christopher muttered, 'But able to buy a ticket and fly to Vienna and find the right hotel room.'

Holloway frowned at his opponent.

'Very well,' Justice Kane said. 'This is my proposal. It is slightly unusual, because the defendant had offered a plea to manslaughter by diminished responsibility, but based on the psychiatry evidence, I am going to regard him unfit to plead at this present time.'

There was a hush throughout the courtroom. Was the case now over, or at least over for some considerable time?

The judge continued talking. 'A fact-finding hearing will take place, starting next Tuesday for three days, and we have Friday if needed, after which the jury will determine whether or not Douglas Wainwright committed the two indictments that we are dealing with. This is without consideration of the defendant's *mens rea*. This is a hearing and is not an adversarial trial, Mr Holloway, so only gentle cross-examination, please.'

Justice Kane rose, everyone nodded to him, and he left the court. It hadn't been a proposal; it had been a decision. Sandy looked around anxiously at both Otto and Linda sitting beside him.

'I have so much to do on Thursday, and Friday is my wedding day. If I could ask Juliet to cover on Friday, I would, but she is coming to my wedding.'

'It might help if you are there as well, though,' Otto chuckled, as they went off to explain to the Barringtons and Wainwrights what the plan was for next week.

Sandy sighed. He just hoped they could wrap things up on Thursday.

Chapter Thirty-Four

The anxiousness Sandy felt all that week didn't go away. His interview on the Friday had gone fairly well, he thought, but had certainly not gone well enough for him to get the role. Whilst most of the practical questions had been straightforward – after all, he had plenty of experience when it came to the day to day – he had struggled with questions about managing a budget. *Oh well*, he thought, *it was worth a try*. He wasn't sure if he would have accepted the offer anyway.

That weekend was Hannah's hen weekend, and a couple of nights in a large, rented property in the Yorkshire Dales sounded like quite sedate fun with lots of drinking, eating and laughing planned. His mother and two sisters were going as well.

His two sisters and their husbands had willingly agreed to take on all of his allotted tasks on the Thursday, which made Sandy feel a little less anxious. When growing up, his sisters had always teased him mercilessly, but in equal measure had adored their big brother. It had always felt like a pedestal that Sandy was worried he would come crashing down from.

The Saturday and Sunday were occupied by Sandy doing some incredibly bad painting, but he had made enough progress so that the main bedroom was at least completed. He had meticulously worked out timings for him to make the Thursday night wedding service rehearsal and then the subsequent rehearsal dinner, factoring in how long it would take to drive from Lincoln with allowances for it being a Friday.

Because Otto was returning from Austria on the Monday, Sandy had offered to drive up the day before the next hearing to keep him company. Mia and Johanna were also now arriving on the Monday, but they were going to use Stamford as their base so they could bring the family to court. Linda Palmer was going to be called as a witness, so she was going to avoid travelling with any of the families, and had enlisted two of her officers to assist Mia and Johanna.

Sandy's Morgan car, which didn't have a great deal of space, was packed to the gunnels with his kilt, his change of clothing for the night of the wedding, his change of clothing for the rehearsal and rehearsal dinner, and his clothing for the days at court, both during and after. His mother had told him what felt like one hundred times now to take her car – which he had declined; to not be late for the rehearsal – which he had assured her he wouldn't be, and to not, under any circumstances, to be late for his wedding. To say she was on edge was an understatement.

Arriving in Lincoln in plenty of time, Sandy and Otto managed to fit in an afternoon tour of Lincoln Cathedral, much to Sandy's delight. The tour included the roof, which was incredible. The cathedral had been in existence for over nine hundred and fifty years, and Sandy almost admitted to himself that the cathedral might possibly be even more magnificent than his own Ely Cathedral.

That evening, they went to what was becoming their usual

drink and meal venue, The Duke William. Otto told Sandy that this was going to be his last case, as he had been offered a role in crime training, and if he liked it, and they liked him, a civilian post would be arranged. His level of knowledge and experience could not just be lost, his boss had told him.

Having got to know Otto during Arthur's case, Sandy was relieved. He knew Otto had made it through the bulk of his career by the skin of his teeth without being burnt out. A salutary lesson not just for Sandy but all homicide detectives, in fact, for all police officers. During their careers, each police officer was likely to encounter between four hundred and six hundred traumatic events, compared to the three or four that an average person normally experienced during their lifetime. Burnout was a real risk, and Otto had been wise to get out before that happened.

∞

The jury selection had already been completed by the time Sandy, Otto and the two families had arrived at court. The timid, quiet and very scared Hazel Wainwright was there with her children, and Johanna, plus a Lincolnshire police officer, was looking after them. Sandy waved to Freddie and then to Andrew and Faith Barrington as he went upstairs into the courtroom. He was surprised to see Douglas Wainwright sitting in the dock with two prison officers either side of him.

He looked clean and smart in his dark suit and dark blue tie. They looked at each other intently as their eyes locked. Not one glimmer of recognition that Sandy had been in his home, then shoved out of it by him, chased – well, followed –

through the streets of Stamford and, much more significantly, had been the man who had saved his life in Rutland Water. Nothing. No acknowledgement that Douglas even recognised Sandy.

When Justice Kane entered and had taken his seat, Christopher stood and addressed the jury, introducing himself and Holloway for the defence.

'Ladies and gentlemen of the jury.'

Sandy looked over. The jury was made up of seven women and five men, with a wide range of ages from a couple of young men, who could only be in their twenties, to at least one man and a woman in their sixties.

Christopher continued. 'You have an unusual duty to perform in this case over the next few days. There are two counts on the indictment: one of attempted murder that took place here in Lincolnshire by the defendant Douglas Wainwright on his wife Hazel Wainwright, and the second, also an unusual duty for you, a count of murder that took place in Vienna, Austria, this being the murder of Arthur Barrington, the fiancée of the defendant's daughter, Emily.'

Mr Coke stopped and paused while the clerk handed out copies of the indictment, and the jury were instructed to place these copies in the folders they had been given.

'His Lordship,' Christopher said, pointing to the judge, 'will advise you at the end of the hearing on the law, but this is a hearing, not a trial. We require you to simply decide whether the defendant carried out these two attacks, one that led to murder and the other that, only due to the skill of our surgeons, the victim survived.' He paused again. 'We do not want you to concern yourselves with what we believe the defendant was thinking or why he did it. We call it his *mens rea*. We do not want you to concern yourselves with what his mitigation could be, for example, his serious mental illness.'

All of the jury swung their heads around from Christopher to the defendant.

'This is a case quite frankly of domestic abuse. Forget everything else, all of the noise concerning his' – he pointed to Douglas Wainwright – 'mental health. We will show a man who violently reigned with terror over his family. Including towards the man his daughter Emily should have by now been happily married to.'

Emily could be heard crying and Johanna gently led her out of the court. Everyone watched her leave.

'For the case of attempted murder, and prior domestic abuse, I call Freddie Wainwright as the first witness.'

After a long pause, the court clerk returned and spoke to Christopher, who then rose and addressed the judge.

'My Lord, the witness is comforting his sister, Emily. I wonder if we might have a short recess so we can get the witness into court?'

Justice Kane rose. 'Fifteen minutes.'

A short while later, as Freddie walked into court having left his distraught sister with his equally distraught mother and Johanna, he passed his father. He deliberately looked straight in front and didn't glance at him. Douglas, on seeing his son, became alert and started to stand, only to be pulled back down by his prison officers.

The smart suit, the undoubted intellect, the incredible way he articulated as he gave evidence, did nothing to hide the fact evident to all that Freddie was a young man carrying the world on his shoulders. Grief, pain and anguish were etched all over in the slump of his body, his face and his expressions.

When Douglas shouted out, 'Freddie, my boy, don't say these things about me, you know I love you. I am so sorry,' Freddie still didn't flinch or look at him. The judge did though, and the solicitor was sent scurrying at lightning pace to keep his client quiet.

The key detail that caught everyone's attention was Freddie describing the coercive control they had been subjected to in the Wainwright household and seeing his father use a chokehold on his mother multiple times.

Sandy had an idea and hurriedly sent a note to Christopher, who asked Freddie, 'Would your father know how dangerous a chokehold could be?'

Looking round at the prosecutor, then keeping his eyes firmly on the jury as he answered, Freddie said, 'Yes. He was trained in martial arts as a young man, until he became sick. He knew exactly the effect of it and if he kept it on longer, even after unconsciousness, the consequences.'

The next witness was planned to be Hazel, but Christopher moved things around, given her distress, and called forward DS Linda Palmer. She described the scene that herself and Juliet had found and the arrival of the paramedics. Linda also described the police records on the reports of domestic abuse, with Douglas as the perpetrator. Surprisingly, as had also been the case with Freddie, not once did Charles Holloway ask any questions.

The last witness before the lunch recess was a consultant in emergency medicine from Peterborough City Hospital. He described how critically ill Hazel Wainwright had been and how she had so nearly died. He believed this had been caused by a compression of her neck. He was unable to describe the mechanism used, but couldn't and wouldn't disagree that it could have been caused by a chokehold.

Holloway did ask a question this time. 'Is it your professional opinion that having reviewed all of the most recent medical records for Mrs Wainwright that she has made a full recovery?'

'Physically, maybe, but I do worry about her eyesight in the future. However, emotionally and psychologically, will she ever recover? I am not a psychiatrist or a psychologist, but I sincerely doubt it.'

Probably not the answer Holloway was looking for, Sandy thought. An old adage for lawyers was to only ask questions when you knew what the answer would be.

The family doctor was not called, but her evidence was read, outlining the treatment for Hazel on three occasions for injuries, one of which was to her neck. A catalogue of medications to treat low mood and feelings of anxiousness associated with being scared to leave her home were cited.

After the lunch recess, Hazel was brought into court through a side door. Screens were positioned so that she couldn't see the defendant and he couldn't see her, nor could she see the public gallery, only the judge, lawyers and jury.

An abridged and agreed version of her evidence was shared via TV screens to the jury and the court. Her description of the life she had led at the hands of her abusing husband was graphic, haunting and quite frankly chilling. The hush and silence in the courtroom was almost suffocating – no one seemed to be able to breathe. On the screen, she told of the incident and how she had refused to tell Wainwright where Emily was going that afternoon, and how he had choked her while shouting "tell me, tell me". Then, oblivion had come. She had passed into another world and was left unconscious.

At the end of this recorded evidence, Holloway rose quietly and surprisingly gently asked her, 'Your husband, Douglas, knows how to use the chokehold effectively, so he never intended for you to almost die, did he? He didn't attempt to kill you, did he?'

As soon as Hazel had said her first few words to answer the question, Douglas Wainwright was on his feet, shouting, 'Hazel, you know I didn't mean it, you know it's the voices I keep hearing, you know it's my illness. I love you, forgive me. I promise I will change. I will change.'

Hazel started crying uncontrollably. The prison officers started fighting with Douglas, who then promptly threw himself down the stairs behind him that led to the cells. His cries of pain could be heard reverberating throughout the court.

The commanding tones of Justice Kane echoed through the courtroom. 'I will not tolerate him being back in my court until he agrees…'

'Question withdrawn,' Holloway quickly said, while the judge was trying to give his instruction.

"… to keep perfectly quiet,' Justice Kane finished. Turning to Hazel, he added much more softly, 'Please, have a sip of water and take your time. If you need us to have a recess, we will.'

Holloway was on his feet in an instant. 'I have no further questions, My Lord. The witness can be released.'

'But we haven't heard her answer to the question you just asked,' the judge said.

He clearly hadn't heard Holloway withdraw his question earlier.

Feeling that she was unable to stay in the court building any longer, Hazel asked for the Lincolnshire family liaison officer to take her home. Emily felt she must stay to honour Arthur, so they set off alone. There were a few more statements that were read in the afternoon and then Justice Kane adjourned court early, ready for the other charge on the indictment, the murder of Arthur Barrington, to be heard the next day.

As Holloway left court, he looked at Sandy and said in a low voice, almost a whisper, 'I have no idea what Hannah Tobias sees in you.'

Sandy smiled inwardly to himself. He had well and truly rattled Mr Holloway. Hannah had acted as his junior barrister on a couple of occasions, and Sandy was sure that she would not do so again.

Chapter Thirty-Five

They were joined in Lincoln that evening by Paulina Steiner, the Austrian crime scene investigator. She quite fancied the Thai restaurant or the Indian restaurant that Sandy had recommended, but Otto only wanted to go to his "local", as he called it, British pub. Juliet had been briefed on the phone that evening and the other case she was working on had now finished, so she was going to tie up loose ends before she and her husband headed to Cambridge for the weekend.

'I hope to be back on Thursday,' Sandy had told her.

'You had better be, sonny boy,' she had told him.

As they walked into court the next day, a quick word with Andrew Barrington showed a man who was not the slightest bit nervous; a man who said he was doing this for his son.

The first action of the day was for Christopher to distribute a photograph of Arthur Barrington for the members of the jury to place in their folders. Sandy had come up with the idea the previous day and was keen for the jury, who had seen Hazel Wainwright in real life and the defendant Douglas Wainwright in real life, to see what Arthur looked like. He was not some name that was being spoken about, but had been a real live person whose young life had been brutally taken from him and his loved ones.

There was no sign of Douglas. It appeared that he had fractured his ankle during his fall, or was it a dive, down the stairs to the cells of the court.

Andrew had given his evidence, strong, clear and with traces of emotion at times. His wife and younger son watched, willing him on, seemingly more nervous for him than he was for himself, though Sandy supposed they were able to be more emotional than he was allowing himself to be.

Holloway rose from his seat and looked at Andrew without speaking for long enough to make Andrew feel uncomfortable.

'You were the prime suspect for Arthur's murder, weren't you? You were even arrested for it.' The jury looked startled at this revelation. 'You had a major row with him, didn't you?'

Fortunately, Sandy and the team had prepared him for a question like this, so Andrew said, 'That was just normal procedure. Clearing the ground from under their feet was how DCI McFarlane described the police action. Other than his killer, I was the last person to see my son alive.'

'You invited Douglas Wainwright to travel with you to Vienna, didn't you? You must have trusted him and known that he wouldn't commit this crime that is alleged. Surely no father would.'

'I didn't know Mr Wainwright. I just believed that, like me, he didn't want the marriage to go ahead this summer.' Andrew looked around at Emily, who was sat with her brother and mother Hazel, and mouthed the word "sorry".

Holloway abruptly sat down, and the statement from Austrian immigration was read by Christopher's junior, before the jury were shown a CCTV picture of Douglas Wainwright in Vienna on the day in question. The statement had identified when he left Austria.

The next witness was a hotel receptionist, who – when shown a picture – recognised Douglas and remembered him asking which room Mr Barrington was in. Otto, when he had found out about this witness, had vowed that he should swing for the hotel manager, who had said that none of his receptionists had seen anything, only the room cleaner had. "Don't rely on others to do detective work," Mia had told him.

Holloway showed the witness a current picture of Douglas, but the receptionist was unable to recognise the now beardless and short-haired Mr Wainwright. Not sure what this proved, Christopher declined to keep the charade going by asking a question about it. The jury had only a short while ago seen the CCTV picture of what Douglas looked like on arrival in Vienna.

Paulina Steiner's evidence was straightforward; she covered the hotel room scene and her finding DNA and fingerprints. One set was Arthur Barrington's, the other set has been confirmed as Douglas Wainwright's. Mr Holloway couldn't argue with this, so he didn't.

With no sign of Professor Von Tripp, Sandy and Otto had quietly left the courtroom to stand outside and wait for him, and at the sight of him running into the castle precinct, confusedly looking for where the court was located, they both let out an audible sigh of relief. Apparently, his train had been delayed from London due to signalling issues. *Nothing new there*, thought Sandy, familiar with the issues that often plagued the British transport system.

With barely ten minutes to spare, the professor prepared

himself and was then called into the witness box. As Sandy had expected, the man was exceptional in giving evidence. His years of lecturing came to the fore and he guided the jury with effortless ease through his autopsy of Arthur and then his findings. He even demonstrated what a chokehold would look like. He had set out what the cause of death was, in his professional opinion, and if any notice had been taken of his long list of qualifications, his professional opinion was undoubtably world renowned.

Professor Von Tripp was then asked to cover the fibre evidence, and he told the jury how he had found the blue fibres on Arthur's neck and then how they had compared to the blue fibres from one of Douglas Wainwright's jumpers. They were an identical match.

The first question Holloway asked when it was his turn to question the professor was, 'An identical match to Mr Wainwright's jumper, you say? Surely only to that same jumper, which might have been part of a batch of many thousands of identical jumpers. So, you can't say it was Mr Wainwright's jumper for sure, can you?'

The professor looked at Holloway in surprise, then a slight grin crept over his face. 'You obviously haven't seen the jumper, Mr Holloway. It is an individual hand-knitted one.'

Even the judge smiled at that, but not Charles Holloway.

He cleared his throat, then continued. 'You say it was a chokehold that was used to kill Arthur. We had only yesterday in court an expert stating that they couldn't identify the mechanism that caused Mrs Wainwright's injury. How can you be so sure?'

That smile appeared again. 'My patient was dead, so I had the benefit of pathology. The other expert was trying to keep their patient alive and that was their priority. I am not sure Mrs Wainwright would have survived if we had sent off slices of her brain to a neuropathologist.' This last comment brought ripples of laughter throughout the court.

The professor made his way off out of the court precinct as quickly as he had arrived. 'A date with an opera in Covent Garden,' was all he said, as he was looking for a taxi to the railway station.

There were a few loose items to finalise in court that afternoon, with very brief speeches made by both Christopher and Holloway, who stressed that they had to be sure that Douglas Wainwright had carried out the actual acts.

They had to be sure, beyond reasonable doubt, Sandy thought. He couldn't see how that could be the situation here.

The judge told the jury that he would be addressing them in the morning. They would then be retiring to consider the verdict of the fact-finding hearing. Justice Kane told them they would have plenty of time and not to rush, as they also had Friday available to them, which brought the butterflies of anxiety straight back again for Sandy.

A trip to their local pub that evening ended with an early night. Sandy's mother and sisters were anxious and stressed, telling him to leave court now and come home. Hannah, on the other hand, was very relaxed, and assured him that his only concern was to be in the St John's College Chapel just before she got there on the Friday itself. Her father Howard and two of her best friends had arrived in Cambridge that afternoon, and they were all enjoying themselves.

∞

The judge kept his word, and the jury were out to consider their verdict in no time. Sandy and Meera explained to both the Barrington and Wainwright families, who were now sitting all together, that this sadly was not the end of the process, but really the beginning, if the verdict came back the way they wanted it to. If not, the release in the short term of Douglas Wainwright could not be ruled out, and that could only be described as a nightmare. Just thinking about it made Sandy nervous, but at least it took his mind off his wedding.

Sat in the dock was Douglas. Everyone was surprised to see him that morning. He had indeed fractured his ankle, and had to be supported by two prison officers to get him into court. They were a bit disgruntled to have to take him back down again so quickly after the start of proceedings. Douglas was not allowed a crutch or a walking stick, as it was considered to be too lethal.

Lunchtime arrived with no verdict. DS Linda Palmer, who had not had many, if any, Crown Court hearings before, wondered if it was a bad sign, but Sandy assured her it wasn't. If it went into Friday afternoon, *then* it would have been a bad sign, on so many fronts. A very bad sign.

As the team walked back towards the court from lunch, which they had eaten nearby, there was an usher waiting for them, as well as Meera.

'Come on, come on, you lot. The jury have a verdict!' Meera shouted as she waved frantically at them.

Sandy's heart missed more than one beat, and he was sure

it was the same for all of the others – Otto, Mia, Johanna and Linda. It was always the same feeling, a mixture of excitement, anticipation and dread, whenever a jury were about to return a verdict. However many times this happened to Sandy, the feeling hadn't lessened.

Just having time to share a comforting word with the Barringtons and Wainwrights, Otto, Sandy and Linda took their seats, leaving Mia and Johanna to sit with the families.

The lawyers were in place, the defendant was in place, the families were in place, the detectives were in place, and the jury were ushered in. Only two of them glanced at Douglas, who was sitting with his leg that was in plaster outstretched. He seemed oblivious to all that was going on.

Justice Kane walked into the room. It was showtime.

The judge didn't even ask Douglas to stand when the foreman of the jury, when asked by the clerk, said in a loud and steady voice that it was a verdict that they all agreed on.

The clerk said, 'On the first count on the indictment, do you, members of the jury, find that the defendant, Douglas Wainwright, carried out the act that led to the death of Arthur Barrington?'

That loud and steady voice again said, 'Yes. A unanimous decision.'

The clerk had to pause before he read the next count, as the pronouncement of the verdict bought loud sobs from both Faith Barrington and Emily Wainwright. The judge was quite happy to let the family express their feelings of grief, sadness and relief. Sandy wanted to punch the air and slap Otto on his back, but there was one more very important decision still needed, and more to the point, he knew that this wasn't a conclusion to the case.

The clerk, now recognising that he had enough quiet to be heard, continued. 'On the second count, on the indictment of the attempted murder of Hazel Wainwright, do you, members of the jury, find that the defendant carried out the act as alleged?'

'Yes, unanimous.'

There was now a hush in court as the judge thanked the jury for their service. 'What you have heard has been deeply distressing,' he added at the end of his speech. 'You have heard about a much-loved, incredibly talented young man having his life brutally taken from him. You have also the catalogue of abuse that the Wainwright family suffered from the husband and father, culminating in Mrs Wainwright almost losing her life to the same man who should have loved and cared for them, but did the opposite.'

After his parting words, the jury were all excused until the following Monday, when there might be another case for them to assist with.

Justice Kane then addressed the defendant, who seemed to be more alert now. Sandy had been told by his solicitor that the heavy-duty painkillers for his ankle were subduing him, as they counteracted with some of his psychosis medicine.

Justice Kane didn't ask him to stand, and was in fact talking to the whole of the court, not just the defendant. 'The only real option I have is a hospital order, which I order now. This will have the impact of detaining Douglas Wainwright in a mental hospital until such time that he is well enough to be released. If that ever was to happen, I also issue a restriction order that he is unable to be released without the permission of the Secretary of State. This should allow time for the CPS and police' – he looked at Meera and then at Sandy – 'to bring him back into the criminal court to be tried. The use of a hybrid order, where I also sentence you, Mr Wainwright, is not available to me in these circumstances, as we haven't looked at your *mens rea.*'

Douglas Wainwright was then taken slowly down into the cells.

The judge now spoke to the families, the Barringtons and Wainwrights. 'For those of you who have not given evidence, you have been in court throughout, and it is all the more personal for each of you. I know it has been very difficult for you to have to hear the evidence. I sincerely sympathise with you all for what you have had to go through during the last few days, and indeed the pain and sadness during this year. For the Wainwright family, almost all of their lives.' He looked around the whole court again and away from the families, but then glanced back at them. 'It is an incredibly sad case on so many levels, and for each of you in such different ways. Thank you for the grace that each of you have displayed.'

Chapter Thirty-Six

Once court was dismissed, there was only just time for Sandy to thank Christopher and Meera, then to hug Otto, telling him to please keep in touch. He caught up with Mia, Johanna and Linda as they were ushering the families into a room. He hugged them and asked each of them to keep in touch with him too. Linda, in particular, as she lived in the neighbouring county.

There was a quietness, almost a sadness and melancholy, in the room. This was a good result and the right result: the person who had carried out the murder and attempted murder had been found to have committed those acts. This wasn't the end, though. He hadn't been convicted of murder or attempted murder, but Sandy was convinced that with the right lawyer in due course, a guilty plea to murder would be attained.

Both Faith and Andrew wanted to hug him and thanked him for what he had done. He shook hands with Freddie, and hugged Emily and Hazel.

For Emily, her grief was overwhelming, and as Sandy left, he could see Faith comforting her and saying, 'Please, Em, for Arthur's sake, don't let this ruin your life. He loved you so much; he always wanted the best for you. You are now free from that ogre of a father. Please, build a life that Arthur would be proud of.'

The tears were flowing for both of them, and for Sandy as he ran to get his car.

He couldn't believe it – the red Morgan Roadster appeared to be almost completely blocked in. It hadn't been like this in the morning when he placed his bags in there. It took an inordinate amount of time edging back and forth, back and forth, to get out, constantly hoping that someone would come into the car park to help, to ensure he didn't scratch his car.

As soon as he was free and constantly glancing at the clock, and as the traffic on the roads seemed to be moving well and the A1 was clear, Sandy started to feel he might just make the rehearsal. He was ignoring the missed calls from his mother, but he did ring Juliet and update her on the court result. Juliet was the lucky one; she was already in Cambridge and was shopping.

The speed of the journey came to an abrupt halt not long after he joined the A14. His father was now ringing him; his mother had obviously got Gregor to phone Sandy as he wasn't answering her calls. He ignored them. He was not going to answer any calls unless it was Hannah.

Cars did start to move, albeit slowly, but any hope of making the rehearsal had long gone. As he parked in the St John's College car park on Queens Road, the call from Hannah arrived.

'I am presuming you haven't run off and aren't going to leave me stranded at the altar?'

'I'm here in Cambridge now,' he said breathlessly. 'Are you walking to Browns for the rehearsal dinner now?'

Hannah was, and was far more relaxed now that her future husband was going to be with her shortly. Sandy knew he wouldn't make the main part of the dinner, so instead took the opportunity to answer a few messages that he had received in relation to the case. The first was to brief his boss, Detective Superintendent Jane Watson, on the outcome and tell her he looked forward to seeing her at the wedding the next afternoon. He messaged his mum and dad to say he was on his way to Browns. He ignored answering his sisters' messages, and finally called Freddie.

'Just checking how you all are?' Sandy said.

'Back in the house in Stamford, not long arrived. A bit shell shocked, if I'm honest.' Freddie did sound subdued. 'Mum has told me to look for jobs elsewhere and is telling Em to go back and finish her A-levels and then go to university. All Em does is cry all the time.'

This was heartbreaking for Sandy to hear, but he realised that tomorrow was meant to be the happiest day of his and Hannah's life. He needed to quickly compartmentalise the Barringtons and the Wainwrights into a professional compartment – normally impossible, but for just a day or so it needed to happen, for himself, for all his family and his friends, but most especially for Hannah Tobias, the love of his life.

∞

They arrived in the chapel extremely early for the wedding ceremony, mostly because Sandy had enlisted the help of a string quartet, the friends of Arthur Barrington's who had played at his celebration of life service. They were incredibly talented musicians and as soon as he entered the chapel, he was amazed by the wonderful sound. As he caught up with them, and prepared for the day ahead, the smiles and feelings of happiness arrived.

Sandy and his best man looked very smart in their kilts, though they did keep being asked, albeit jokingly, what they were wearing underneath.

Hannah had kept very close to her school friends and they were now arriving along with friends from university and work colleagues. Juliet came and gave Sandy the biggest and longest hug; she was so proud of him. Arriving soon after were Jane Watson and Rich Singh, whose wife wore the most beautiful sari. Lofty Dobson hadn't grown any shorter and towered over Sandy. Barrister friends of Hannah's were all arriving and Sandy was especially pleased to see Ebony Forbes-Hamilton KC.

Sandy's Grandad Tom had told him to enjoy every part of the whole day and not be caught up in what was happening – soak it all in, he'd said. The method appeared to be working, for Sandy really was having a wonderful time greeting everyone.

When Sandy's mum and dad arrived and took their place at the front of the chapel, Sandy's leg involuntarily started to tremble. This was it. His mum had whispered that Hannah and her father were here. It was really going to happen. He was going to be marrying Hannah Tobias.

With such a talented string quartet and the resident organist, how could Hannah's entry music not be to anything but Pachelbel's Canon in D major. Hannah slowly, gracefully and beautifully walked up the aisle with her arm through her father's. She smiled at everyone as she went. If there were any nerves, they were certainly not showing.

Her dress was a combination of the traditional and the modern. It had a plunging neckline and was made of white satin and overlaid on the bodice with lace. Although she had a veil, it was not a full veil. As Sandy said when he first saw her come and stand beside him, she looked beautiful. The smiles they greeted each other with said it all. All of this was just about them getting married to each other. The rest was an added bonus.

The marriage service was very traditional, with readings and hymns, but happiness radiated from all eighty people in attendance. One of the readings was, of course, 1 Corinthians 13:1–13, which was all about love, read by the eldest of Sandy's two sisters, Aileen.

After their "you may kiss the bride" moment, as they went to sign the register, Sandy couldn't stop wanting to kiss Hannah over and over, and tell her how beautiful she looked and how much he loved her.

The taking of photographs after the service seemed to take an inordinate amount of time. Sandy only really wanted to have a drink and eat canapés, but more than that, talk to their guests, but he did as he was told.

Howard's speech was humorous and engaging: being a university lecturer, he was well practised. He mostly told funny stories of Hannah growing up. However, everyone, especially Hannah and her dad, got emotional when he talked about her mother and how terrible it was when Hannah had lost her mother to cancer as a child. He said how proud she would have been to see who Hannah had become and she would have given anything to have been there at her wedding.

Breaking tradition, he asked for a toast to Hannah's mother, which everyone enthusiastically and emotionally obliged.

When Sandy rose to his feet, the speech he had prepared went out of the window. He had too much emotion swirling about inside him from after the last few days: the wedding that never was for Arthur and Emily, the loss many years ago of Hannah's mother, but mostly his love for Hannah. So instead, he spoke of their first meeting, though he did get some laughter when he mentioned them being set up by his grandfather. He talked about how attracted to her he had been, both when it came to her beauty and her brain, and how he had almost lost her through his own stupidity and stubbornness, and how grateful he was that she had given him another chance. Finally, he simply thanked Hannah for agreeing to want to spend the rest of their lives together.

After the speeches and meal had been wrapped up, they managed to get away for a few moments to be by themselves. They paused as they walked over the Wren Bridge, and even though Sandy had seen it probably hundreds of times before, they both marvelled at one of the most incredible features of St John's College: the Bridge of Sighs, definitely one of the most recognisable pieces of architecture in the whole of Cambridge.

They found a bench to sit on out of the way in the Fellows' Garden. Hannah and Sandy were not really meant to be in this garden, but they needed a few moments to themselves. After sharing a long, passionate kiss, Sandy switched his phone on, as did Hannah, to catch up on their congratulatory messages.

Sandy saw that he had a number of missed calls, and one was from a Huntingdon number. His phone rang then, and he wasn't going to answer it, but saw it was that number again.

'DCI McFarlane?' the female voice said, as Sandy stood up and walked away from Hannah.

'Yes, who is this calling?' he asked.

'I am the Deputy Chief Constable of Cambridgeshire. I've got some news that I hope you will be pleased about.'

'Yes…' was all Sandy could say.

'You have been successful in your application to become our next detective superintendent of our major crime department.' Not getting a reply from the stunned Sandy, the DCC carried on talking. 'The post won't be available for a few months, and we have put together a development plan to help and support you to manage a large department.' Still getting no reply from Sandy, she said, 'You are pleased with this news, aren't you?'

'Absolutely,' Sandy said. 'Just a bit surprised. Today is in fact my wedding day.'

'What are you doing talking to me then? Congratulations! Go and enjoy yourself. Give me a call when you return from your honeymoon to give me your formal reply, but if you say yes, you must commit to coming to work for us.'

Before Sandy could tell Hannah what had just happened, he saw Juliet wandering towards them.

She whispered to Sandy, 'The families in Durham for the two deaths in Singapore want to see us when you get back – they have a possible lead to pursue.'

No sooner had he had a chance to begin to process this, and the news from the DCC, his two grandfathers wandered up.

'Sandy,' John said, pulling him away from going back to

sit with Hannah. 'I wonder if when you get back from the honeymoon, you could spare time to talk to your grandfathers about a new case we have picked up.'

'What new case?' Sandy said, a bit bamboozled by what was going on. The quietness Hannah and himself had been seeking was not happening; it felt more like Piccadilly Circus what with phone calls and Juliet and now his grandfathers. 'What new case?' he said again.

'We have been asked to look into the case of some items from The Fitzwilliam Museum that might have been misplaced, lost or even stolen,' Tom answered, before the two of them wandered off again.

Shaking his head in bemusement, he returned to Hannah, but as he opened his mouth to explain what had just occurred, Hannah said, 'There is something I want to and need to tell you.'

Still somewhat overwhelmed, Sandy simply nodded for her to continue.

'I'm pregnant,' she said, smiling tentatively at him.

Sandy let out a choked sound of overwhelmed delight, pulling Hannah into his arms. He couldn't stop repeating how delighted he was, and how it had put the cherry on top of an incredible day.

They sat in personable silence then, simply holding one another.

Hannah chuckled to herself, then whispered to Sandy, 'I have researched if Morgan do an SUV version of their car, but they don't.'

Sandy burst out laughing at that, even though in the back of his mind, he immediately started working out how he could somehow keep his beloved car.

Finally deciding it was time to return to their guests, they stood and walked back arm in arm back to their families and friends, to the most wonderful wedding day that anyone could have imagined.

AUTHOR'S NOTE

The inspiration for this story came from the life of Alfred Lord Tennyson. His best friend and his sister Emilia's fiancée was a man called Arthur Hallam. Arthur died suddenly in a hotel room in Vienna in 1833. The poem "In Memoriam" with its immortal line "It is better to have loved and lost than never to have loved at all" was written by Tennyson about him following his death.

Obviously, my work is all fiction and the work of my imagination, but what if there was more to Arthur's death than him dying suddenly? He was, after all, only twenty-two years old.

Tennyson's father George was a troubled man who suffered from mental health most of his life, not paranoid schizophrenia as the father in my story, but attributed to his epilepsy and his taking of drugs and alcohol. Unlike in this story, there are no reports of him being a perpetrator of domestic abuse, though we still struggle now to understand coercive controlling behaviour, and in the early 1800s, I am sure they had no concept of this whatsoever. The fact that the Tennyson family would scatter when he was in a dark mood said it all to me.

In honour of Arthur, I kept the name Arthur for my victim who died in Vienna, also a twenty-two-year-old. I gave his friend the name Freddie as a tribute to Alfred Tennyson and the fiancée and sister as Em, but for me Emily rather than her real name of Emilia. Alfred and Arthur did attend Trinity College Cambridge and in fact his father George actually spent many years at St John's College, Cambridge, my fictional detective's college.

The idea for the scene of the President of Austria's attempted kidnapping stemmed from a real-life case. I came across this when I was working abroad in a European capital. We had to take a day out of the work we were doing and I had the privilege to watch drone footage of the police there following a vehicle on its way to kidnap a member of the country's royal family. They were spooked and it never happened, but the vision, excitement and adrenaline rush never left me.

The entry into the wrong side of an apartment was also a true case and involved an international kidnap that I was part of investigating. In this, another European capital city, they did go into the wrong apartment, only to find the right one was on the exact opposite side.

I did also miss my wedding rehearsal as I was kept on duty. Being a police officer sadly means a catalogue of missing special occasions.

Everywhere I looked I kept seeing cases of paranoid schizophrenia and murders, including one I was personally reviewing. The one that really tugged at my and the nation's heartstrings was the murders of two 19-year-old University of Nottingham students, Barnaby Webber and Grace O'Malley-Kumar, along with Ian Coates, a 65-year-old caretaker on his way to work, who were all killed by Valdo Calocane. This happened in Nottingham on 13th June 2023. He suffered from paranoid schizophrenia. Even though I have dealt with a hundred plus cases of serious crime, neither myself nor any of us, I am sure, can imagine the grief and despair that their families must have felt, and must continue to feel.

When the prosecution accepted the plea of manslaughter by diminished responsibility, it was widely reported in the media that the families felt that Calocane was getting away with murder, hence the title of my story was born. I hope to have respectfully dealt with this sort of crime in the story, which is a fictional story. My further hope is that we learn to intervene earlier in cases of those suffering from severe mental health before a crisis arrives, such as them committing murder or taking their own life by suicide.

I spent over thirty years as a police officer and the majority of these years were as a detective. I served as a detective in every rank, finally as the detective chief superintendent (head of the detective branch) of the Cambridgeshire Constabulary. As a detective, I led over one hundred major crime cases, a number of which were homicides or suspicious deaths. I absolutely loved this opportunity. The rank I enjoyed most, though, was the rank that Alexander McFarlane holds, that of a DCI. I am best known for my work as a detective around the UK for my role, over many years, as the national policing lead for the investigation of child death, as well as for my role as the senior investigator at the deposition site for the recovery and forensic investigation into the deaths of Holly Wells and Jessica Chapman, two ten-year-old girls from Soham, who were murdered by Ian Huntley.

In October 2019, my wife Debbie and I had a chance encounter in a remote hilltop village in the Atlas Mountains

(Morocco) with a couple from Melbourne – Professor Anne Buist and her partner Graeme Simsion. They are both authors and were working on a romantic comedy novel together. Graeme authored the bestselling novel, *The Rosie Project*. When I told him I had a detective crime novel in mind, he proceeded to give me a fifteen-minute masterclass on how to author a novel. Coincidently, both Professor Buist and I were to be keynote speakers at a conference two weeks later in Melbourne, relating to children who had been murdered by a parent. This chance meeting cemented my thoughts to author the novel I had been talking about for years.

This didn't occur, however, until the first lockdown arrived due to the COVID-19 pandemic. Even though I was still busy with my safeguarding work and writing a number of reviews, I decided to write a first draft of a novel during this period. That novel, *Greed is a Powerful Motive*, and the subsequent ones, *Missing But Not Lost*, *Death at Chateau Peveril* and *Body Overboard*, have been published by my brilliant publisher Cranthorpe Millner, to whom I am immensely grateful for all they do for me.

This is the fifth novel in my DCI Alexander McFarlane series and I am not sure I will write any more. I have some other ideas, including a spin off with his two grandfathers, to think about next.

Acknowledgements

To my wife Debbie, who is and has always been my greatest supporter in all that I do. Debbie was the first to read this novel and then painstakingly helped me to carry out a first edit for every page of it. For this and everything, I am truly grateful.

To all my family: my children Daniel, Rebecca and Matthew; and my father-in-law Sydney Barton and sister-in law Ruth Chaplain-Barton for reading and commenting on the story.

Also, to my close friends, who have taken the time to read the novel and to give me feedback. Thank you to Judi Richardson, Lorri and John Kendall (my Canadian family), Joanne Procter, Andrew Harrison (my writing and sourdough buddy), David Marshall (my work buddy and for all of his anecdotes that I include from time to time), Angela and Mark Craig (my friends, but also my daughter's wonderful mother- and father-in-law), Gary Etherington, Jane Ashton, Glenys Johnston, Mike Richardson, Janel Pike and Wendi Ogle-Welbourn. I would also like to thank the brilliant Dr Nat Cary (forensic pathologist).

Finally, I'd like to also thank Kirsty Jackson and her team at Cranthorpe Millner, including Victoria Richards, my senior editor, and Shannon Chapman for her creative cover designs and the marketing prowess of her team.